UNNECESSARY DRAMA

ALSO BY
NINA KENWOOD

It Sounded Better in My Head

UNNECESSARY DRAMA

NINA KENWOOD

FLATIRON
BOOKS
NEW YORK

UNNECESSARY DRAMA. Copyright © 2022 by Nina Kenwood. All rights reserved. Printed in the United States of America. For information, address Flatiron Books, 120 Broadway, New York, NY 10271.

www.flatironbooks.com

Designed by Devan Norman

The Library of Congress Cataloging-in-Publication Data is available upon request.

ISBN 978-1-250-89444-1 (trade paperback)
ISBN 978-1-250-89442-7 (hardcover)
ISBN 978-1-250-89443-4 (ebook)

Our books may be purchased in bulk for promotional, educational, or business use. Please contact your local bookseller or the Macmillan Corporate and Premium Sales Department at 1-800-221-7945, extension 5442, or by email at MacmillanSpecialMarkets@macmillan.com.

Originally published in Australia in 2022 by the Text Publishing Company

First U.S. Edition: 2023

10 9 8 7 6 5 4 3 2 1

FOR
ABBY

UNNECESSARY DRAMA

ONE

There is a mouse in the corner of my room. A mouse. In my bedroom. Where I sleep. It's sitting on its little haunches, frozen in fear. I'm in bed, also frozen in fear.

We are making direct and intimate eye contact.

It's funny because seconds ago I was so cozy and comfortable in my bed, feeling safe and wrapped up and pleased with myself—*here I am, in my new house, an adult at last, independent, free, worldly, some might even say sophisticated*—and now, my shaking hand is reaching for my phone, ready to call Mum and say come back and get me right this second.

I don't know how to end this standoff. Should I lie back in surrender, showing my belly like a dog? Or stand my ground, slowly wave my arms so it recognizes me as a human and backs off? That's what you do if you encounter a bear, along with blowing a whistle. I memorized how to survive an encounter with a bear when I was ten, for no reason other than that I suddenly woke up one day with a pit of anxiety deep in my stomach about encountering a bear. I was also very worried about quicksand and the fact that I didn't know how to tie an unbreakable knot or start a fire using nothing but two sticks. My ten-year-old self was earnestly imagining a future in which I would need these skills, even though I was a strictly indoors child who once cried because I was *almost* stung by a bee.

The thing is, I am a person who prepares. The very *essence* of who I am is my preparedness, my to-do lists, my thorough research, my above-and-beyond reading, my color-coded spreadsheets, my first-hand-in-the-air-I-know-the-answer energy. Before I moved out, I had a typed, itemized list of things I needed to buy, grouped by store, and then each item assigned to a person, so Mum and my older sister, Lauren, and I could get through the Boxing Day sales with the most efficiency. (Lauren looked at the list when I handed it to her and said, "No. Absolutely not. Brooke, why do you do this? I'm not coming anymore.") And yet I didn't research what to do when a mouse appears in the bedroom of your share house in the middle of the night. I should have screamed. But I didn't scream when I first saw it, and it really feels like the appropriate window of time in which to scream has now passed.

This is my first night living away from Mum, Lauren, and Nanna. The first night of my shiny new university student life in a shiny new city. Is turning on a lamp and seeing a disease-carrying rodent a bad omen? Not necessarily. This can still be a good sign. Maybe the mouse and I will become friends, have little adventures together. He'll travel around in my pocket, I'll call him Cornelius, it could be a charming period of my life that I will write about when I'm older.

I shift my arm ever so slightly and the spell is broken. The mouse races off, and even though it's going away from me, I finally scream. Louder than I thought I could scream. I jump up into a defensive standing position, legs slightly bent, hands in a ready-to-strike pose I vaguely remember from year-seven self-defense class. The mouse has very quickly gone from my friend Cornelius back to foul creature again.

"Brooke?" There's a knock on my door and Harper pokes her head in. "Are you okay?"

"There's a mouse. It was in the corner and then it ran out the door," I say, trying not to sound like I'm on the verge of tears. I don't have any pants on, just an oversize T-shirt and underwear, and I think the T-shirt is long enough to provide me with a tiny bit of dignity, but I still hope we can both pretend in the morning that Harper never saw the uppermost parts of my thighs.

Harper is a year older than me and her family owns the house. She has a small, lovely flower tattoo on her shoulder, she wears lots of delicate gold rings layered on her fingers, her dark, curly hair perfectly frames her face, her eyeliner skills far exceed anything I will ever be capable of, and she mentioned two bands I'd never heard of in our first conversation this afternoon. I'm hoping this mouse incident doesn't ruin my already slim chance of becoming her friend.

"Oh. God. Sorry. I've never seen one in the bedroom before." She frowns, runs a hand through her curls.

Which raises a question: Where *has* she seen them? She can see my face clocking her words, thinking about the possible number of mice she has seen in the house, and she shakes her head.

"No, no, don't worry. We don't have a mouse infestation or anything. I saw one in the backyard last week, that's all. The house is pretty old. Tomorrow we can put foil and steel wool in the floorboard cracks," she says.

She already warned me that the gap in the back door means the lounge room can get cold but you can plug it with a towel and it's mostly fine. And that the tap in the bathroom drips unless you turn it so tight you can almost not turn it on again. Also, the back gate lock sticks because the gate is warped, there might be just a touch of mold in winter, the oven rattles and shakes and sometimes turns itself off, the towel rack and the toilet-roll holder fall off the walls constantly and we just need to ignore the weird smell in the hall cupboard that you can never fully get rid of.

All that but she never said anything about mice.

I ignore my pounding heart and smile at her, dropping my hands back to my sides, and say, "Sounds good. See you in the morning." I lower myself back into my bed, as if I might sleep again tonight, rather than immediately googling "diseases you can catch from a mouse."

TWO

It's seven a.m., and the house is silent. I miraculously managed to fall asleep after learning through extensive research that the mouse probably wasn't carrying any diseases and also that mice can't see very well, so the meaningful eye contact between us that was haunting me might not have been as intense as I imagined.

Today is the day our other housemate will arrive. His name is Jeremy and I know nothing else, not even his last name, because Harper wasn't forthcoming and I'm trying to masquerade as a very relaxed, easy-to-live-with person who doesn't anxiously ask too many questions. *Oh Jeremy, no last name, no other identifying details? No worries, not a single worry here, no follow-up questions at all.* As if it's normal to agree to live with a guy—in close quarters, sharing a *bathroom*—and not have at the very least a short dossier on him, just a brief little overview of his family history, his friends, his past relationships, his school marks, his medical history, his politics, his problematic social media posts. And yet, here I am.

I am debating whether to quickly switch bedrooms before he arrives.

Being the grandchild of the owners and the first one to move in, Harper naturally has the biggest room. It has an ornamental fireplace and space for a queen-size bed and a desk and two bookcases, plus an enormous number of plants and a few other random items that don't actually fit but she's squished them in anyway, like an ugly hat rack that is not currently holding any hats and a heavy mirror propped against a wall. Her room is messy and overflowing with clothes, trinkets, furniture, Polaroid photos, vinyl records, jewelry, a bowl of crystals, books. There were four glasses of half-drunk water, two mugs of half-drunk tea, and an open bottle of Powerade on her desk, all dangerously close to her open laptop. It makes me itch to tidy it up. Just a really quick spruce here, a little neaten-up there, and a total and complete reorganization of her closets, that's all. And I can't even think about where she's put things in the kitchen. Mugs and glasses in a bottom drawer, plates and bowls on the very top shelf—it all feels wrong to me, but I am trying my best not to take over.

Harper gave me the choice of the other two rooms when I arrived. I picked the room with better light and fewer ceiling cracks, but it also apparently harbors a mouse. Mystery guy Jeremy has the room next to mine, which is slightly bigger, but it's a weird shape and has a big, faded stain on the wall that made me immediately think of blood splatter. I started thinking of it as the Murder Room as soon as I saw it, and that kind of name doesn't just go away once your brain attaches it to a place.

Murder or mouse, it's a conundrum.

I'm thinking it over in the shower when there's a knock on the bathroom door.

"Hello?" I call out, my voice high and stressed like I'm answering the phone to an unknown number.

Harper yells something but it's too muffled to hear. Is she

telling me to get out of the shower, to stop wasting hot water, to hurry up? Have I done something wrong, broken a rule? I don't even know the house rules yet. Surely not. I've been in the bathroom for only five minutes. I feel resentful of her possible bossiness, even though I have spent most of my life banging on bathroom doors and yelling at Lauren to hurry up. But that's different. That's sister stuff. That's justified, because Lauren will spend forty minutes in a shower if you let her, using up every single drop of hot water while she treats her hair with fancy products and exfoliates every inch of her body with a skin scrub she paid way too much money for.

Harper being the default leader of the house is disconcerting for me. Lauren might be my older sister, but I was always the one in charge of things at home. I was my school's arts captain, codirector of our year-ten play (alongside the drama teacher, so I had equal authority with an adult, an unprecedented situation; I even bought a black beret to wear, which, in hindsight, I will concede was the wrong choice), founder of our school's Jane Austen Book Club, secretary of the social justice committee, leader of our Model UN team. I am very comfortable in leadership roles.

But fine. Harper is in charge here. I'll settle for being vice-captain of the house, maybe. I won't say it to anyone out loud, but I'll definitely be thinking it in my head.

I crack the door and peer out of the bathroom. I left my dressing gown in my room by mistake, because I've never had to think about covering up as I go from bathroom to bedroom before, and now I have to dash through the house in a too-small towel.

I hurry down the hall, almost running as I get to the kitchen, but I skid to a halt when I see a man and a woman standing there holding boxes, as well as a preteen boy sitting on the floor in everyone's way, playing a Nintendo Switch, and a younger girl wailing, "I'm thirsty, Mum!" and a redheaded toddler holding a Barbie doll that is missing its head.

Harper widens her eyes at me, and I realize she had been knocking to warn me that there were people in the house.

"This is Brooke," Harper says.

They smile and nod and say hello, busying themselves with bags and boxes and crying children, politely averting their eyes from my almost nakedness. I assume they are new housemate Jeremy's family. Both of the adults look very familiar: I've seen them before, but I can't place them.

I maneuver past them in the kitchen, fake smiling, acutely aware of the towel sitting barely a centimeter below my butt cheek and also dangerously low across my boobs. This is the second time Harper has seen my upper thighs in the space of twelve hours. I am all for body positivity—when you're the less attractive sister in a family you really need to be across that from a young age—but my upper thighs are the body part I'd rather not *lead* with when getting to know people. They're just not opening-act material.

The toddler runs over to me, grabs a handful of towel, and yanks, which makes the almost naked situation even more precarious. I bend down awkwardly to remove his chubby little fingers, which have locked on to the towel with some kind of powerful death grip. I did not know children were so strong.

"Bottom, bottom! It's a bot!" the toddler yells, pointing under the towel. Oh my God, *where* is this child's mother? I look around in desperation.

"Oh, here he is," Harper says as someone else walks into the house, a teetering pile of boxes obscuring their face. "Brooke, this is Jeremy. Jeremy, Brooke."

I am too distracted by the toddler's attempts to humiliate and dominate me to be really paying attention.

"Oh, no one calls me Jeremy," he says.

My head jerks up. Wait. I know that voice.

The box lowers and a pair of eyes appear.

Those eyes.

Then his whole face. Long nose, broad shoulders, shaggy brown hair tucked behind his ears.

It's Jesse.

THREE

My heart is pounding and I'm trying to keep my face calm. My jaw suddenly feels locked and frozen. I'm trying to move it and I can't, but no, I'm not going to panic. It's fine. It's fine! Yes, Jesse is moving into my house, but I will process this information calmly and rationally, and my jaw will unlock itself any minute now, my heart will slow down eventually, and *everything is fine*.

"Jesse," I say, my voice strained.

"You two know each other?" Harper asks. "I guess that makes sense: my grandmother found you both." She laughs but emphasizes the word "grandmother" just a little too hard, and I sense lingering resentment that she was not given the choice to find her own housemates. Harper's grandparents live in my town, and they know my mother. And, apparently, Jesse's father.

"We went to the same school," I say, managing finally to get the towel out of the toddler's tight little fist, but he immediately reattaches himself with both hands and yanks on it even harder. I look around helplessly for someone to intervene. If there was a checklist for the ideal babysitter, I would tick every single box for even the most overprotective parent, but despite this I have no practical experience and I really do not know what to do with small children. Are you allowed to pick them up if they're not yours? Will they obey you if you speak in a firm, authoritative voice, like a dog might?

"Brooke, of course, you're Michelle's daughter," Jesse's dad says, seemingly unconcerned about the battle I am engaged in with his child. His tone sounds disapproving, but it's hard to tell if that is his voice's natural cadence or a pronouncement on my mother, or both.

"Yes. Michelle's daughter. Hello." I'm dripping water onto the floor, and I try to casually wipe it with my bare foot and continue edging toward my room, toddler in tow.

Jesse still hasn't said anything. He's just holding the boxes, watching me floundering, an inscrutable look on his face.

"Jesse, for God's sake, you haven't even said hello," Jesse's father snaps. "How 'bout you set a good example for your brothers and sister once in a while, huh?" That heavy disapproving tone again. I have a sudden memory of Nanna describing Jesse's father as an unpleasant man. Admittedly, she has said this about at least half of the men in our town (including the lovely local GP who doesn't charge her for visits, the smiling brothers who run the butcher shop and give us extra meat for her Siamese cat, Minty, and a widower who lives on our street who politely asked her out to lunch), but I think her assessment in this case was accurate. There's a moment of silent awkwardness.

"Sorry. Yeah. Hi, Brooke," Jesse says, clearing his throat.

I last saw him maybe three months ago, on graduation night, but he somehow seems taller now.

"Hi Jesse," I say, trying to look nonchalant and dignified while semi-naked and battling a toddler.

Jesse puts his boxes down and walks over to me. I'm worried about what he's planning to do, but he leans down, says,

"Come here, you," and scoops up his brother, throwing him over his shoulder in a way that makes the boy scream with delight.

Jesse glances back at me, and our eyes meet. I narrow mine the slightest, slightest bit, a message to him that . . . what? That I don't want us to be housemates any more than he does, but I got here first and if one of us is going to leave then it should be him, that what he did to me five years ago remains the greatest betrayal and humiliation I have ever endured, that I still haven't forgiven him and I never will. That's a lot for a momentary, barely noticeable narrowing of eyes to communicate, but I feel like he got the general vibe.

I hurry into my room, shutting the door with relief and then putting several heavy books in front of it in case the toddler tries to come in for round two.

I wonder if Jesse is going to back out. Will he turn to his parents and ask to leave? Well, good. I'm not going to leave. I can't leave. I've already paid my bond and spent a night here and made peace with the idea of the mouse and made loose plans to go to the market with Harper and started setting up a vision board and bought a Myki and told everyone in my life that I'm living in an amazing share house in Melbourne while I study economics with the aim of working for the UN while also being a best-selling author on the side and maybe writing an Oscar-winning screenplay.

This is my dream. I'm not giving it up. I spent months searching for somewhere affordable and half-decent to live. I interviewed with an older guy in his midtwenties who described himself online as a "philosopher, feminist, pacifist, entrepreneur, craftsman, communist, artist, lover, soul seeker," and then he said, when we chatted over the phone, that he liked living with younger women because he felt he had so much to teach them. I talked with three girls who assured me that "the room is small and a bit unconventional but *really* nice," which turned out to mean that the room was an area of carpet behind a couch, surrounded by a "privacy curtain" (a sheet pegged to a clotheshorse). Then Mum told me a couple in our town was looking for someone to live with their granddaughter. The relief was overwhelming.

I have nowhere else to go if this house doesn't work out. I don't want to live with a creepy guy or behind someone's couch. And I can't move home. I can't fail within forty-eight hours of leaving. I am simply not the kind of person who fails.

I get dressed slowly, automatically thinking, *I'll avoid Jesse until he leaves*, until I remember he's here because he's moving in. There's no avoiding. I read a book on my bed for a while, but I can't concentrate on the words. I try playing on my phone, but it makes me hyperaware of the fact my hands are shaking a little. I start to worry that Jesse will bond with Harper while I'm hiding in here, and they'll go to the market without me, and I'll be the one on the outer.

I poke my head out of my room. Everything is quiet. Jesse's family have gone. I heard them leave not long after I went into my bedroom. Because it's a long drive back to our town and they needed to get one of the kids to karate and another one needed a nap and the third was crying, they hustled out the door in a flurry of stress and yelling and I don't think they even said a proper goodbye to Jesse. I try not to compare that to yesterday, when Mum cried three times before leaving, Nanna solemnly gifted me her precious St. Christopher medal, and Lauren pretended she didn't care but then made Mum stop the car so she could run back in and hug me one more time. My family is perhaps a touch too codependent.

I find Harper in the kitchen.

"I bought bagels if you want one," she says.

"Yum, yes, please." My voice is oddly high-pitched. Everything I say sounds just a little bit not right, not me. I need to calm down or at least give the appearance of being calm. A physiotherapist once told me that she had never seen someone as incapable of relaxing their shoulders as me, which I chose to take as a compliment.

"So, do you and Jesse know each other well?" Harper says, cutting the bagels in two on the table, no chopping board, letting the knife scrape the wood, which makes my eye twitch.

Do we know each other well? The simplest question and I have no idea how to answer.

"Um, sort of. Not really. Well enough, I guess," I babble.

Harper lowers her voice a little, leans forward, ringlets falling across her forehead. Her earrings are gold, in the shape of beautiful tiny little skulls. I have the urge to run to my room and start googling "where to buy gold skull earrings." As if I could pull off skull earrings.

"So, what's he like?" Harper says in an almost whisper.

My heart glows a little. The way she says it, inviting intimacy, like we're already friends. But I need to be careful, I need to stop myself from immediately gossiping about him. Jesse lives here now. Harper doesn't know either of us. I don't want her first impression of me to be negative.

"He's. Um. He's nice," I say, still flailing. "He's fine, he'll be good to live with, he's really . . . nice." I am acutely aware I said "nice" twice but my mind is suddenly empty of all other adjectives.

"Okay. Yeah, I chatted to him a few times, he does seem nice," Harper says, looking disappointed at my dull reply. She was probably hoping for a sign that her grandmother hadn't stuck her with two boring duds. She gave me an opening, and I gave her nothing.

Harper puts cream cheese on the bagel and hands it to me. I try not to worry that she licked cream cheese off her finger and then that finger touched my bagel, and I wonder if she'll think it's rude if I get up for a plate. I settle for holding my hand under it to catch the sesame seeds falling.

Jesse walks into the kitchen, looking much more relaxed and happy without his family, and Harper offers him the other half of my bagel. He seems unbothered about her hands or the lack of plates or spilling sesame seeds.

"So I thought we'd go over the house rules," Harper says.

I sit up straighter. This is the conversation I have been waiting for. I imagine she's typed them up, laminated them, or, if it were me, put them in a lovely, nonthreatening binder. I'm ready for a deep discussion, possibly a friendly debate. I'm ready to make concessions, to compromise, to be flexible and very accommodating, but also to gently steer them in certain directions, toward a higher cleaning standard, a schedule, and to use the shared shopping list app I researched and have already downloaded onto my phone.

Harper starts talking, and I realize there's no laminated list, nothing written, just verbal rules. That's fine. I can take notes. Maybe I'll make the binder later.

The house rules are: no pets; no romance between housemates; and no unnecessary drama, in general.

She stops, and I wait. Is there more? Surely there must be more? What about division of chores, sharing of food, late-night noise, having guests over, parties, TV usage, sleep schedules, paying bills, checking the mail, bin night, using the dryer, fridge space, communal food, internet usage, length of showers, preferred scent of handwash? And these are just my top-level questions. I have subcategories. And sub-subcategories. Who is in charge of what? How does this household *run*, at a granular level? What are we each responsible for *doing*? There are already two drinking glasses and a knife covered in cream cheese in the kitchen sink and we have no established plan of when they will be cleaned or by who. I am sweating.

"So that's it. Pretty basic. We can figure everything else out as we go along. Any questions?" Harper asks, smiling. She's warm and friendly, which, for a person with natural charisma, she really doesn't need to be, so I especially appreciate it.

"What does 'no unnecessary drama' mean?" Jesse asks.

"No arguments, no tension, that sort of thing," Harper says. "Everyone just being chill and getting along."

"Sounds easy enough," Jesse says, not looking at me.

My heart is racing. This is going to be a disaster. I am holding my bagel in a death grip. I will my fingers to relax. I am not going to be the uptight one, I am not, I am not, I am not.

"Absolutely," I say, lowering my shoulders, wiggling my neck a little.

"Oh, and I thought, once you both get settled, we could have a housewarming party," Harper says.

"Sounds great," I say. How long will it take us to get settled? Are we talking three weeks, four, five? I need a timeline, a deadline, for this party so I know how long I have to make a lot of new friends, buy some cute clothes, deep-clean the house, and get my whole life in order. I try my best to not let a hint of these thoughts show on my very relaxed, very serene face.

"I can't wait," I add.

FOUR

After our house rules discussion, Harper tells us she's going out to see her girlfriend, Penny. She doesn't specify if or when she'll be home, which is normal for housemates, I guess, although I personally would love to implement a system so we can know when to worry about each other, so I don't have to default to worrying all the time.

Harper leaves, and Jesse and I are left alone for the first time. I walk into the lounge room and sit on the couch. I should get up and go and read. Organize my stationery. Start preparing for my uni classes tomorrow. Finish setting up my room. Make a list of things I need to buy for the house. Pick out my clothes for the week. Go for a walk and fall in love with the city. (Can this be done in one quick walk, or will it take three or four? I've never fallen in love with a place before. Or a person, for that matter.) And I'm still itching to rearrange the kitchen and clean the dirty dishes. All these things I need to do, but I can't move.

I miss home.

I feel like a needy little dog, trembling, huddled in a corner, away from its owners for the first time.

I'm not good when I'm out of my comfort zone. When I

couldn't sleep over the summer, and my heart was beating fast with fear about moving, I would watch old sitcoms, like *Friends* and *New Girl* and *How I Met Your Mother*, to reassure myself. This is what it will be like living with other people. We'll be instant best friends. I'll be different from the person I have always been, because no one will know anything about me. I'll be free to rewrite my own character, pretend I have a whole team of people giving me great dialogue and lots of plot and a roster of romantic entanglements. We'll have dinner parties and watch horror movies and sit up talking all night, have picnics in parks and start a netball team and go to concerts and restaurants and art galleries. And I'll be a runner (in these fantasies, I'm always very fit) and good at yoga and playing goal attack in netball. I won't worry about anything, because I won't need to: I'll be too busy and happy and successful.

But now it can't be like that, not with Jesse here, his very presence reminding me who I was, who I am.

I used to spend a lot of my Saturday nights sitting with Nanna and her cat, Minty, watching British crime dramas while simultaneously creating to-do lists, study plans, meal ideas, tracking books I want to read and the books I have read, and analyzing my sleep, exercise, study time, screen time from the previous week, logging it all into my apps and spreadsheets, making graphs, observing progress. It was a soothing ritual, having the numbers, knowing the data, seeing where I've been and where I'm going. I felt better being in control of everything.

I have always been the friend who remembered all the birthdays and organized the group present and paid for it and nervously and politely chased everyone else for their share of the money. I was the helper, the doer, the bringer of positive energy. I was the designated driver, the guarder-of-drinks, the holder-back-of-hair, the minder-of-bags, the lookout-for-parents, the one keeping track of who went where with who and how drunk they might be and when I should check on them.

I knew exactly what to do when there was a knock at the front door late on a Saturday night and two boys were standing there with Lauren. One had her shoulders and the other had her feet, and she swung between them, eyes closed, drunk and limp and dangling like a dead body. Mum at work or asleep, Nanna in the granny flat out the back, it was up to me and the chattering of my familiar internal monologue, *I hope nothing has happened to her, I hope these boys are trustworthy, I hope she doesn't need her stomach pumped, I hope she isn't going to vomit all over everything, I hope she doesn't wet the bed.* I would get towels, a bucket, a plastic tumbler of water (plastic, not glass, never glass), help Lauren to the bathroom, find her clean pajamas, put her to sleep on her side. Then I would sit in her room and listen to her breathe for hours, and make sure she didn't vomit in her sleep and choke to death, anxiety shooting through my body like a rocket, zooming up and down my arms and legs, looping circles in my stomach.

I did this so many times. With Mum sometimes, but sometimes on my own.

"You should be studying nursing," Mum said once, not understanding anything at all. I wasn't doing this because I loved looking after people, I was doing it because I loved Lauren. I was doing it out of duty. I was doing it because I loved Mum and she needed someone to carry the stress of it with her. I was doing it because we didn't want Nanna to know. I was doing it because there was no one else. I was doing it because it seemed to me to be women's work, the intimate work of caring and worrying and touching and looking after someone else's body. Mum didn't understand that I actually *hated* this, I hated it so much it made me feel almost dizzy when Lauren went out to a party or a friend's house or a concert or just a "quiet" night with girls from uni, and I started anticipating what might happen when she came home. Part of the reason I needed to move away so badly was that I wanted to be free of this responsibility; I didn't want to see it anymore. I didn't want to just be the person who cleaned shit up, who saw the worst parts and never the good parts. I wanted to find the good parts for myself, whatever they might look like.

This is the year when I am going to reinvent myself and find the good parts.

Jesse walks into the lounge room and sits on the couch across from me. Both the couches belong to Harper, or her family, I guess, and they're not new, but they are nicer than I expected. One is mustard yellow, the other faded gray, both very well-worn, but comfortable. I try not to think about when they were last cleaned.

I glance at Jesse and then look away. He's annoyingly tall. I'm not good at estimating heights, but I would say six two, maybe six three. He has very broad shoulders, and he takes up a lot of space, which makes me feel irrationally irritated.

"So," he says.

"So," I say in reply. If he thinks I'm going to do the work of making small talk, he's wrong. I will give him exactly as much as he gives me. No, wait, from now on I will give him just a little bit less. I will be cold, harsh, I will freeze him out, I will squash every single natural urge I have to fill the silence and be polite and friendly and make a joke. I might be a people pleaser, for teachers, for parents, for friends, for the imaginary person analyzing my social media likes, for my future great-grandchild who might one day unearth my diaries, but not for him. Never for him.

"We're living together." He's tapping the couch with the

fingers of one hand and I can tell he's nervous. He can't rely on flashing me his dimple-in-his-left-cheek smile, a look that served him well throughout high school—he knows I am impervious to his charm. I've seen him turn on his don't-you-just-find-me-a-little-bit-irresistible persona plenty of times before. Once at a party, he played a few chords on a guitar and held it while looking contemplatively at the sky, and people acted like he was an actual rock star for years after. Guys have it so easy. We're always looking for ways to find them hot, charming, attractive, interesting, talented. We'll take one small element, one moment, one single look, and build a whole fantasy around it.

"Look, so you know, I had no idea you were the other housemate when I moved in," I say, the words bursting out of me. "I had no idea your real name is *Jeremy*. If Harper had said Jesse, I might have had a clue or asked more questions or something. I mean, since when is your real name Jeremy? I hear the name Jeremy, and I think of a history professor in a bow tie. Saying your name was Jeremy was very misleading. This is all your fault. I would never voluntarily live with you. I had no idea you were even planning to move to Melbourne—you knew that was always my plan. But what's done is done and to avoid any unnecessary drama, I think—"

I take a breath. Okay, so the ice-queen plan didn't last long. I've gone in the opposite direction, complete verbal meltdown. But, I can recover this. I just need to be firm and take charge. I swallow, lower my voice, bring it a few notches down from hysteria.

"I think we just need to act friendly to each other when we're around Harper," I finish, folding my arms.

"Sorry, can we back up a second? You heard the name Jeremy and you thought you were going to be living with a *professor*?" Jesse says.

"A very young one, yes, maybe." I really wish I had not said that part.

"Who wears a bow tie?" he says.

"Yes. And a tweed blazer. With those leather patches on the elbows."

"You spent quite a bit of time imagining this Professor Jeremy," he says, and I can see a smile tugging at the edges of his lips.

"I was imagining him as a mentor," I say huffily. I was actually imagining him as a handsome, floppy-haired, bow-tie-clad postgrad student who loves the library and has a posh accent and would bring me a strong cup of tea every afternoon while I was studying and we would make intellectual and deeply insightful jokes about Hemingway or some other dead author I haven't read yet, but no one ever need know that level of detail.

"Mmmm. I'm sure," Jesse says.

"Anyway. The plan. We're nice to each other when we're around Harper, and we get through this year—"

"I told you my real name was Jeremy," he interrupts.

"No you didn't."

"Yes I did. We were sitting together on the bus, and you said if you ever published a book, you wanted it to be under your nanna's name, which I'm pretty sure you said was Evelyn or something like that, because you don't like your name, even though you have a perfectly fine name, and I said if I ever did, I would publish it under my real name, Jeremy."

He's right. The memory floods back instantly. I remember not just the conversation, but the way we were sitting, turned toward each other, elbows bumping, and that it was afternoon and we were heading home. We were fourteen, and our friendship was new and exciting in the way it is when you suddenly and unexpectedly click with someone and you feel like you could talk forever.

I push the memory away as fast as possible. "I don't remember that," I say, looking away.

"Okay," he says.

I'm not sure he believes me.

"So what about when we're not around Harper?" he adds.

"What do you mean?"

"You said we act friendly to each other around Harper. How do we act when we're not around her, when we're just on our own?" he asks. We look at each other, and for a second, just a second, I feel, absurdly, like I might cry. I push my fingernails into my palms, and the feeling passes.

I frown at him. "We ignore each other," I say.

He nods and tucks his hair behind his ears.

"All right. So if you're home, and I'm home, but Harper's out, and I walk into the kitchen, do I literally pretend you're not there or can I say something?" he says.

"It depends," I say.

"On what?"

"On what you might say."

"I will probably say 'Hi.' Or 'Excuse me,' if I need to reach around you to get to the fridge. Or 'How was your day?' if I'm feeling really bold," he says, and his face is serious but I can see his eyes twinkling a little. This is a joke to him. I'm a joke to him.

"They're acceptable options," I say, keeping my face impassive. "But no follow-up questions. If you ask me how my day was, and I say 'Good,' that's it."

"Should I submit a full list to you of things I might say, for you to approve ahead of time?" he says.

"Yes. You should," I say, still not giving him a hint of a smile. Let him worry I am being serious. Let him worry how far over the edge I have gone. Let him sweat.

He gives a short laugh and shakes his head. "Come on, Brooke," he says.

"Come on, what?" I say. I will not let him weasel his way back into my life. We are not friends.

"Fine. Sounds good. We will silently endure living together and stay out of each other's way as much as possible," he says, sighing and standing up.

I stand up too, because I don't like the imbalance of him standing and me sitting, even though he still towers over me when we're both standing. We hold eye contact for a beat longer than is comfortable. Is this a power play? Am I winning or losing? I need to have the last word in this conversation.

"Shake on it," I say, holding out my hand, which I immediately regret, because he could refuse to shake it, and then what will I do? Oh God.

But he doesn't refuse. He reaches out and shakes my hand, lets it go, and then we turn and walk into our separate bedrooms.

FIVE

Jesse and I met when we were fourteen. It was the middle of term three in year eight and my homeroom teacher asked me to show a new student around. This was the kind of job often given to me—look after the new kid, read the book out loud while the teacher had to duck out and get something, collect all the assignments off the desks and bring them to the front.

The new student was Jesse, and he stood leaning in the doorway waiting for me. He was tall, but lanky and thin, in the way of teenage boys who haven't filled out or got comfortable in their bodies yet and seem kind of permanently surprised about it, like they've just woken up in a new stretched-out body. I knew the feeling. I'd had my growth spurt early. I was the tallest girl all through the last years of primary school, which made me feel oversize and on display, under pressure to be a good goalkeeper in netball, bend my knees a little in every group photo, and pretend I didn't mind when people said, "*You're* Lauren's little sister?" with surprise.

I walked him around the school. He told me he'd just gone from living with his mum to living with his dad, but he said it in a way that didn't invite more questions, so I changed the subject and gave him my ranking of the teachers from nicest to most likely to say something sexist.

A few weeks after that, we were paired up in English class for an assignment where we had to write a short story with an additional creative component. We spent all of the class talking about ideas, and on the bus on the way home, he sat down next to me, as if it were the most natural thing in the world, as if we'd always sat together. From the day he'd arrived, he'd been welcomed by the various groups that sat toward the back of the bus, so walking halfway down to my spot in the middle was noteworthy.

He said, let's figure out the plot together, and then you could write the story and I could illustrate it with a map.

He showed me a book full of sketches—houses and castles and towers. When I saw the lines and details and intricacies of his work, I could suddenly see the fantasy world we were creating. I had that itch in my hands, a buzz in my stomach, almost a taste in my mouth, that I got when I couldn't wait to start writing.

I'd been writing stories since I was little. Mum and Nanna have stacks of little booklets I produced when I was seven, eight, nine. Stories about animals, many about horses, a chestnut pony called Star, specifically, that I thought I could manifest into reality out of sheer willpower. Then, as I got older, I started getting more serious, self-importantly thinking of the stories as "short stories" and plotting out potential novels. When Dad first moved to Perth and Lauren was busy with her high school friends, I would spend whole weekends writing. I instinctively felt I was good at it, but despite this belief, I was too scared to ever show anyone my work. It was my private triumph, too fragile to be entrusted to others.

But planning this story with Jesse gave me confidence. When I showed him what I had written so far for our assignment, he said with real awe and sincerity, "You're a really good writer." It sent a jolt into me. It made me feel like I mattered. His map was amazing, beautifully and perfectly detailing the world we created together. We handed in the assignment and got an A+. Our teacher pinned the map up on the class notice-board for everyone to admire. Jesse was mortified, but I was delighted.

After that, we always sat together in English. Sometimes on the bus home, he'd wait until Frances and Lakshmi, the girls I usually hung out with, got off and then he'd come and slide into the seat next to me for the last fifteen minutes of the trip. If we passed each other during the school day, we'd grin. We texted all the time, jokes and memes and links and random thoughts. A few times, we walked his family's dog together. Our friendship wasn't hidden, exactly, but it felt like a little bubble of secret happiness in my day. I would sit in class and look at the map on the wall and smile.

Lauren teased me that I liked him, which made me yell at her, but privately, I wondered. The mechanics of crushes—desire, emotions, lust—were all still confusing to me. Lauren had her first kiss when she was eleven, she'd had three boyfriends by sixteen, and I had just turned fourteen and had never been kissed and it was not something I saw happening in my immediate future. Lauren was the kissable sister, I was the one who read about it in my sister's diary. *Did* I like Jesse in that way? How did you know what was just friendship and what was more? No one had ever liked me, so I had no baseline data. I needed a pro–con list, a deep-dive YouTube series, a twenty-page quiz, a how-to guide, and a relationship coach before I could work it out.

Feelings were scary. I knew that much.

One weekend in November, Gretel Morewell invited the whole year level to her fourteenth birthday party. She lived on a five-acre property, and her parents were there to supervise, but they holed themselves upstairs, and fifty or so of us spread out through her house and yard. There was a firepit, and she'd put speakers in her windows so you could hear the music outside. There were endless boxes of pizza laid out on the counter, and we had free rein until ten p.m.

It was the first real party I'd been to that wasn't a sleepover with three or four other girls, and I went mostly out of curiosity. I knew everyone there, but the air crackled with the thrill of possibility of being with your classmates at nighttime, away from school. I drifted from group to group, until I found myself sitting next to Jesse on the couch inside. We chatted for a while, and when there was a lull in the conversation, I turned to him, about to tell him how much I loved the song that was playing ("Sign of the Times" by Harry Styles, which had come out six months earlier and I was still listening to it semi-obsessively every night). Jesse turned to me at the same time, our eyes met, and he leaned down toward me. It took me a second to realize he was leaning in to kiss me. *I was about to be kissed.* I sat up straighter, thrilled and nervous, ready for my life to change.

It wasn't, by any definition, a good kiss. It was barely a kiss. He leaned down way too fast, then hesitated, then kept going at the same time as I leaned in too, so we almost bumped heads. Our lips fumbled together, and the angle of our heads was all wrong. It occurred to me as it was happening that I had no idea what exactly you were supposed to do when you were kissed. One of my hands hovered awkwardly in the air, because I was too afraid to put it down anywhere in case it was wrong.

But still. My first kiss. With a cute boy. While my favorite song was playing. This was the stuff dreams are made of.

After a few seconds, we broke apart. I blinked and looked up at him, willing him to do it again, but slower, so I could improve, or at least figure out what to do with my hand. I started to lean in toward him, then panicked that I looked too eager, so I jerked backward just as he was moving in to meet me. His face went red and he mumbled something that I couldn't hear.

A burst of laughter interrupted us, and I turned and saw Gretel and a bunch of boys from our class standing in the doorway.

"What's going on here?" Gretel said, her voice both delighted and dangerous. "Jesse, do you like *Brooke*?"

The implication in her tone was clear. I was not worthy of being liked, as least not by Jesse.

Jesse's face was very red now. He stood up quickly, without looking at me, which was my first clue as to what would come next. He looked at Gretel and the five or six guys standing behind her, and laughed and shook his head and said, "Do I like Brooke? No. *No*. Fuck, no."

I stared up at him, shocked.

"No offense," he said, looking back at me and quickly away again, rubbing his hand over his mouth. His eyes looked desperate, there was a sheen of sweat on his forehead. My mouth was dry. I had no idea what to do or say. I felt like my insides were liquefying. I had emotional whiplash. Kissed and publicly rejected within the time span of a Harry Styles song.

"That's harsh, man," one of the guys said to Jesse. "She's not that bad." But then they were all talking about something else, complaining they hated the song, and Gretel picked up her phone to skip it. Jesse walked over to help her choose another song, leaning his head in extra close to hers, and I was left still sitting there, alone.

I pulled out my phone with shaking hands and texted Mum to come and get me. She would be at least half an hour, maybe longer, and I considered sitting by the dirt road in the dark to wait for her, which I calculated carried about a fifty percent risk of murder but still seemed better than being here. Gretel's mother came downstairs to get more wine and took one look at me, sitting on the couch pale faced and trembling, and brought me upstairs to sit awkwardly between her and her husband and watch *Midsomer Murders* with them until my mum arrived.

On Monday morning, I ignored Jesse on the bus. I had thought maybe he would text me over the weekend, but he didn't. I had typed and then deleted so many messages to him that Mum and Lauren both demanded to know what was going on. I didn't tell them. Later, I would let Lauren know that Jesse and I had had a fight, but I never gave her the details. It was too personal. It was too humiliating.

I was the last one out of our homeroom after the bell rang for lunch that Monday, and I hovered at the noticeboard, looking at his map—our map. All the effort, all that detail, all those hours of work. I really loved the little world we'd created. I reached out, and I only meant to touch it, but something vicious came over me. He'd ruined not just my first kiss but my favorite song. I pulled the map off the wall and tore it in two. It felt so good, I ripped it again.

I heard a noise behind me and turned. Jesse was standing there watching me.

"Brooke," he started to say, running his hands through his hair. "Listen."

"No," I said, shaking my head. "Do not talk to me. Ever again."

"I—"

"I said, don't ever talk to me again." My voice was as cold and hard as I could make it. I needed him to get away from me, fast, in case I cried. Or in case I changed my mind, because underneath everything, I already missed being his friend, and that made me angrier. I was determined not to show an ounce of weakness. I scrunched his map into a ball, threw it at his feet, and walked out of the classroom. And it felt good, so good, *amazingly* good. Anger, it turned out, was more satisfying than sadness or humiliation.

I couldn't resist looking back, though. Just once, just quickly, just in case he was really upset. Our eyes met. He'd picked up the map from the ground and held the torn, scrunched pieces in his hands.

"I don't care about this. It was a shit story anyway," he yelled at me.

That was it. I turned and walked away.

The next year, at the year-nine social, I told Georgia Crowley not to kiss him because he was a bad kisser, which was the cruelest thing I could think to do, and she reported back to him that I said that (but she did not heed my advice, because by then he was the boy everyone wanted to kiss). After that, it became a thing, a known, established thing, that we didn't like each other. "Keep them separated," I overheard a teacher say once, "Brooke and Jesse don't work well together."

That night at Gretel's party didn't ruin my life in any measurable sense. It didn't leave me friendless and alone. I went on to have a boyfriend and a reasonable approximation of a social life. But it was one of those moments that lingered. It lodged inside me like a shard of glass, and if I moved the wrong way, I would feel it, a sharp, unexpected jab.

Do I like Brooke? No. No. Fuck, no.

When I finished school, I thought, *Thank God I'll never have to see Jesse again.*

SIX

I'm early for my Creative Writing: Ideas and Practice class, which means I am sitting awkwardly alone in the room with our teacher, PJ Mayfield.

This is my heart class, the one I picked with hands shaking with guilt and trepidation, because I was doing it for pure enjoyment and that's not what studying is supposed to be about. Enjoyment? Enjoyment is frivolous, and I am here to learn, to achieve, to figure out a serious career path. But every time I've stepped into the room for our creative writing class, I've had to bite back a smile of pure happiness at the prospect of being here, on campus, in a room with high ceilings, big windows, and a general aura of importance and significance, with people who just want to talk about books and writing.

PJ Mayfield is an author. She wrote a very bleak, critically acclaimed book two years ago. I hadn't heard of it, but I bought it when I saw she was in charge of the course. It's very good, in that literary way where most of the characters are sad and depressed and say cruel things that are funny but not in a way I am comfortable with laughing at because I'm worried I don't actually get it. There is a horrible scene in the middle of the novel involving the grisly death of a dog left alone in a hot car that made me put the book down for days and debate whether to keep reading or even take the class. Almost every review alludes to this scene, often with trigger warnings. "IF YOU LOVE DOGS, OR ANY ANIMAL, OR EVEN JUST SORT OF LIKE THEM, STAY AWAY FROM THIS BOOK!!!!!!" wrote one Goodreads reviewer. I have to agree with them, and I almost liked their review, but then I'm worried PJ might be neurotic enough to monitor this kind of thing and trace that like back to me.

PJ doesn't seem bothered that I'm here early today. She's reclining in her chair, eyes closed, her Blundstone-clad feet on the desk, balancing a book facedown and open on her chest. I would assume she was asleep except she stretches her neck from side to side occasionally. She is just firmly determined not to open even the slightest crack of opportunity for enthusiastic early arrivers to engage with her.

I have leaned forward as subtly as I can to try to see the title of her book, but I can't. It's slim, with a minimalist cover. It looks European. Maybe something obscure translated from German. Or maybe she's reading it in German. She seems like someone who can read fluently in German. Or, oh God, Russian. *Latin?* I'm too scared to take my book out of my bag, in case she judges me for reading a bestseller written in English, even though I'm at a really good part and dying to finish the chapter.

I have a latte on my desk, and I sip it very slowly, playing with my phone, trying to pretend I am possibly taking notes for a novel I am going to write, instead of looking through my photo reel and wondering if it's true that your nose keeps growing for your entire life and if I can see that growth in photos of me over the last five years. (I think I can.)

I've been living in Melbourne for almost a month now. It's going well, really well. Sort of. On the good side of things, I have successfully managed to avoid Jesse most days (I have memorized his schedule to make sure mine is slightly different and we're never in the kitchen together or on the same tram in the mornings), I enjoy most of my uni classes, and I have forged the tentative beginnings of a friendship with Harper and her girlfriend, Penny. I think. It's hard to tell. Harper was very enthusiastic about the chocolate-chip cookies I made yesterday, but she might just love chocolate-chip cookies.

On the negative side, I can relax enough to poop only when I think the others are asleep, so I've had to adjust my entire digestive schedule. I wake up every night, heart pounding, convinced the mouse is back. I had a trial at a local café for a casual waitress position and they never called back despite the fact I smiled the whole time, even when a man made me repeat his order back to him twice because he didn't believe I could remember that he wanted his latte *very hot*. I bought two tickets to the movies last weekend because I was going to see if Harper wanted to come with me, but then I chickened out of asking her. It felt too presumptuous and cringeworthy, to have already bought the tickets, and the opportunity to just casually ask her never naturally arose, so I ended up going on my own, and I sat in a near-empty cinema and felt like the depressed but beautiful main character of an indie film, which made me feel very adult and mysterious (maybe a cute quirky guy was watching me from nearby, appreciating my haunting allure), but also a little sad.

The things I have learned living with Harper and Jesse are that they're not as shy about the toilet as me, they don't mind their clothes sitting wet in the washing machine for *days*, they will squish things down and jenga a piece of rubbish on top of a teetering bin rather than take the garbage out, they haven't appeared to notice I do all the vacuuming, and they can't cook. Harper goes out a lot at night to see Penny, but when she's home, she eats takeout or plain pasta with cheese. Jesse seems to eat cereal for dinner as his main option, sometimes two-minute noodles, sometimes a banana and a giant tub of yogurt. Occasionally he'll cook a steak and eat just that, a hunk of meat alone on a plate, sitting in its juices.

When I cook, I put any leftovers in the fridge with a note encouraging Harper and Jesse to help themselves, listing the ingredients (in case of allergies) and the date it is good until, adding a smiley face and an exclamation mark to make it all seem very friendly and relaxed and low drama. I even bought purple Post-it notes because they seem less uptight than the standard yellow ones.

I have the purple Post-it notes with me now in class, because they also seemed the most appropriate for creativity, but now I'm suddenly worried PJ will judge those too. She seems like a strictly no-nonsense yellow-Post-it-only person. I subtly slide them off my desk and push them back into my bag. Finally, other students start arriving, including Sophie, Justin, and Ruby, the three students I sit with every class and who are the closest I have come to making friends with at uni so far. I always have a moment of fear when they arrive, that they won't sit with me today, and I curse myself simultaneously for putting myself in this position by arriving early and for being so pathetically insecure to even worry about it, but they smile and head in my direction, and I almost slump in relief.

PJ always starts the class with a kind of rambling lecture on her thoughts on writing and publishing books. Today she tells us: it's hard; it takes years and years to write anything half-decent; if you think you've written something great, you'll come back to it three months later and realize it's not; there's absolutely no money to be made, especially in Australia; it's lonely; it's a form of torture, really; most people won't get published; if you do get published, you'll be utterly disappointed at what an anticlimax it is; writing talent is rare, but even rarer is a talented writer who can take on feedback and actually do the work to make their writing better. But, despite all this, if we want to write, if it calls to us in the dark of night, if it's in our very *bones*, then we should face down the inevitable heartbreak and do it anyway, because nothing else will ever feel as nourishing to our souls. Making art, she says, requires courage and fortitude. Oh, and exercise helps. Helps what? someone asks. Helps everything, she says gravely.

I dutifully write it all down in my new notebook: *hard, lonely, no money, great suffering but possible happiness. Start running?*

Sophie has been making a pained face at Justin throughout this lecture. Justin is grinning back at her. Ruby is sipping on a giant iced coffee, using one finger to slowly scroll through a clothing website on her laptop. Sophie, Ruby, and Justin all think PJ is too cynical and bitter. They roll their eyes and make fun of her in the group chat we set up, while also remaining completely terrified of her in person. Obviously, we are all desperate for her approval. But I like her. I like the way she combines no-bullshit honesty with a flair for the dramatic. I like that she tells us it's going to be terrible but we should do it anyway because it might also be wonderful.

At the end of class, I say, "See you on Friday," to Sophie, Ruby, and Justin and then brace myself, because Friday is our housewarming party, and I am expecting the three of them to give me blank looks or make excuses for why they can't come. But they all cheerfully say, "See you then," and, once again, I am flooded with relief. I don't remember ever being this nervous or neurotic about making friends in high school. Back then, I had a group I sat with at lunch, and I had other groups that my group was friends with, friendships that were wide and shallow and safe. Things weren't perfect, but I knew who I was and where I fit. I am out of my depth here. I'm always on edge that I'll be exposed as a fraud in some way.

I invited eight of my school friends to the housewarming party. Two said they would try to make it after something else, which means they won't be coming. The other six are working, or can't get to Melbourne, or have other plans. The trouble with my school friendships now is that even though we all still talk and text, everyone is so eager to meet new people and forge new post–high school lives, it's easy to slip away from each other. And when you're holding a party, and you need to invite people to said party and be sure they actually *show up in person*, it's like a friendship exam. I don't want to fail the exam. I *can't* fail the exam. When Sophie, Ruby, and Justin all said yes to the invitation straightaway, I almost cried.

On the tram on the way home, I am gazing out the window when I see Jesse get on. We go to different universities but they're close to each other, his in the city center, mine a few minutes farther out, but we are on the same tram line home. I glance away, hoping he doesn't see me. He's halfway down the tram, and there are five people standing in between us. I sneak a look at him. He has headphones in and a backpack on, and for a brief moment, my heart softens a little. There's something about him standing there alone, one hand gripping the pole, in a crowd of people, that makes me feel like maybe we're the same, both floundering a little in a new city, trying to meet people and learn the public transport system and not get lost or overwhelmed or homesick.

He looks up and we make eye contact. *Damn it.*

He awkwardly raises a hand, and I give a small nod back.

No smile. We are not at smiling stage. The people standing between us get off, and now it's very hard to ignore him. Will he move closer to me, or should I move closer to him? What is the protocol here? I take one small sideways step toward him and then pretend it was nothing more than adjusting my balance. The tram stops again, and several more people get off, leaving a double seat empty between us. A glaring empty seat right there, beckoning, an invitation for us both to sit down. I don't want to share the seat with him, it's too much like sharing our bus seat in high school. But if I sit down first, he'll be the one left with the dilemma of what to do. He seems to be thinking the same thing, as we both make a move for the seat at the same time, bumping into each other.

"Sorry," we say at the same time. He smiles. I don't.

"After you, m'lady," he says, using, for some reason, a ridiculous British accent and giving a grand, sweeping hand gesture.

"Thank you," I say, frowning a little, because I suspect he did the accent to try to trick me into smiling, and I need him to know I will not be won over so easily. I absolutely do not find him charming or cute.

I sit down and he sits down next to me. I get the sense he's regretting the fake accent. I would be. I vow not to speak to him, to hold firm, but not speaking to someone is much harder when you are sitting right next to each other. We're not touching, but I'm acutely aware of every inch of his body beside me. My mind keeps slipping back into memories of us chatting and laughing on the bus in high school. *No. Do not think about that.* The silence stretches on, and I stare resolutely out the window. *Do not make small talk. Do not look at him. Do not.*

Jesse clears his throat.

"I know we're supposed to ignore each other when no one else is around," he says. "But I have to tell you—"

My heart catches, just for a second, as I wait for him to finish his sentence. Maybe he's feeling nostalgic too. Maybe he's going to try to rekindle our friendship. I brace myself for an emotional confession. To coldly remind him we are not friends and can never be again.

"—that your foot is touching something disgusting," he says, pointing at the floor.

Oh. I look down and he's right. Under our seat is a discarded McDonald's bag and my shoe is resting on what appears to be a squashed junior burger, the sauce squirting out and onto my sneaker. I lift my foot, and a sticky mess follows it, with the burger wrapper and a pickle now stuck to the sole of my shoe. I wipe my foot against the wall, but the wrapper won't come off. Jesse watches on as I struggle with the mess.

Finally, he leans down and grabs the dirty wrapper off my shoe with his hand.

"I didn't need your help," I say huffily.

"Sorry. I will never help you with anything again," he says. He doesn't visibly roll his eyes but I can feel a sarcastic eye roll in his tone.

"Good," I say, folding my arms.

"Glad we're agreed," he says, folding his as well.

We don't speak again for the rest of the ride home.

SEVEN

It's the night of our housewarming party and I am in the kitchen, chopping fruit into decorative shapes and artfully arranging cheeses and jamming toothpicks into rolled-up salami slices with what I am sure an outside observer would describe as a manic energy. I told Harper and Jesse I would prepare the food for the party, because it calms me to have a job and because I like to make things special.

They thought I would dump a few packets of chips into bowls, but I have created fully stylized grazing platters. This just seemed nicer than a tub of hummus and a few packets of water crackers. Although now I take a breath and stand back and look at it all, I'm starting to worry I might have gone overboard. I am putting the finishing touches on my kiwifruit cut into flower shapes when Harper and Penny walk into the kitchen.

"Oh wow!" Harper says, smiling. "You've really gone all out."

I can't tell if she thinks that's a good thing or a bad thing.

"It's no big deal," I say, hoping they can't tell from looking at me that I spent all morning watching instructional YouTube videos on how to create charcuterie platters. I want people to be deeply impressed, but I also don't want anyone to know how hard I am trying for their approval. It's a complicated balance.

Penny is carrying a bottle of champagne and wearing an adorable jumpsuit and bright lipstick. Her chestnut hair is spilling in every direction, and her chunky heels are so high I want to study the mechanics of how she walks so effortlessly in them. Harper is wearing high-waisted black jeans, Converse sneakers, and a cropped red top with the word "cheese" on it in blocky white type. I don't know if "cheese" is an obscure reference or if it's completely random, but I do intuitively know that it makes the top very cool. I don't know which outfit I wish I could pull off more. I'm wearing a loose black dress that feels very dull in comparison, and now I'm worried I look like a waitress.

"You should start a catering business," Penny says, which makes me definitely want to get changed. "You have talent."

Harper laughs and grabs a carrot off my platter. "Stop telling everyone they should start a business," she says to Penny.

"I can't help it. I see potential everywhere I go," Penny replies.

"She listened to one podcast episode on young women launching start-ups and now she's unbearable," Harper says, and I laugh. I resist asking which podcast, because I don't need the pressure of trying to think up a successful business idea right now.

Penny picks up a strawberry and looks at me intently. "How are you settling in?" she says. Her voice is kind, and I worry I am giving off out-of-my-depth-small-town-girl energy.

"Good, good," I say. "I love it here. It's—" I pause and try to think of something very *Melbourne* to say, something worldly, chic, cultured. "It's a really nice area," I finish.

"Brooke is so organized," Harper says to Penny, still chewing on the carrot. A very ambiguous statement. Is that a good thing? A bad thing? A neutral thing?

Harper and Penny smile at me, and my heart is beating very fast in the silence that follows. I feel personally responsible for the lull in the conversation. Why am I suddenly so bad at this? Without the structures of school, the security of a minor leadership role, and the safe haven of my family, I am struggling. I actually had the sad thought the other day that I miss my school uniform. Now I spend hours scrolling through social media to find girls of my body size and type (tall, wide hips, strong thighs, a non-flat stomach, hair that swings between mousy brown and dark blond depending on when I last went to the hairdresser and if I am under flattering light, pink-toned skin with a tendency toward eczema and extreme dryness but that will turn oily as soon as moisturizer touches it) who dress well, so I can copy their style. Penny is tall and about my size, but she's operating at three fashion levels, at least, above me.

I hear the front door opening and voices in the hallway.

"Oh, someone's here," Harper says, and she and Penny go to see who it is. It's their second year of uni, they grew up in Melbourne, and they're part of a whole interconnected social group. Harper said she has twenty or thirty friends coming tonight.

Within minutes of people arriving, it's clear that Harper's friends and Jesse's friends are very different types of people. Harper's friends are artsy, politically engaged, sitting in our lounge room like a big clump of intimidating coolness, drinking wine and debating the merits of a French TV show that I have heard of but didn't realize anyone my age actually watched, and they all have great hair, somehow, which seems statistically unlikely, but there it is.

Jesse's friends are a mix of shy and sweet engineering students and old school friends who are living in a share house in

Geelong in what appears to be a mostly nocturnal life, where they play video games all night, eat Meat Lover's pizza six times a week for dinner, shower on average once every four days, and recently started a small fire by putting a pizza, cardboard box and all, in the oven to reheat it.

I fuss around, putting food out, tidying the kitchen, refilling drinks, trying to look busy while I anxiously wait for Ruby, Sophie, and Justin to arrive. I'm sweaty and flustered. I stand in front of the open fridge for a second, trying to cool down.

In the lounge room, Jesse is sitting on the couch next to one of Harper's friends, a pretty girl with waist-length caramel-colored hair and a nose ring. They're deep in conversation, leaning toward each other, knees almost touching. It makes me feel a little bit sick. And betrayed. Here I was thinking we were both nervous and tentative in this new life, that we were equals, both *in between*, but he has so many friends here, old and new, and now he's casually flirting, and he's never looked more relaxed in his life. He cannot integrate into Harper and Penny's friendship group before me.

I approach them with a tray of food.

"Hi, I'm Brooke," I say to the girl.

"Amber," she says in return. She looks at the platter of food I'm offering and exclaims with delight, "Oh my God, the detail! This looks like the kind of thing my mother spends all day making for her book club."

"Oh, um, thanks?" I say. I don't really know how to respond to that.

Amber smiles at me cheerfully as she piles food onto a napkin. "You know what? I think my mum actually owns that dress too!" she says, gesturing to my clothes.

I am really hoping her mother is very young and very fashionable.

Jesse has just put a chip in his mouth while listening to our interaction, and he wrinkles his nose.

"What am I eating?" he asks.

"A turmeric-flavored lentil crisp," I tell him.

"Ugh," he says. "It is not good."

"It's an acquired taste. For a sophisticated palate," I say, trying to sound worldly and disdainful. In truth, I bought them because they were on special at the supermarket.

"How long does it take to acquire a taste for it?" he says.

"For you? It'll take a while," I say.

"Brooke!" a voice calls.

I turn, and squint. I don't immediately recognize the girl walking toward me. But I can't really concentrate on her face because she's wearing an animal onesie. One of those all-in-one animal-patterned onesies that have hoods and are sometimes sold as costumes and sometimes as novelty pajamas. I think this one is a cow because it's white with big black patches and, I think, yes, definitely, there are pink udders hanging off her stomach, and a little cow face on the hood, and a tail trailing at the back. Is that *Ruby*? Why is she wearing that? Oh God.

"Hey, Brooke," Ruby says, walking over to me.

Her voice is slightly slurry. I am an expert in knowing when and how drunk someone is, and I would say Ruby is currently happily buzzed but heading toward the unsteady and messy phase.

"Hey!" I say. I give her a quick hug, even though we've never hugged before, but the cow onesie has thrown me. Her soft udders squish against me in a disconcerting way.

"I like your place." She waves a hand around vaguely.

"Thanks. Thanks for coming," I say. I pause and wait for her to explain the onesie, but she's been distracted by the food and is busy picking at the grapes.

I can see Amber and Jesse taking in the costume, Amber with raised eyebrows and wide eyes and Jesse looking like he wants to laugh.

I frown at him. *Grow up.*

If my friend wants to dress like a cow at my party, well, she can. I'm interested to know why, of course, but really, it might be none of our business. It might be a very personal emotional situation.

"Hey guys, over here!" Ruby yells as Sophie and Justin walk in. They are also wearing animal onesies. Did I tell them it was a costume party? No, I didn't. *Did I?* No. Definitely not. Of course not. Is this a . . . sexual kinky thing, maybe? Or a Melbourne thing? A creative thing? Or is it a joke? An ironic joke or a prop comedy joke? Am I the butt of the joke or am I in on it? My hands are clammy. I'm definitely not in on it.

Sophie is in an orange kangaroo onesie, and it has a little pouch with a joey poking out. Justin is in a lime-green dinosaur onesie, with felt spikes all down his back and a long tail. He is pink cheeked and sweaty and looks like he might be overheated. His suit zipper is pulled down a little and I can see a patch of bare chest. He's wearing underwear, though, surely. I don't dare look down at his dinosaur crotch.

"Hey, hey, hey, girl," Sophie says, shimmying up to me.

"Hi! I'm so glad you came. You all look so fun!" I say, my hands clasped tightly together. I sound like an uptight fifty-something-year-old interacting with the local neighborhood teen-agers for the first time. Or Amber's book-club-hosting mother.

"Oh yeah. We had pizza and pre-drinks at Ruby's before we came, and she has a bunch of these onesies because her school had an animal-themed muck-up day, and we put them on as a joke, and then we thought, why not keep wearing them, you know, I mean, when you think about it, why do we, as a society, even wear *clothes*, they are just a social construct," Sophie says.

"Sure, sure, that makes sense," I say.

"We are no longer going to conform to society's arbitrary, bullshit 'beauty standards,'" Ruby says. "Well, at least not tonight. I do have to look good tomorrow morning in case that cute barista is working at the coffee shop."

"Fuck society and fuck society's expectations," Justin says, vigorously fanning his hot face and unzipping his suit a few more centimeters. "But yes, that barista is hot. You should wear that cute skirt you just bought."

"Oooh yes," Sophie says.

"Can I get you all a drink?" I say.

"We're good. We brought our own. And we drank quite a bit at home," Sophie says. She has the soft, gooey eyes of an emotional drunk who'll start crying later.

"Oh wait!" Ruby yells. "I forgot. We brought you a onesie too!"

"Yes," Sophie says, clapping her hands, and together they rummage through a grubby bookshop tote bag filled with clinking bottles until they pull out a bundle of cheap, fluro-yellow material with a flourish.

"Ta-da!" Ruby says. "It's a chicken!"

"Oh," I say. "Thank you." I hold it in my hands and consider what to do next. I am touched and pleased that they thought to include me, but the chicken suit looks pre-worn and I have no faith that Ruby has washed it since someone from her school might have worn it last year. Also, it's a *chicken suit*.

"Put it on," Jesse says gleefully from behind us, where he has apparently been listening to everything from the couch with great amusement. That makes me determined not to put it on.

"It might not fit," I say. I think I see some sweat stains on the fabric.

"It's one-size-fits-all," Ruby assures me.

"You don't have to," Sophie says kindly, touching my arm. "You look quite sober."

"Yeah, what are you drinking?" Justin says. His hood has fallen forward and the stegosaurus eyes are goggling at me.

"Oh nothing. I mean, nothing right this second."

"You need to catch up. Someone get this girl a drink!" he shouts.

"It's fine."

"No, no, you need a drink."

"I'm fine, truly."

"It's your party. You have to drink."

"I will, I will," I say.

I lead them to the corner of the room, where there are two beanbags. They recline on them and laugh and throw their legs over each other with a comfort that makes it seem like they've been friends for years. When we all first met in class, they asked me what school I went to (the first question everyone asks in every single class, I discovered), and when I told them, they all nodded politely, having obviously never heard of it. They went to big Melbourne private schools and had mutual friends and experiences and jokes, because Justin's ex-boyfriend was friends with Sophie's sister and Ruby had hung out with Justin's best friend one time, and they had an instant built-in scaffolding for their friendship. They were a threesome and I was an outsider from day one.

I perch awkwardly on the edge of one of the beanbags, still holding the chicken onesie, now folded neatly, in my lap. Do I sit with them for the rest of the night? Am I in charge of them, like a babysitter or a parent or, let's be generous, a fun, young aunt? I'm starting to think I would actually feel better if I was wearing the onesie.

Jesse comes over, holding the Polaroid camera that Harper told us was for taking photos of the party. That she insisted we use and take lots and lots of pictures.

"We'll put them all over the fridge," she said. "It'll be our house's thing!" She'd tried to take a photo of Jesse and me, but we both backed away.

"Let me get a picture for the fridge," Jesse says to us now. I am immediately suspicious that he's making fun of me, even though his tone is mild and friendly.

He holds the camera up and Ruby, Justin, and Sophie pose in increasingly silly ways against the wall, completely at ease in their costumes and with each other and the world, giggling joyfully at half jokes that make sense in their drunken minds, and I am filled with an overwhelming desire to be part of the group. Or part of Harper and Penny's group. Any group. I wish for anything other than what I have: my three new sort-of friends laughing uproariously while I hover anxiously to the side.

I think of Lauren saying to me once, "But don't you want to let go? Don't you want to *unclench*, just once?"

Unclench, unclench, unclench, I tell myself, but saying those words makes me clench my insides, my stomach, my jaw, my eyeballs, my mind, harder.

"Brooke, get in the picture," Jesse says, his eyes shining and his dimple-smile working overtime to charm everyone.

"Oh, no, I think I'm okay here," I say, fake smiling at him.

"Brooke, get in!" Sophie shouts. "Put the onesie on and get in."

"It's important for the future of this household that I get a shot of you in the chicken suit," Jesse says, grinning.

I narrow my eyes. Does he think I'm *afraid* to wear the

costume? That I'm scared of the judgment from him, and Amber, and his school friends and everyone else here? That I take myself so seriously I can't wear a chicken suit in front of strangers at my first party in Melbourne? Well, I'll show him. I determinedly haul the chicken onesie on over my dress and zip it up. I expect my self-consciousness to magically disappear once I am standing alongside the others in costume but, unfortunately, it doesn't. I can't let Jesse see that, though. He's only going to see the most carefree version of Brooke ever.

Justin, Ruby, and Sophie surround me and make funny faces for the camera and I smile wide—*unclench, unclench*—being a good sport, laughing along, and hamming it up. But secretly, I'm hot and itchy and overstimulated and a little bit tired, and I want to rip the suit off, go to the kitchen, and start tidying up while listening to a long podcast about a random topic like medieval nuns or the history of bread. A deeply absorbing activity where I can just relax and forget I even have a body or a to-do list or a "things I want to achieve this year" plan or big friendship-shaped holes in my life or sharp spikes of anxiety that I keep catching myself on or the memory of *Do I like Brooke? No. No. Fuck, no.* I just want to sink deep into my brain like it's a pristine empty swimming pool.

I'm not Fun Drunk Chicken Suit Girl, I will never be Fun Drunk Chicken Suit Girl, I know that, and everyone else here probably knows it too.

EIGHT

The thing about parties, especially parties with new people, is I always have to eventually face the Question. The Why-Don't-You-Drink Question, my least favorite question of all time.

You would think I would be used to it, after being asked endlessly all through high school. Even by people who know I don't drink, even occasionally by other people who don't drink themselves, by people who have known me for years, people who are expecting me to drive them home but who just can't help themselves in asking "But why?" and "But just this once, Brooke," and "Come on, Brookey, come on," and "BB, you would be so funny to see wasted, come on," and "Oh my God, can you imagine Brooke drunk?" and "We love you, come on, just for us."

I have a few different responses to the drinking question, depending on the situation.

"I'm on antibiotics, so I can't"—can be used only once or twice without inviting questions about what kind of ongoing medical issue I might have.

"I'm driving"—if I'm sure I won't be later hassled about driving them home.

"I don't like the taste"—never works.

"I'm not really a drinker"—people see this as a fun challenge.

"I *am* drinking!"— works only if I am holding something that looks like alcohol and runs a risk of me being exposed as a liar.

"I don't want to"—can lead to arguments or probing questions or "But why?"

"I had a bad experience once"—people want the story, they always want the story.

"No thanks, I'm not feeling well"—leads to people not wanting to be near you in case you're contagious.

"I'm pacing myself"—no one respects someone pacing themselves.

"I'm allergic to additives"—people start googling what drinks are available that you can have.

"It's against my beliefs"—then I either have to lie about being religious or create some kind of elaborate belief system that sits outside of religion.

"I'm on a cleanse"—sadly it's one of the most accepted excuses, although you need a detailed list of information about the cleanse because they always want to know what you are eating and drinking and more important *not* eating and *not* drinking and *exactly* how much weight you've lost and if it's worth it and how long it takes and how fast they would lose that weight if they were to do this imaginary cleanse and suddenly you're supporting someone else's disordered eating.

I don't drink because, well, the simplest explanation is, I don't want to. Of course, it's more complicated. It's layers of complication. First, there's Lauren. And Dad.

I have spent a lot of time googling "how to know if someone has a drinking problem." Reading books, reading forums, reading life-advice columns. But when so many people around you binge-drink, it's hard to know what the problem is—the person, or the small town, or the country, or the culture, or my age, or my personality, or my family, or my issues, or a very specific combination of it all.

After a big night, Lauren will emerge like a little fawn, unsure on her legs, but smiling, doe-eyed, innocent. It's all a funny story to her. Then I start to feel crazy. *Was* it funny? Am I remembering my dread, my jagged anxiety, my disgust, all wrong? Everyone else loves this thing, everyone else does it, and I don't, and I am the only one walking away with dark memories and trembling hands and a stomach that aches when I think someone I love is going out and might not be safe and in control. I must be the one in the wrong.

When I was growing up, people would say, "Your dad is fun." And he was. But he was the kind of fun that gave me an aching jaw from holding my mouth tight. He was the kind of fun that made me not trust having fun. I have never relaxed around Dad. I didn't actually realize that until I realized the clenching I feel about Lauren I first felt about Dad. Well, it's not quite the same. With Dad, it was *I don't like who you are when you're drinking, even though everyone else does*. With Lauren, it's more *I am so tired of being scared of what might happen to you*.

I need to be sober to make sure everyone else is safe. I need to feel in control. Being in control of myself is the most important factor to me feeling *okay*. If I don't feel like me, true me, real me, then I feel out of sync with the world in a way that makes me feel like I might fall off the planet or stop breathing. I need to be grounded in my me-ness to exist, to keep going, to not get sucked into an am-I-good-enough-have-I-done-enough-will-I-ever-be-enough anxiety tornado. Being drunk would be messy, dangerous, out of control. My worst self might come out.

NINE

It's two a.m. and Ruby, Justin, and Sophie have just left, and I am finally alone, in my room. I'm still wearing the chicken onesie, because taking it off before the night was officially over seemed like admitting defeat—although keeping it on hasn't exactly felt like a win.

Justin, predictably, asked me a lot of questions about not drinking, and I deflected by asking them how their short stories for class were going, which then triggered Sophie into a full spiral about her story ("I read back over it and I realized, nothing happens. It's about *nothing*. Nothing! There's no climax, there's no conflict, there's no plot. It's literally just people talking and a dream sequence!"), which has now triggered me into my own spiral about my story, because all of Sophie's problems are my problems, and I'm torn between getting my laptop out right now to read over it or going to the kitchen to do a quick tidy first because I can't sleep knowing there are empty bottles sitting around not in the recycling bin and I should double-check a drunk person didn't turn on the oven, just for peace of mind.

I'm walking out of my bedroom when there is a bloodcurdling scream and a crash, and Jesse and Amber emerge from his room, disheveled and yelling incoherently.

Jesse is shirtless, something my brain eagerly notes. *No. I refuse to acknowledge he is attractive, I refuse to acknowledge his body, even in the privacy of my own mind.*

"Oh my God, oh my God, oh my God," Amber is screaming, and then she launches herself at Jesse, trying to climb onto his back, arms and legs flailing.

"What is going on?" I say.

Harper and Penny arrive in the hallway, both in pajamas: Harper in a loose black tank top and pants and Penny in a gorgeous green silk matching singlet and shorts. Penny is holding a bottle of lotion, and she's rubbing it into her arms as she looks on with concern.

"What happened? Are you okay?" she asks.

"There was a motherfucking mouse!" Jesse yells. Amber is now on his back, in a full piggyback, her arms squeezing his neck so tight that I'm surprised he can breathe.

Harper and I make eye contact.

"It's probably the same one we saw," she says.

"In my bedroom," I add.

"You saw a mouse? And no one told me?" Jesse yelps.

"We were worried you'd overreact," I say, which is a lie. We just forgot to tell him, but seeing him and Amber emerge together from his bedroom has given me the sudden urge to be mean.

Amber gives a little sob. Her top is only halfway on, and I'm worried about a nip slip, so I look away respectfully.

"Brooke was much calmer when she saw it than you two," Harper says, and I smile at her. You know what, I *was* calm and dignified, in hindsight.

"It's probably not even the same mouse! There could be hundreds of them for all we know," Jesse says, frantically looking around like a plague is about to come swarming down the hallway. "And I am calm," he adds, his voice deepening.

"Don't drop me!" Amber shouts at him, tightening her grip on his neck. She looks at Harper and Penny. "I need to leave. You don't understand. I hate, hate, hate mice."

"Okay, okay, we understand," Penny says soothingly, snapping the lid back on her lotion bottle. "I'll get your things."

"My bra is on the floor by Jesse's bed, and my bag is on the couch!" she yells as Jesse piggybacks her outside. She looks at me. "And could you maybe bring me a glass of water and are there any of those little food platters left? Because I'd love, like, a grape, a single grape, right now."

"Um," I say. "Sure." I don't love being treated like a waitress, but she *is* upset and I know the pain of seeing a mouse in a bedroom. I get her a glass of water and a bunch of grapes (putting a single grape on a plate felt like a step too far), and I even add a lemon slice to the water, and carry it all outside, where everyone is waiting for Amber's Uber.

"Here you go," I say. Even braless and in distress, Amber looks pretty and put-together. I am acutely aware that I am still in the chicken suit.

"Thanks, sweetie," she says, taking the glass and drinking the water. I try to keep my face impassive even though it makes my eye twitch to be called sweetie by people my own age.

"Oh my God, this is one of the most traumatizing nights of my life," Amber says, picking grapes off the plate I am holding. "I am never going in your plague house again."

Harper looks offended and I give her a sympathetic smile and escape back into the house. I clean the kitchen, wash my face, and get changed into my pajamas. On my way to bed, I pass Jesse, now wearing a T-shirt, peering under the couch with his phone torchlight.

"Still worried about the mouse?" I say.

"Just checking where it might be."

"You made quite the scene," I say.

"You can talk, in your chicken outfit," he says, glancing up at me and holding eye contact for a beat too long.

Later, while I'm trying to sleep, having stuffed a towel under my door just in case the mouse comes back to my room, Jesse's shirtless body pops into my head, and I squash it down. No. Do not think of that. Do not think of his shoulders, or his chest, or any part of him. Even if we didn't have any history, he's not my type. Not anymore. My type is, well, I don't know exactly. I thought it was Tristan, my ex-boyfriend, but I think I thought he was my type only because he liked me, and "person who likes me" seemed like a useful type to have.

Tristan was cute. He photographed well, he always smelled nice, he smelled *clean*, he was the kind of guy who always washed his hands before eating, he wore button-down shirts, he got regular haircuts, he had excellent manners. Both his parents are psychologists, and he is their only child, the focus of their lives. He rarely swore. He helped me at school. When I had a lot on, when I overcommitted to things, he would say, "What can I do?" And he wasn't just saying it, he really meant it. He was organized, and smart, and he challenged me. He was the best study partner I ever had.

Tristan was also good at romance. Or maybe not good, but enthusiastic. He wrote me a poem once, which on the surface sounds like a beautiful gesture. But when he handed it to me to read in front of him, I felt my soul briefly leave my body. Reading a poem in front of the person who had written it for me was my worst nightmare, I suddenly realized. And Tristan didn't even like English, he was a science and maths nerd. Whenever I talked about books, he would remind me that he read *The Lord of the Rings* every year, or he said he did, although sometimes he just watched the movies instead. That was the extent of his involvement in literature. But maybe he was a poet. I don't know who gets to decide these things. I also don't know how you know if a poem is any good, but I didn't want to try to figure that out while someone was watching me.

I thought maybe the poem would rhyme and be sweet and fun. My darling Brooke, my heart swells at just a look—something like that. I could enjoy that.

The poem wasn't rhyming.

I read it, twice, in respectful silence, and then looked up at him. I still remember it, line for line.

> *The sky, limp and gray*
> *The ground, damp and hard*
> *My life, plain like an empty field*
> *And then you came along*
> *And made my buds bloom.*

He was leaning forward, his face open, excited to hear what I think.

"I love it," I said, swallowing and smiling hard.

"I thought you would," he said.

I didn't love it.

I loved that he'd written it for me. No, that's not true either. I *wanted* to love that he'd written it for me. I definitely *appreciated* that he'd written it for me. Some people will go through their whole lives without someone writing a romantic poem for them and now I could tick that box off, nice and early.

There were just so many words in it that I didn't like. Specifically, the word "limp." And the word "damp" right near the word "hard." And I definitely wish I had never seen the word "buds" in there. I *made* his buds bloom. It's a very aggressive image. Especially when you factor in that I had touched the penis of the person who wrote it.

And it was just printed on regular A4 paper. Arial font, size 12, left aligned at the top of the page. Then his name and, for some absurd reason, the copyright symbol after it.

Did he choose that font and presentation, or just go with the default when he opened a Word doc? I thought maybe he might have bought some nice thick, creamy paper, increased the font size, framed it, laminated it, just put more effort into the final product. Now I had a loose piece of paper to deal with, and I wasn't sure if I should fold it up or keep it crease-free and put it in a manila folder or something. I had a home laminator, but I didn't want to commit to lamination.

In a fit of mistaken need, I shared the poem with Mum, Nanna, and Lauren. Mum said, "Before anyone says anything, let's remember that we like Tristan." Lauren screamed with laughter and committed it to memory almost instantly. Nanna asked to read it on the page and spent a long time staring at it. "Do not marry this boy," she said to me. "If you do, do not let him read this at the wedding, because he'll want to." I was then in the awkward position of defending this poem that I didn't even like, but I felt obliged to not let Tristan become an object of derision among my family.

Tristan made me anxious when we were alone, because I was worried about him saying "I love you" and then me having to say it back. I felt deficient as a girlfriend, maybe as a person, that I didn't love him. Because Tristan was a sweetheart, perfect for me in every way, so who was I to not love him? Did I think I could do better than him? Certainly not. But I didn't feel it. Whatever *it* is. The spark. Chemistry. Love, the beginnings of love.

The whole thing was complicated because while I was afraid that he liked me too much, I was also deathly afraid that he didn't like me enough. I didn't want him to love me but I didn't want him to *not* love me, because that would be worse. It was kind of a lose-lose situation.

When I posted a picture of the peonies he bought me for our three-month anniversary on social media, it was my most liked post all year. When I put up pictures we took in one of those little photo booths, our faces squished together, being as cute as possible, people posted love hearts in the comments. It felt so good to not only feel like I was adored, but to have others witness it. In my head, secretly, I was still escaping the incident with Jesse. *Look, everyone, look at my life, my enviable life. Look at how much Tristan loves me, even though he has never actually said that and the thought gives me anxiety sweats and nausea late at night, and I'm terrified I am not capable of either giving or receiving love.*

And then, Tristan caught me off guard.

He said we needed to talk about something serious. *Here it comes*, I thought. I braced, ready to receive his declaration of love.

"I'm in love with someone else," he said.

I almost laughed, I was so shocked.

"Who?" I said in disbelief.

His childhood friend, Kendra. They'd been best friends for years. I knew her, but she didn't go to our school, so we'd met only a handful of times. He had been in love with her for a long time, he said. As long as he could remember. He'd just never admitted it to himself until now.

It was a gut punch. Tristan was my emotional safety net. I had thought he was the kind of guy who would never leave me, never hurt me, never choose anyone else over me.

But he had never truly wanted me at all.

TEN

This is it. Today is the day I am going to start running. I will officially be a *runner* in about an hour, after I complete a lap of the Tan, the running track that is both conveniently nearish to my house and the first result when I googled "best place to run in Melbourne." I'm trying to keep my expectations reasonable, but there's a lot of pressure on this first run. It needs to be my first step toward fitness. It needs to unlock all of my creativity. It needs to turn me into the kind of person I imagine a runner to be: strong, energized, arrogant but in an attractive, powerful way. I am also hoping it will cure my insomnia, expose me to enough sunshine to instantly increase my vitamin D levels, stop the weird ache in my lower stomach that I woke up with this morning, and squash the anxiety that comes with my new, all-encompassing crisis of the day: Dad is in Melbourne for work and wants to have dinner with me tonight.

Lauren said, "Don't go, just say no. Tell him you're busy—he's only given you twenty-four hours' notice." But I haven't seen him in almost a year—no, wait, it's been more than a year—and I'm not busy. And what kind of daughter pretends to be busy to get out of dinner with the father she never sees?

"You'll regret it," Lauren said.

"I won't," I insisted. The sun is shining, I'm about to *go running*, my life is full of potential, and maybe everything will be different. Maybe Dad and I will go out for dinner and we'll laugh and bond and have a surprisingly great and normal time.

When I was younger, I would prepare a list of topics to discuss with him on phone calls, a minimum of ten, because several of them would not lead to anything beyond an "Oh that's interesting, sweetheart" from him and then I needed to scramble to the next thing when he asked no follow-up questions. Now I don't bother with that, I just ask him about his favorite topics (wine, his fantasy football team, flying drones, paddleboarding) and nod along.

At worst, tonight's dinner will give me some new funny stories to share with Mum and Nanna. Lauren and I like to give Mum little offerings of the most out-of-touch things Dad says, as a reward for raising us mostly on her own. At best, though, Dad and I might really connect. Despite all his flaws, I still love him. The fun I had with him growing up was not when he was socializing and having what he thought of as fun, but the times when we played chess together, or he taught us how to play poker, or pretended to be a monster and chased us screaming through the house, or when we watched movies on a Saturday afternoon and he set up a barrier of couch cushions that Lauren and I could hide behind in the scary bits. I hold on to these memories tightly, as proof. I secretly hope that maybe he's the kind of person who struggled with the responsibility of being a parent to kids, but now that I'm eighteen and living out of home, an adult of sorts, there's less pressure on him, and he could do better. He didn't have to tell me he was in Melbourne, I would never have known. He *wants* to see me.

I walk from our house to the Tan, do some stretches, pull my shoulders back. The plan is: walk for two minutes, run for two minutes, and continue like that around the whole loop. Maybe even run for three minutes if I'm feeling good. Simple.

At first, it works well. Apart from a weird stomach pain, I feel okay. I push a bit on my two minutes of running, thinking the harder I run, the faster I will find solutions to my life. Or the sooner I will feel the famous runner's high. I could really do with that right now. Except my left hamstring starts to hurt, and two minutes is suddenly a *very* long time, and my right hamstring is also hurting but in a different way to the left one, I am sure I can feel two—no, wait, three—blisters forming, my bra isn't really giving me the kind of support I want, and the stabbing pain in my gut is getting more and more intense.

I'm slowing right down, my face getting hotter and sweatier, when I look up and see Jesse running toward me. Fuck. He's running fast, and smoothly, and no, there's absolutely no way I can let him see me right now, death would be preferable. I look around for somewhere to hide. There's nowhere, of course.

I can't see anything clearly with sweat pouring into my eyes but I am certain he's seen me and he's probably smirking too, I can just sense it. Maybe I can still fix this, I can still look good. I start running faster, my legs feeling like wobbly sticks of butter, melting and shuddering with every step, my shoes gripping my toes like a bear trap, my pelvis crunching with pain, my face feeling three times its normal size. I have forgotten what I am supposed to do with my hands and arms while running—they feel like they are swinging too much. Despite all this effort, I might actually be going slower than I was before.

We've almost reached each other now. I'm going to visualize myself as cool and calm. Fake it until you make it, and who knows, maybe I actually look really good right now. Maybe I look like the sleek Lycra-clad women who keep flying past me. I really could be going much faster than I realize.

Is he going to say hi to me? Am I going to say hi to him? This is worse than the tram situation. Maybe just a head nod. That seems like something runners do. I am arranging my face into an expression of polite disdain, when the pain in my abdomen sharpens suddenly, like someone has slipped a knife into my side and now they're turning it.

I swallow a yelp and stop shuffle-running and bend over, walking to the side of the track and then kneeling down. I don't want to be kneeling. It feels very dramatic, and I especially don't want to be kneeling in front of *Jesse*. I would almost rather die. But I don't have a choice, the pain is bending me in two, and I very well might be dying.

Jesse is suddenly beside me, panting and sweating over the top of me.

"Are you okay?" he asks, sucking in air and pushing his hair back.

"I'm fine," I say, suppressing a moan.

"You don't look fine," he says.

"My stomach hurts a bit, that's all." I say stomach but it's lower. My ovaries, my uterus, my bladder maybe. Something in that vicinity. I don't want to give him this level of detail. My pelvis is my private business.

"Like a stitch?" he asks.

"Sort of. Not really," I say. I want to be magically transported home to my bed and not have anyone look at me or be near me while I crunch in pain under a blanket and cry. Which is how I often feel on the first few days of my period, but this pain is sharper and more intense than anything I've ever had before, and my period isn't due.

"Do you know what a stitch feels like?" Jesse asks, which I find to be a very condescending question.

"Yes, I know what a stitch feels like. I played netball for years," I say. He's not the only sporty one here. He doesn't need to know my chief contribution to the team was making sure we had substitute players when people didn't show up and paying the team fees on time.

He blinks and makes a noise in his throat in response to this, or maybe in response to my tone, which was snappy, and for a second I think he's going to turn and continue on with his run, and panic fills my chest. But he squats down next to me.

"I'm trying to help you," he says in a gentle voice. "I know you said you never wanted my help again, but I think you need it." Now he kind of sounds like he's talking to a frightened dog.

"It's not a stitch," I say to him. I am trying to sound firm and authoritative, but my voice has an edge of desperation now.

"Is it a sharp pain or a dull pain?" he says.

"It was dull when I woke up this morning and now it's sharp," I say. Kneeling isn't giving me enough relief, so I lie down and press the painful side into the grass, and the pressure helps a bit.

Maybe it's a UTI. A kidney stone. A blockage or a rupture in the small intestine. I remember reading an article where a man swallowed an AirPod in the night and I panic for a second until I remember that I don't own AirPods. But could I have swallowed something else? Every medical show I've ever watched comes screaming into my mind. Maybe I've given myself a stomach ulcer through stress. How embarrassing. I'm still in my first semester of my first year. I haven't even had any exams yet.

The pain is getting worse.

"You look really pale. I think I should call someone," Jesse says, pulling out his phone.

I have no idea who "someone" is in this context. I have no

one in the city to call. Dad? The very thought is a joke. The idea of him helping me in a medical crisis involving my pelvis is . . . no. It's taking all my optimism to picture us having a pleasant dinner together tonight. Mum? She's away with her two best friends for a weekend in Daylesford, a long overdue birthday present that she's been saving for and planning for months. I am not ruining her weekend and asking her to drive two hours to me for what might be a weird flash of period pain, or bad gas, or simply my body violently rejecting the idea of being a runner.

I'm writhing a little in the grass now, which sounds like it could be sexy, but it's most definitely not. I can't get comfortable. I shimmy around until I'm holding myself at an odd angle, grimacing.

"Don't call anyone," I say.

A new thought hits me. A nightmarish thought. What if I'm one of those people who got pregnant without realizing it and now I'm about to give birth? No, not possible. Tristan and I had sex a total of four times last year, and each time we did, we were incredibly careful. We were so careful we were smug about it. I even took pregnancy tests to be doubly sure. And I've gotten my period every month, heavy and unpleasant and like clockwork, for the past year. But, but, but. All those horror stories they told us in school. That one video I saw online. That you can get pregnant even when using a condom, you can get pregnant even if they pull out, even if you're on the Pill. You can somehow be pregnant and not have a single symptom or gain any weight or notice anything different or lose your period or get a positive pregnancy test. Yes, all of those things at once are extremely unlikely but not *impossible*. I could be the outlier. Someone must be the one in a million, and it's me and it's now and my life is over.

I look up at Jesse and try to imagine saying, *I'm giving birth.*

Or worse. *I'm giving birth and there's no time, you'll have to deliver the baby, here, at the Tan, with attractive runners passing us in their matching bike shorts and crop tops—please limit the number of people who will see my vagina.* I can feel a rising hysteria, which might flow out of me as laughter or tears, I'm not sure which. I'll be the girl who gave birth at the Tan. My child will be known as the Tan Baby. The story will go viral, and worst of all, Jesse will be the hero.

Stop. Calm down. Think rationally. This is not labor. I know I am not pregnant. I know this isn't labor.

"Where exactly is the pain?" Jesse is kneeling down beside me.

"Here," I say, pointing to the right side of my pelvis. "And also my whole stomach, I guess. It's kind of radiating out."

"Hmmm. Okay." Jesse pulls out his phone and starts typing.

"What are you doing?" I look up at him pathetically.

"Googling all the major organs," he says.

I lie back a little and close my eyes. I picture myself dying, ascending to the clouds. Except I can't die right now. I am the least popular and least successful I have ever been. I need to hold on until I get that big assignment back so I can see if I get a 100 percent. And I bought that new mascara online that had its delivery delayed.

"Well?" I say, looking up at him. "Which organs are we worried about?"

"Well, there's your heart."

"My heart is up here, you have no idea what you're doing, give me that phone," I say, holding out my hand and groaning a little. I do not have the patience for his incompetence.

"Yes, I know where your heart is, but my aunt had a heart attack, and her only symptoms were a sore arm and stomach pain," Jesse says. "We can't rule anything out yet."

Jesse zooms in on something on his phone, squints, looks at me, zooms in again. What is he *looking* at? Then he squats next to me and takes my wrist in his hand.

"I'm going to check your pulse."

"Okay." That seems proactive, at least.

We sit in silence as he counts my heartbeats. A little concentration line appears between his eyes. It's very intimate, I realize, the counting of heartbeats. His hand on my wrist. His lips move slightly as he counts. I smother a little whimper of pain.

"Is it too fast?" I say.

"I don't know yet."

We wait, and then he looks up.

"It's fine. Beating at a normal speed. Normal-ish."

"Normal-*ish*?"

"Well, you've been running. So, it's going pretty fast."

"So it could still be a heart attack?"

"Technically, yes."

"Look, I think it's just really bad period pain or something," I say, turning away from him. It's not that the words "period pain" are inherently that embarrassing, but it's humiliating to say them to Jesse while lying out dramatically on a bit of grass during the first run I have ever attempted. Being in pain, in public, feels intensely personal and revealing. I don't have control of my body. I am trapped inside something that is malfunctioning. And that is scary as hell.

"Should I call an ambulance?" Jesse says. "It could be your appendix bursting."

"No!" An ambulance. How ridiculous. You need to be screaming in pain for an ambulance. I am only in lightly writhing, soft-moaning pain.

"What then?" He sounds frustrated but he puts his hand gently on my arm, and it feels surprisingly warm and soothing.

"I'll just lie here until I feel better." My voice is shaky.

"I'm not sure that's the best plan."

"Well, it's my plan. So get on board."

"Okay," he says. I curl into a ball and deep breathe, and he sits next to me, and I can hear him breathing in tandem with me, his hand on my back. It's extremely comforting to know I am not alone out here, to have his hand on me, but I don't want him to know that. I don't want to feel that. I want to hate his hand on me, I want to hate his very presence, I want to be strong enough to not need anyone right now, but especially, especially not him.

I squeeze my eyes shut as tight as possible and count to thirty. By the time I reach thirty, the pain seems to be receding a little, and then a little more.

"It feels a bit better," I say. I'm too scared to move.

"Okay. Here's what we'll do. My car is parked not far away. I'm going to run and get it, pick you up, and drive us home, okay?" he says.

"Okay," I say. "That sounds good." I know I should say thank you, for being with me, for getting your car, for not dismissing my pain, for checking my pulse, for comforting me, for not leaving, but I can't quite bring myself to. It's too much, to be lying on the ground in a public place and then to have to be grateful to him. *This does not make us even. I do not forgive you.*

ELEVEN

I have changed outfits four times for this dinner with Dad. Which, when you consider the fact that my pelvic pain has remained fairly intense all afternoon and I am walking around with a heating pad pressed to my stomach, is the equivalent of changing outfits ten times or more. I texted Dad a list of restaurant options, all of which look nice and trendy but are reasonably priced, in case I need to pay. I won't need to pay—he'll pay, I'm sure he'll pay—but I like to be prepared, just in case. Everything with Dad is *just in case*.

He didn't reply to any of these messages. Then I offered to pick a place and make the booking. Still no reply. It's midafternoon now and we have no plan, no restaurant, no time. I need to know where I'm going, figure out how I'm going to get there, what I'm going to wear, look at the menu online ahead of time and decide what I will eat. I imagine this is what dating is like when you're an adult. Or maybe even now, as a semi-adult. Just desperate hopeful text messages, sent out into the ether, and nothing. Being ghosted by your own father is surely worse than being ghosted by a date.

I text Lauren, who replies with, "I told you not to do this dinner," and, "It's Dad, none of this is surprising." Which is not helpful, but it's also soothing—that she knows, that someone knows. I remain stubbornly hopeful.

Lauren and I talk about Dad, but only in small ways, making fun of him, gently nudging against our issues, but never really delving into it all in a meaningful way. Lauren doesn't enjoy delving into things as a general rule. But sometimes I want her to, sometimes I wish we could share every memory, every screwed-up thing, get it all out and recorded and signed off on, stamped and official, into the Dad files, and then we put it away, close the book on it, maybe start a new chapter.

When I was seven and Lauren was nine, a few years before he moved away, Dad came to pick us up from a birthday party. It was an after-school party for a friend of Lauren's, and I had been allowed to tag along. Dad had been out for a long work lunch, and when he got there, he was wearing sunglasses, and his nose was red, and he was slurring his words a little. A few of the other mothers noticed, and they got together in a huddle and then told Lauren and me that Millie's mum would drive us home, and they wouldn't let Dad take us in the car. Dad was angry, and there was a scene. Not a big scene. He didn't swear or scream. In fact, he was kind of sweet and charming about it at first. That was his thing—when he was drunk, he was funny and appealing, people tended to like him. But not on this day. The charm didn't work. He got annoyed, then he got nasty. I could see it in his eyes, the flash of concealed anger. He said they were being over the top, that they were out of line, that we were his kids, he was fine, he'd had a glass of wine with lunch. But the mothers held the line, and when Millie's mum dropped us at our house, Dad said nothing to her and nothing to Mum. It was like it didn't happen.

There were so many moments like this that we just absorbed, never mentioned to Mum, never talked about.

I brought that one up to Lauren once, when we were teenagers, and she said she vaguely remembered, maybe. I couldn't get over that. "How can you not remember?" I said.

"I remember," she said. "Of course I remember. I remember that time and all the others. I just don't want to dwell on any of it."

"Dwelling is healthy," I assured her. She didn't think so.

So, we don't talk about it.

At four p.m., Dad messages me to say that he has made a booking at a restaurant on the other side of the city. An upscale, expensive steak house, the kind of place that has $55 steaks and their accompanying sauces on the menu and nothing else, the kind of place that I definitely can't afford and will be difficult to get to and doesn't really fit with my complicated relationship with red meat (I don't eat it except when I'm craving a burger or a cheap sausage in bread). But there is a plan, at least. An inconvenient, annoying plan, but a plan nonetheless. I need to look on the bright side, to manifest a positive outcome. I imagine Dad and me laughing over hunks of meat.

I take some painkillers, and now I'm sitting on the couch, heat pad on my abdomen, convincing myself I am not really in pain, not *desperate* pain anyway, when Harper and Penny walk in.

"I bought us a lamp from IKEA!" Harper says. "And this blue-and-pink-striped pot, or maybe it's a vase. I'm not really sure what it's for but I like the look of it." She pauses and looks at me. "Are you okay?" she says, seeing the heat pad.

"Fine, I just have some cramps," I say. "I'm getting ready to have dinner with my dad."

Jesse appears in the doorway. "It's more serious than she's saying. It might be her appendix," he says as if I can't hear him.

"It's fine." I frown at him.

"You collapsed at the Tan," he says, glowering back at me, arms folded.

"Collapsed!" Penny gasps.

"He's exaggerating. I sat down on the grass, that's all," I say. Jesse's insistence on making this a big deal is making me determined to prove that it isn't. *You're wrong, and you don't know me.*

"Brooke, that sounds serious," Harper says. "You shouldn't go out."

"It's fine, really. Plus I haven't seen my dad in a long time, and he's really excited to have dinner," I say. "Really excited" might be an exaggeration but I have no proof that he's *not* really excited, so I'm running with it.

"It could be your gallbladder. My mum had gallstones and she said it was worse than childbirth," Penny says with concern.

"My dad thought he had gallstones but he had a hernia. Is there anything, like, pushing out of your stomach?" Harper asks.

"No!" I say, horrified at the thought, but I touch all over just in case. Why does everyone have to have a bad story? Why can't one of them say, "My cousin had really bad pain one day and it turned out to be absolutely nothing at all and the next day her skin was glowing and she met the love of her life and adopted a puppy"?

Penny frowns and looks at Jesse.

"You should drive her to the restaurant," she says.

"Yes," Harper says.

"No!" My voice is close to shouting. "No," I say again, more calmly. "I'll get an Uber." I can't really afford an Uber, but I do not want Jesse to drive me.

"I can drive you," Jesse says, and he grabs his keys off the table.

Penny and Harper smile encouragingly at him. Ugh. Saint Jesse. Martyr Jesse. He'll be giving himself feel-good credits for helping me out: he'll go to sleep tonight thinking, *I'm such a good person for helping poor, pathetic Brooke today.*

"It's fine, really," I say, sitting up a bit and trying very hard to keep my face neutral, no annoyance, no pain. Let nothing show.

"Don't be silly, let Jesse drive you," Harper says, looking at me with concern. I open my mouth to reply but then think of the "no drama" house rule.

"Fine," I say to Harper. "I appreciate your help," I say to Jesse, hoping he picks up the dark undertones in my words.

He smiles. "Happy to give it," he says. "Not a big deal."

It might be the pain I'm in, but his face, I realize at this moment, has a very slappable quality.

I walk slowly out to the car behind him.

"Have you taken some painkillers, or an anti-inflammatory?" he asks.

I want to scream, "Stop helping me! Stop pretending you care!" I don't say this, obviously, but the urge to be mean, to test his niceness—to prove how flimsy it is, that he'll turn it off at the slightest obstacle, that he'll abandon me—is overwhelming.

"Yes," I say, trying to sound pleasant and also walk normally, even though I really need to press into the painful area with my fingertips to take the edge off the pain.

"I wasn't doing anything tonight anyway," he says, getting in the car. "It's not a big deal. Driving you."

"When you keep saying something isn't a big deal, it makes it sound like it is a big deal," I say, opening the car door.

"Well, when you keep resisting help and telling people you're fine, it makes it sound like you're not," he says, starting the car.

I show him how to get to the restaurant and then look out the window and ignore him until my guilt kicks in. I huff out a sigh.

"Thank you for driving me, and helping me earlier, and checking my pulse and all of that," I say in a rush, because I don't want to seem ungrateful, and I also don't want him to have any possible reason to think he's a better person than me.

"You're welcome," he replies.

We drive in silence and I tap my fingers on the seat, which I know is annoying, but I can't help it. I'm a finger tapper, a pen clicker, a nail biter, when I'm nervous. And the closer we get to the restaurant, the more nervous I feel. I want to get my phone out and double-check what I look like—Dad hasn't seen my face in person in so long—but I can't do that in front of Jesse, so instead I tap my fingers and practice in my head the things I'm going to say. I even spent some time this afternoon googling drones and paddleboarding. I can do this. It's good that I'm going to do this. We're going to bond, we're going to have fun, the whole night is going to be better than I expected, and I'm just going to casually keep one hand inside the waist of my pants and pressed into my pelvis while eating to reduce the pain.

We're almost there when my phone lights up with a message from Dad.

Hey darling, I'm really sorry to do this last minute, but I'm caught up with work people. Can we reschedule, do brunch tomorrow instead? Thanks, Dad xxx

Of course. Of course, of course, of course.

Of course he canceled at the last minute.

TWELVE

I do have this recurring fantasy about Dad. One where I'm not picturing repairing our relationship, or starting over, or finding common ground—all the things I try to keep at the forefront when I think about him. This other fantasy is about having a fight with Dad. The Fight. Where I yell at him in ways that make me feel ashamed to think about. I imagine reaching deep inside and touching anger, nothing but intoxicating anger, all the way down. I imagine just letting go and saying the cruelest things—things I won't be able to come back from, things that would hurt him so badly, things that would haunt him, things he would never, ever get over, and saying it all in front of his girlfriend and his work friends and strangers and Mum and Nanna and Lauren and anyone else I can think of. Really letting loose. And, God, it would feel so good.

That anger, that imagined fight, the perfect punishment, comes to me again now as I sit in Jesse's car, still heading toward the restaurant, looking at Dad's text, my abdomen on fire. Except now I'm starting to worry that even if I screamed every nasty, dark thought I'd ever had at him, threw every barb and weapon I have, it wouldn't affect him at all. He might just shrug and move on, and this huge power I imagined I secretly had over him is no power at all.

"Um," I say, clearing my throat a little, not really sure whether to tell Jesse that my dinner is canceled or just get dropped off at the restaurant and pretend everything is fine.

"Yeah?" Jesse says, looking over.

My face is red, I can tell. I'm hot with anger, and embarrassment, and pain, and I'm not very far away from crying, even though this is the kind of thing I have vowed never to cry over, and it's not even in the top ten of ways Dad has let me down. It's nothing, it's just a dinner, I can go home and lie in bed with a heat pad now, I should be happy, I am happy, I just need to get past all the other feelings first.

"Do you want me to park or just drop you out the front?" Jesse continues when I don't say anything.

"Well, my dad just texted me to cancel, actually, so you don't need to, we can . . . we can just drive home," I say, babbling, not knowing how to finish the sentence.

"*What?* Your dad canceled your dinner? The one we're driving to right now?"

"Yeah, he's caught up with work stuff. We'll have brunch tomorrow."

We won't have brunch tomorrow. Dad knows it, and I know it. He'll be busy or hungover or something will happen. I roll my eyes at Jesse, so he can see that this is a minor annoyance but mostly nothing. It's nothing, no problem. "Not a big deal," as Jesse would say. My face still feels warm, I know my skin is betraying me right now, and I'm chewing on my thumbnail.

"That's really shit," Jesse says. He's looking at me with pity eyes. I do not want pity from him, not now, not ever.

"What can you do?" I say, shrugging, looking out the window, pressing into my abdomen.

"I get it," he says.

I turn slightly toward him.

"Get what?" I say after letting the silence hang for a while.

"What it's like to have a shitty dad," he says. If he thinks I'm going to ask him questions, be his therapist, he can think again. I don't want him offering me crumbs of his own trauma.

"Congratulations. Let's start a club," I say.

"Great, I'll be president and you can be secretary," he says, and I can't stop myself from glaring at him, at the very idea he would have the leadership role over me in our fictional club, even though I know he said it only to get that very reaction.

He looks at my face and laughs.

He thinks he knows me so well. I swallow down the sarcastic remark I was going to say in return. I don't have the energy.

We drive in silence for a few more minutes, now heading back toward our house, before he speaks again.

"You're in a lot of pain," he says. For a minute, I think he means emotional pain, about my dad, and I'm about to yell at him to mind his damn business, but then I realize he probably means the abdominal pain.

"It still hurts, yes," I say.

"That's it. We're going to the emergency room," he says.

"No!" I say.

"Yes."

"I can't! I don't have anything on me."

"What do you need?"

"Clothes! And, other stuff." I can't think of exactly what I need right this second, but I know I can't go to the *hospital* like this, without a big bag of stuff, without a plan, without hours of consideration and a pro–con list, without my mum, my GP, and a nurse on call all approving the decision.

"Harper can bring you clothes if they want to keep you overnight."

Oh God. Overnight in hospital. I am sweating.

"I can't just *go* to the emergency room. It's for people who are bleeding and dying."

"It's for people who are in need of urgent care. You might be bleeding internally. We don't know."

"I'm not ready!"

"It's the emergency room. By its very nature, people who go there aren't ready."

I start making a list in my phone of all the things I will need at the hospital. My skin cleanser, my moisturizer, my good pajamas, a hairbrush, a toothbrush, at least six pairs of clean, sensible, full-coverage underwear, a cozy cardigan, a blanket, a clean pillowcase, the book I'm reading, a backup book, a second backup book because who knows what kind of mood I'll be in, my laptop, my laptop charger, a water bottle, snacks, my passport maybe, or even my birth certificate (I'm not sure why but I want the highest form of identification), a cute T-shirt and maybe headband in case I need to do a hospital-bed selfie with bad bed hair. Wait, do I even own a headband? Or know where my birth certificate is? I put question marks against these items on my list.

We get to the hospital and into the emergency department. I feel like a fraud walking in, but Jesse steers me up to the counter. He sits in the waiting room while someone takes my details, asks me questions about the pain, my periods, my history, if I could be pregnant. Am I sure, am I really, really sure, they'll check for me anyway but am I sure? I answer as if my answers are getting graded. I would like an A+ on my emergency room form, please.

"Okay, head over there and we'll call you when someone is free. You're lucky, it's not busy right now, you'll be seen in a couple of hours," the woman says, sounding bored. This is nothing to her, this is her working day.

I walk back to Jesse, who is sitting in the corner, away from the myriad other people.

"It could be a while," I say. This is his opening to escape, to leave.

"How are you feeling?" he says.

"I'm okay. It hurts, but the worst pain was on the run. It's probably nothing."

"Should you call your mum?"

"I don't want to ruin her weekend away. She'll freak out. I'll call her when I've seen the doctor."

"Okay." He looks at me like he thinks this is a bad idea. He also doesn't look like he's about to leave.

"You really don't need to wait with me," I say. Obviously, I will cry if he leaves me alone, but I also must push him to leave.

"I'll wait," he says cheerfully, like it's a fun prospect for a Saturday night.

"You don't *need* to, though." This clarification is important. I am not asking him to stay. I am not asking Jesse for help. I do not owe him anything. *Let it be noted on the record, let the history books reflect the truth of the matter. Let me have this technicality, Your Honor.*

"Brooke. I'm not doing you a favor. I want to wait here," he says.

"Oh sure. Everyone loves hanging out in the emergency room. It has such a lovely, upbeat atmosphere," I say.

"Exactly. The smell, the people, the sounds, the germs. I'm just excited to soak it all up."

I hide a smile. I pull out my phone and start googling phrases like "sudden abdominal pain death" and "top ten signs you are going to die" and Jesse looks over my shoulder and sighs.

"You're going to be fine," he says.

"You only say that to someone if you think there's a chance they won't be fine, so it actually reinforces the idea of being not fine."

"So what should I say instead? You won't be fine?"

"Yes. I am the kind of person who appreciates an acknowledgment of the reality of the situation."

"Okay. You're not fine. I think something might be seriously wrong."

There's a beat of silence between us.

"Huh. You know what, I didn't like hearing that either," I say.

"Yeah, it sounded horrible when I said it," he says.

I keep scrolling through search results.

"This says I have a seventy-five percent chance of dying," I say, holding up my phone.

"What will distract you?" he says, putting his hand over my phone screen.

"Nothing," I say dramatically, and I put my head down in the crook of my arms.

"I'm good at distracting people. Ask me anything," he says.

"There's nothing I want to know," I say, still with my face in my arms.

"This is your chance. To find out my darkest secrets, the biggest scandals of my life," he says, using his most exaggerated voice.

"There have been zero scandals in your life." If we ignore the scandal of his betrayal of me. It feels like we are edging dangerously close to that.

"You'll never know if you don't ask," he says.

"Fine. Tell me about your shitty dad," I say, sitting up. He wanted to tell me before, now is his chance.

"Oh. Okay. Well, um . . ." He clears his throat and makes a face like he's about to give a presentation to the class. "Where do I even start?"

"You're already bad at this. Start at the beginning."

"I thought you were going to ask me a fun question. Okay. My parents split up when I was five, and then they both remarried and both had more kids with their new partners, and I've always felt like . . ."

He pauses. I think he's going to stop, because it's weird, it's definitely weird to be confiding in me about this. It's weird to be sitting in the emergency room together, but he looks at me, my wincing-in-pain-but-also-trying-to-be-a-supportive-and-good-listener face, and he decides to keep going.

"I've always felt like I didn't really fully belong with either family. I'm the odd one out. I'm the mistake my parents made before they started their real lives. And Dad and I really struggle to get along, which makes it worse."

I knew that his parents had split up and had kids in their new marriages, he told me that back when we were friends, but I hadn't really thought how that would *feel*, what it might be like. No matter what happened with Dad—how many times he canceled plans or didn't show up, how he talked of super-fun holidays we knew we'd never take, how obvious he made it that spending time with Lauren and me was always his second or third choice, never the thing he *really* wanted to be doing—I could deal with it because I had a real home with Mum, the kind of home you hold in your heart forever, a secret locket around your neck that protects you when things are going wrong. Jesse doesn't have that. I regret asking him about it now, because I don't want to know this: I don't want the sadness of it, I don't want the intimacy. I can't hold him at arm's length as easily when he tells me things like this. I can't hate him as easily.

"That sounds hard. I'm sorry," I say, and I mean it. "What do you and your dad argue about?"

"Huh. Well. Nothing big. My stepmum, Bree, she likes things done a certain way. That's fine. I get it. She's got a house of six people to manage. But whenever I do something that annoys her, she gets Dad to come and tell me what I've done wrong. I stacked the dishwasher the wrong way, I was too noisy when I came home and I woke the baby—you get the picture. And Dad gets stressed by Bree getting stressed, so he yells at me, and I yell back, and we're stuck in this stupid loop of arguing about things that don't really matter. I just wish he would be on my side, just *once*, you know?"

"Have you ever told him that?" I say. My pain is impeding me from talking much.

"Nah. He's not really receptive to parenting advice," Jesse says, and laughs. "Anyway, it's fine now I don't live there anymore. They can just forget I exist."

"They haven't forgotten you exist," I say.

Jesse looks at me. "Has your dad? Forgotten you exist?"

"Ah . . ." I pause. Jesse is being nice. This is *nice*. It feels like before, back when we were friends, but that's the problem. I don't trust him. I can't trust him and this doesn't change anything. And I don't talk about my dad with anyone.

"My dad hasn't forgotten me. He's just . . . he's just not great at being a dad."

I bend over in my seat a little more, trying to get comfortable. God, I hope they give me strong painkillers.

"Let's play Words with Friends," Jesse says suddenly.

"Yes. Wait, no." I love Words with Friends but I'll lose to him if I play in this state.

"I feel like a competitive word game might be your best distraction."

"All right, let's play but you have to remember I am in a weakened state, so you can't judge me on this performance. My losses won't count."

"We'll delete all evidence that we ever played if you lose."

"No, that sounds pathetic. I'm not a sore loser. My losses will count."

"Fine. We'll make a permanent record of it."

We play on our phones, round after round, and it helps, and even though I don't win as much as I should, I win enough to lift my spirits. Jesse is a good loser. He wants to win but accepts the loss.

"Brooke Williams!" someone shouts, just as I'm about to make a big move and get rid of my J and X in one go.

Jesse looks at me, touches my arm, then quickly removes his hand.

"You're up. Do you want me to come with you or wait here?"

"Um . . ." I pause. "No. Thank you, but no. You should go. Home. I've already wasted so much of your time. I'll get a cab home," I say, and turn quickly, before I regret saying it or he sees how scared I am.

THIRTEEN

I have a ruptured ovarian cyst.

A cyst has been growing on my ovary and it must have burst during the run, and that's what the pain was. They examined my ovaries on ultrasound, saw the fluid from the ruptured cyst in my pelvis, and now they're giving me painkillers. They'll observe me a bit longer before sending me home.

"Ruptured cysts are fairly common, you'll be fine, the pain might take a few days to go away. We'll give you a referral for a follow-up ultrasound appointment to check it's healed in a few weeks and you should see your GP," a tired and harried-looking doctor says.

"Okay," I say, nodding, processing. I was imagining it would be like *Grey's Anatomy*, which I binge-watched all last year late at night when I couldn't sleep from exam stress, and watching people with bigger problems than mine felt soothing. And now I'm waiting for a bunch of attractive young interns to come and crowd around my bed, and maybe we will flirt, or at least they will flirt among themselves and then loop me in on all the interpersonal drama.

Instead, my doctor leaves, and it takes me a full minute to

realize that's it. She's not coming back. I have so many questions, I didn't know my window for questions was so small. Can I still have kids? Is this a sign of anything else? Will there be more? What does it mean in a bigger-picture sense? Can I still go running? Will it affect my period? Why did it happen? What do I do if I feel that pain again? Could it have been caused by the time I accidentally left a tampon in for twenty-four hours and then remembered and spent all night googling toxic shock syndrome symptoms?

I call Mum.

"Mum?"

"Honey, how are you?"

"I'm good," I say automatically.

"I'm having such a lovely time and Tricia and I went to the cutest shop today—"

"Mum, wait. I'm not good."

"What's wrong?"

"I'm at the hospital. But I'm fine! I mean, not the *best* I've ever been. But it's not an emergency. Well, technically I did go to the emergency room. But it wasn't an emergency in the traditional sense. I didn't have a heart attack. Or a baby."

"What!!"

"I had bad pain and they did an ultrasound and it's a ruptured ovarian cyst."

"Oh my God. Why didn't you call me earlier?"

"I'm okay! I feel good now. A little groggy. They've given me meds for the pain."

"Who's with you? Is anyone with you?"

"Jesse is here. Was here. Is here." If I say I'm alone, she'll come, and she can't come—this is her weekend away.

"Jesse! Who's Jesse?"

"Mum. Calm down. *Jesse*. My housemate."

"Is anyone else with you?" Mum doesn't trust men in emergency situations.

"No."

"What hospital are you at? And what did the doctors say exactly?"

I tell her as much information as I can.

"I'm on my way."

"Mum, *no*. You're in the middle of a weekend away that you've been looking forward to all year. You have a full day of massages booked tomorrow. There's no point driving up tonight. I'll be home and safely in bed asleep before you even get here. Everything is fine. I will give you constant text updates. The cyst has burst, it's gone, there's no internal bleeding, all I have to do now is rest for a few days."

I take a moment to appreciate how calm and mature and adult I sound.

I'm trying to be brave, and my rational brain knows everything I am saying is right, but my irrational brain, the part of my brain that reverts to being five years old, the part of my brain that is lonely and scared and homesick, that part wants Mum to come. That part wants her to drive at full speed up the highway straight to the hospital, screeching through yellow lights, taking corners too tightly, parking in a spot reserved for doctors, not caring about anything but me, me, me. I want her to sit in the chair next to my bed and watch me sleep, staying awake all night, and then I want her to hold my hand and cradle my head the whole time, stroke my hair like when I was little. I thought I was homesick before this, but now I am mum-sick. I need her so badly. I want to smack away anyone who is not her.

There's no way I can do this a second longer without her.

"Okay, well, call me as soon as they tell you anything else. *Anything* else, okay? My phone is on. And call Lauren. She can drive up."

"I don't want Lauren here, she'll stress me out." I do kind of want Lauren here, because Lauren is as much comfort as Mum in many ways, but Lauren also makes me tense. She'll say something inappropriate. She'll flirt with doctors and nurses. She'll go off somewhere and not come back for ages. She'll be loud and boisterous and disturb the other people in the room, or maybe she won't do any of these things, but there's the possibility, the unpredictability, the tension that comes with being around Lauren. And then she'll need to stay at my house, I don't want her to see . . . I don't want her to see or to know, what I have here. My world is still too small and fragile.

"Are you sure you'll be okay?" Mum says.

"Yes. I'll be fine."

"I'll call you again a bit later okay?"

"Okay."

"Love you, sweetheart."

I hang up and, without warning, there are tears in my eyes. She's not coming. I pretend I urgently need to fiddle with the remote-control thingy that operates the bed, but really I need a distraction to stop the tears. My ovary hurts and I've never been in a hospital before and I'm scared of the pain meds they've given me and I want my mum.

"Brooke?" Jesse is at the door.

"Oh, hi," I say, pinching my arm under the blanket to push my tears back. "You're here. I mean, you're still here."

"I'm still here. Are you okay?" He sounds really worried. He probably thinks I've been given some horrible terminal diagnosis.

"I'm fine," I say, and quickly wipe my eyes, swallowing hard, clearing my throat, using my most upbeat voice. "It's a . . . a ruptured ovarian cyst!"

That was maybe a little too upbeat. Especially because cyst is a very ugly word when you say it out loud.

"Oh, okay. Is that serious?"

"Sometimes. But they think mine is fine. I can go home soon."

"Good, good." He looks awkward.

There was an ease between us when things felt urgent, but now, with me in a hospital gown and in a bed, with a diagnosis and a cyst—well, a former cyst—and him hovering there, it feels strange. We are not friends. This is way too much. We've level-jumped from nemeses to hospital buddies. No. I need to find a way to roll this back.

"You waited all this time?" I ask. It's been hours since I left him. My heart is softening, but I'm in there, building the barriers back up as fast as they crumble.

"Oh yeah. I went to the canteen and had a coffee, and then I, um, I went to the, um, gift shop." He's holding a bag with the gift shop logo on it, but he doesn't offer any more information.

"What did you buy?" I ask, looking at the bag.

"Just something to fill time," he says.

"What is it?" I prompt, because he's acting weird and I have no idea what's in the bag.

"Okay. Look. I bought something for you. I was really worried, you know. That you were going to die. Or have emergency surgery or something," he says. He's flustered and I wish I didn't think his flustered face was as cute as it is.

"Okay," I say. He's still not showing me what's in the bag.

"I'm going to return it," he says.

"Show me what it is first."

"I don't want to." He scrunches up his nose.

"God, what is it?" Something sick and twisted. Something perverted. Do they have perverted things in a hospital gift shop? My eyes are wide.

"Nothing. It's nothing, it's just, giving it to you has turned into a big deal now, so let's just forget it." He's clutching the bag to his chest like it contains his greatest shame, and I have to hold back laughter.

"Give it to me right now," I say, holding out my hand. He is not leaving this room until I know what is in the bag.

We look at each other. I'm in a hospital bed. He knows he has to do what I say right now.

He sighs. "Fine." He hands me the bag. "It was a panic purchase."

Inside is a stuffed toy dog wearing green scrubs with the word "Dogtor" embroidered on them and a little stethoscope around its neck. It's completely cheesy and also totally adorable.

"Thank you," I say. Should I hug it? I want to hug it. Hug him? No, and no. I hold it in a way I hope looks appreciative. I am appreciative, not just of this toy, but of everything he's done all day. Appreciative and supremely irritated that I have such a long list of things I have to appreciate about the person who once crushed my soul.

"I felt like I needed to buy something, I was in the shop so long," he says, as if I have accused him of something.

"It was a good purchase. I love it," I say. I put the dog on the table next to my bed, and we both stare at it.

"Would you trust a dog doctor or a cat doctor more?" I ask, mostly to fill the silence and possibly because the painkillers have softened my brain.

"A cat," he says, putting his hands in his pockets.

"Me too," I say. "They're smarter."

"A dog would have a much better bedside manner, though," he says.

We nod, like this is a perfectly normal conversation to be having.

"Brooke?" says a voice from the doorway, and it's Harper.

"Hi," I say, feeling a bit shy.

"Oh my God, are you okay?"

I go through the whole spiel, and Harper nods sympathetically.

"Bodies suck. Here, I packed you a bag, just in case," she says.

"Thank you." I'm too scared to look inside. Everything about this feels kind of shameful. That she had to go through my things. That I am an inconvenience to everyone. That I need to be mothered when I usually do the mothering.

"Well, I guess I should go then," Jesse says, looking uncertain. Harper will probably go with him. My stomach twists. *No, don't leave me, don't leave, don't leave.* But who knows when they'll discharge me, the paperwork might be hours, I can't ask them to wait.

"Thank you for bringing me here. And waiting with me. And for the dog," I say to Jesse. If they are going, I need them to leave urgently, before I start crying again. A big cry is coming, I can feel it building.

Sobbing into the pillow and hugging my new toy dogtor and really feeling bad for myself and examining my swollen puffy eyes in horror afterward kind of cry.

Jesse looks at me. "Are you really sure you're okay?" He's all furrowed brow and intense eyes and I think it's the pain meds, because it's doing something to me when I look at him. *Take your pleasing face and your height and your sparkly smile and your lovely hair and your concern and leave this room right now, sir.*

"Yes, fine. You go, you've been with me all night," I say.

"Is your mum coming?" Harper asks.

"No, she's away for the weekend," I say.

"Is anyone else coming?" she asks.

"No," I say, and my voice wobbles the tiniest bit. "I have no friends" is the unspoken bit.

"Are you hungry?" Harper asks. Her tone is warm and gentle.

"A bit," I say, looking up at her pathetically.

She looks at Jesse and they seem to be having a silent conversation with their eyes, because suddenly Jesse is going off to find Harper and me some food, and she's settling into the chair, and neither of them is leaving, they're going to stay until I'm discharged and drive me home, and my body sags with the relief of it, of not having to be alone, of not having to pretend to be strong, of not having to get a taxi home, of having two people in my life who are willing to help me. It feels so lucky, to have this.

FOURTEEN

It's Monday night, and I can't sleep. My ovary still hurt, not too much, but enough to be distracting, and I'm thinking about Dad. More accurately, trying hard not to think about him. We didn't have brunch yesterday. As predicted, he texted me saying he had woken up with a sore back (one of his many euphemisms for a hangover), and I said feel better soon, and then he called me that night and I didn't answer, because I didn't want to have to tell him about my burst cyst or any of that. He left me a voice mail saying he would transfer some money into my bank account, and I didn't reply to that either, because I was afraid he would ask how much money I wanted from him, and I didn't want the pressure of saying a figure.

So I'm awake thinking about Dad and also about my essay that I need to redo, and my short story that I can't finish, and my failure to be a runner, and worrying about Lauren, who didn't respond to my text tonight so I assume she's out drinking and that old kick of anxiety still hits me. Sometimes it's harder being farther away, having even less power to help her.

When I can't sleep, in the moment, it can feel like a catastrophe. It's not, and a small, rational part of my brain knows that, but generally it goes like this: I will look at my phone and see 1:45 a.m. (I can still get plenty of sleep, it's fine), 2:00 a.m. (still can get four or five hours, that's heaps), 2:30 a.m. (I should get up, read a book, but instead I might scroll through social media, even though I know the phone itself is probably largely responsible for my insomnia, and I alternate between funny videos that hype up my mind and scary news reports that set my heart racing), 3:00 a.m. (now I'm feeling weepy, and furious at my brain: *just sleep, please just sleep*, but I feel wide-awake, hours away from possible sleep), 3:30 a.m. (a sleep podcast, maybe, but where are my headphones, maybe I need a glass of water or to get up and pee, even though I know doing all of that makes me more awake), 4:00 a.m. (you've got through a day with no sleep before, you can survive this), 4:30 a.m. (I want to scream because I'm so furious at this body that won't sleep: *just sleep, stop thinking, you trash heap of a brain*), 5:30 a.m. (I might have dozed off for five minutes, this is good, I got some minutes of sleep, I'll be totally fine!), 7:00 a.m. (wake from a deep sleep as the alarm goes off, eyes feel gritty and like they are full of sand, head feels like it's wobbling on a stick).

When I'm anxious, I can't sleep. But when I'm tired, I get more anxious. Who designed this crappy system that loops in circles? That's what I want to know.

The last time I was stuck in this loop, I spent an hour before bed cycling through sleep meditation podcasts, trying to find someone with a voice I like. I find a lot of the male voices unsettling, like there is a man in my room whispering in my ear. The podcast everyone recommends with the man who tells a long, rambling story that is supposed to make you sleep because of how boring it is, just stresses me out, because I keep waiting for him to get to the point, and I get worked up with how frustrating I find his diversions.

I finally found one that seems nonjudgmental, where a woman says, "You're not asleep, but you're resting, and that's good too. Enjoy your rest," and it calms me to know that this anonymous woman on a podcast is telling me it's okay if I have failed at falling asleep but resting and lying quietly is good for me too. *Thank you, lady on the podcast, for giving me permission not to get furious at myself, for letting me give my body and my brain a little encouragement, a B+ for resting, for trying hard.*

Tonight, I decide to follow the advice I read on a forum for insomniacs, which is to "change up your environment." Leave your bedroom for an hour and then go back. Even if you are tired, try to force yourself to stay awake for that hour. So I get up from my bed and head for the lounge room. It feels like the right time to bring out my secret weapon. It's time to start rewatching one of my top-tier comfort TV shows from the very beginning.

I take my laptop and set it up on the coffee table. I am settling in, wrapped in a light blanket, when I hear someone in the kitchen, boiling the kettle, pouring hot water, and then footsteps coming toward me.

"What are you doing?" Jesse asks from the doorway. He's wearing glasses. I've never seen him wear glasses before.

"I'm watching a show," I say.

"It's pretty late." He's leaning against the doorjamb, blowing on his tea.

"I know. I can't sleep."

"Me neither," he says cheerfully, in the way of someone who doesn't have insomnia or maybe doesn't have high expectations for what they want to do the next day and can treat a night without sleep as an interesting occurrence rather than the torturous cage of pain.

"Are you drinking my sleepytime tea?" I say, squinting at his mug. Which isn't his mug, but my mug, oversize and polka-dotted, my second-favorite mug.

"Oh yeah. I thought it belonged to the house." He gives me a quick smile. He is not good at lying. The green tea belongs to the house. The black tea belongs to the house. My expensive, made-on-a-farm-in-Byron-Bay-with-certified-organic-ingredients sleepytime tea, with the typed label "Brooke's sleep tea" on it is special. It is to be portioned out like medication. But, fine. We've been in a weird truce, a sort of almost friendship, since the hospital. The barriers got knocked down, and I haven't been able to build them up as high again. I guess we're at the sharing-my-good-tea stage.

Jesse walks over and sits on the couch next to me.

"Is your ovary hurting?" he says, then makes a face. "Sorry. That's weird. That's a weird question to ask."

"It's a bit sore but okay," I say.

"I'll watch whatever you're going to watch with you," he says.

"No." I shake my head. "Absolutely not."

"Why not?"

"Because I am about to rewatch a show I know you wouldn't be interested in."

"How do you know? I'm interested in lots of things." He sips the tea, makes a disgusted face. It is a tea to be endured, not enjoyed. "What is in this?"

"Flowers and herbs."

"Huh." He sips again, swallows, and looks pained. "Is this like that turmeric chip from the party—an acquired taste you learn to love?"

"No, it stays pretty bad." I sit back on the couch and fold my arms, waiting for him to leave.

"Just tell me what the show is." He squishes a pillow behind his back, wriggling to get more comfy.

"No."

"Brooke. I'm not as judgmental as . . ." He trails off.

"As who?" I say.

"As nobody." He pretends to be very interested in his tea.

"Were you going to say not as judgmental as *me*?" If he thinks this is my first rodeo, my first time being told I'm judgmental, my first time hearing criticism, then he's a fool. I grew up in a household of women, a household where faults and flaws are discussed freely, sometimes shouted at you mid-argument (Lauren to me) or itemized on a piece of paper slipped under your door (me to Lauren).

"I mean, you're not *not* judgmental."

"People think I'm judgmental because I don't drink," I say, which is true. I think sometimes people hate me for not drinking because then I'm just there as a sober witness to everyone's mistakes, and that really kills the vibe, I know it does.

"It has nothing to do with you not drinking," Jesse says.

"Then why do you think I'm judgmental?"

"You're not. Forget it."

"You don't need to protect me. I know all the reasons people don't like me, don't worry."

"That's very self-aware of you."

"I'm uptight, I'm controlling, I'm anxious, I worry about things too much, I'm not 'fun' . . ." I tick them off on my fingers as I go.

He is watching me with a kind of fascination.

"You're really hard on yourself," he says.

"Is that an observation or a flaw to add to my list?"

"Um, both, I guess?" He smiles.

"Too self-critical. Got it. Adding it in," I say.

He shakes his head. "That's . . . No. Wait. I'm scared to say anything now in case you add it to your list," he says.

"I think it's healthy to know your flaws," I say.

"Okay. Do me," he says.

"Do you what?"

"Do my worst traits."

I look at him, that eager face, every feature somehow enhanced by his black-rimmed glasses.

"I can handle it," he says.

"Fine," I say.

He looks excited. That there might actually be a best and worst trait. That he's so confident in his likability and charm he thinks hearing his worst traits will be entertaining.

"You're kind of a slob. You care too much about what other people think. You have a big ego. And—" I pause. I was going to say something that alluded to what he did to me. You're a traitor, maybe, or you're cowardly, or you can be cruel, you abandon people, but I can't quite say it. If I do, it will shift the mood entirely, but more than that, I don't want to delve into it right now. It's like touching an old injury that never healed. Discussing it will make it all real again.

"And?" Jesse says quietly. His demeanor has changed, softened, and I can feel it, like he's opening a door, willing me to bring it up.

"And nothing. That's it." We look at each other for a moment.

"Brooke," he says. "About what happened in school. I never told you how—"

"No," I say. "I don't want to talk about that."

There's a beat of silence, and I see him wavering, wondering whether to push it, but my expression must warn him off.

"Well. Okay. I have some questions about your list, then," he says, his voice returning to its light, jocular tone, putting his tea down on the coffee table.

"Ask away. I am ready to give you answers."

"Do I really have a big ego?"

"You're tall. All tall guys are conditioned to have big egos, so it's as much society's fault as yours. But yes. Of course you do, it's not even in question," I say.

"But growing up, I was actually a really small kid."

"So?"

"So I developed my sense of self back then."

"That was overridden by the time you were sixteen, six-foot-whatever and sitting in the back seat of the bus, making fun of other people."

"I never made fun of people," he says, looking slightly outraged.

"You sat with people who did, and that's the same."

"Really? When?" He seems honestly confused.

"Here's an example. Two years ago. It was winter, and we had a casual-clothes day at school. I'd saved up and bought a new jacket, and it was brightly patterned, not the black puffer I usually wore. Your friend Nathan yelled out, 'Nice jacket!' in his most obnoxious voice in front of everyone when I got on the bus."

"Nathan is not my friend. We just sat sort of near each other. And I don't remember that."

"Well, I do. And it made me feel like shit."

"I'm sorry."

"You should be."

"I didn't say it!"

"You didn't stop it," I say. I want to add, "And you *caused* it." Nathan was there, in the room, standing behind Gretel, when Jesse said, "Do I like Brooke? No. No. Fuck, no." Nathan is a douchebag and, frankly, a loser, and he probably would have yelled, "Nice jacket!" at anyone wearing anything that caught his eye. I can accept the logic of this, but my brain still thinks it all started that night at Gretel's, that Jesse gave him permission in some twisted way.

"You're right. Nathan was a dick, but I don't think I ever told him that."

"Well, it's never too late."

"Should I call him right now?" Jesse holds up his phone.

"Yes," I say.

"I don't actually have his number," Jesse says.

"Send him a DM." I smile and blink innocently at him.

"Feels a bit out of the blue. I've never messaged him in my life," Jesse says. I knew he'd try to weasel out of it.

"It would be really cathartic for me," I say. Jesse gives a small snort, then squares his shoulders a little.

"Okay. What should I say?" he says.

"You made fun of Brooke's jacket on the bus two years ago and you were wrong. It was a great jacket and she looked amazing in it."

He opens a message and types it up, exactly as I said. Two formal little sentences sitting there, and he even puts a full stop at the end.

"Should I send?" he says, raising his eyebrows.

I start laughing. "Yes! Send."

He does, which makes me laugh more. We watch and wait for a response.

"He's probably asleep," Jesse says. "Oh wait. A reply!"

He holds it up. The message says "wtf" and nothing else.

Now we're both laughing.

"What now?" Jesse says.

"I don't know. I'm panicking," I say.

"I mean, it's fairly self-explanatory. Does he really need more information?"

"Can you imagine what he's thinking, getting this message out of the blue at one in the morning?" I say, and we're both helplessly laughing, the kind that moves into hysteria the more you try to stop it, the kind that is impossible to explain to anyone not there in the moment with you.

"See, I think this proves I don't care about what other people think," Jesse says.

"No, it doesn't. The idea of not being cool terrifies you."

"I'm *not* cool, though," he says.

"Oh please. You only say that because you think a cool person would never admit to being cool. That a cool person wouldn't identify with the word 'cool' at all. Which is true, a cool person wouldn't, but someone worried they're not cool also wouldn't."

"Help, I'm trapped by your logic."

"Just accept my psychological assessment and adjust your life accordingly."

"Okay, but you know what wasn't on my list of flaws?"

"What?"

"Making fun of other people's TV shows."

"Oh that's on there. It's just not in your top three. It's, like, number twenty-two on the list."

He laughs. "How long is this list?"

"It doesn't have a definite end point yet."

"I think the fact you are too scared to put on a TV show in front of me tells me *you* are the one actually afraid of what others think."

I sit with that for a second. Damn. He's probably right.

"Okay. Fine. You win. But I'm only afraid of your judgment

because girls are taught to be ashamed of the stuff they like. I'll put on my show."

"Do I get to know what it is before you press play?"

"No."

"Brooke," he says, and I determinedly squash down my body's reaction to how cutely he says my name.

"Fine. It's *The Vampire Diaries*. A show I have rewatched every year since I was twelve. It's very important to me, on an emotional-support level. And I don't want to hear whatever you're thinking," I say. I am trying to sound very stern.

"I'm not thinking anything," he says.

"I saw your face when I said the word 'vampire' and then also your face when I said the word 'diaries.'"

"My face was neutral!"

"Your face was not neutral."

"I won't ruin your vampire-journal show, I promise," he says, grinning.

"You will ruin it. Saying that, right then, already puts you right on the edge of ruining it." I fold my arms.

"What if I watch one episode with you, and show you how nonjudgmental I can be?"

"No."

"Just the pilot."

"The pilot is quite bad," I say.

"So skip to a good episode."

"I don't ever skip the first episode. I love the first episode."

"You just said it was bad."

"For you. A newbie. Not for me. Because I know where it's going. I know in six episodes it will get better, and then in ten episodes it will be wonderful, and in seventeen episodes it will be perfect."

"Sorry, *how* many episodes are there?"

"Twenty-two a season, give or take."

"And how many seasons are there?"

"Eight."

"You rewatch all that every year?"

"Well, no, I don't rewatch every episode."

"Which ones do you watch?"

I look at him, in his glasses, looking eager to hear all about it, not realizing this is my private ritual, one of my most soothing escapes, and the only person I've ever shared it with is Lauren.

"Okay, so I have a system."

"Of course you do."

"I watch all of season one, and all of season two, which is the best season, then all of season three except for one particular episode that I hate, then the first part of season four and the final three episodes, then three episodes from season five, and then most of season six, and then two episodes each from seasons seven and eight."

Jesse is nodding along like he finds this all very fascinating and normal.

"You don't ever rewatch shows?" I fold my legs under me.

"Well, yeah, I'll put on a comedy I've seen before if I just want to relax, but I don't rewatch with that kind of . . . plan."

"I like plans, sue me." Everything I do has a plan.

"I like that you like plans," he says.

"Well, get ready for your first episode of *The Vampire Diaries*."

"I'm excited," he says with too much false enthusiasm for my liking.

"Stop smiling."

"I can't *smile*?"

"No. It's condescending."

"Come on, Brooke."

"You can smile if something funny happens. *Intentionally* funny. You can respond to scripted humor. *Only* then."

"Is this something you do with all your friends?"

"What do you mean?" I say. I am not going to acknowledge that he said "friends" as if he and I have definitely moved into that category. Maybe we have. But fourteen-year-old me is screaming, *Remember, remember.*

"Give them permission to smile," he says.

"No, that's just a rule for you," I say.

"Okay, but does this new rule supersede the old one of not talking to each other when Harper's not around? Because you've been breaking that one a lot lately." He's grinning at me.

"I'm starting the show," I say.

I press play and try to pretend he's not there. He leans forward and picks up his tea again. We watch in silence, and then he makes a noise in his throat—a kind of guttural choking-laughing sound—and I turn my head.

"What was that?"

"Nothing." He makes a faux innocent face.

"You made a noise." I point my finger at him accusingly.

"I was swallowing."

"A judgmental swallow."

"It wasn't. It was just a regular swallow."

I press play, and then, the throat noise again.

I hit pause. "No! I can't do this. We've just started and you are already ruining it."

"I'm sorry, I'm sorry! I'm trying not to. It's just . . ." Jesse presses his lips together, like he's trying to suppress a smile or stop words coming out of his mouth.

"What." I fold my arms again. For God's sake.

"I didn't realize there would actually be *vampires writing in diaries*."

"That *is* the title." I can hear how huffy and defensive I sound. How dare he make me huffy and defensive about my own show.

"I thought it was more symbolic than literal."

"Well, it's not."

"Okay."

"Can you deal with that?"

"Yes. I have accepted the diary writing and will not be commenting further." He adjusts his glasses.

"Good." I press play again, then immediately hit pause, because it's suddenly bugging me.

"Since when do you wear glasses?"

"Since I was sixteen."

"I've never seen you wear them."

"Well, my eyesight isn't that bad. And I usually wear contacts during the day."

"Why?"

"Well, it's easier to run in contacts and less hassle, I don't have to worry about forgetting my glasses, and, I guess, I look kind of dorky in the glasses." He looks a little flustered, like he didn't mean to say that last bit. There it is. Hello, ego.

I almost say, "I told you so," but I swallow it down.

"You don't look dorky," I say without thinking.

He grins and looks at me in exaggerated wonderment.

"I think that's the first nice thing you've said to me. A compliment from Brooke." He sighs, puts his hand on his heart. "Wow, wow, wow."

"It was hardly a compliment." Now I am flustered. I don't like being accused of giving compliments. He knows about my favorite comfort show and my exploding cyst and I've now said something too nice, and the whole night is practically ruined because I am being exposed and he is not.

"What was it, then?"

"I was just stating a fact."

"It's a *fact* that I look good in glasses?" His eyes are wide with delight.

"I didn't say that. But yes. Most guys do. And girls." He is not *special*. I like glasses. The right pair of glasses can elevate everyone.

"I think that's definitely a compliment."

"Well, you are free to take it that way."

"I am going to."

"But just so you know, *I* don't consider it to be. And as the compliment giver, I really should be the one to know."

"Noted. But it's still going in my compliments journal."

"Go for it."

"It's a journal I keep under my bed, and every day at the end of the day, I write down all the compliments I get. Then first thing in the morning, I wake up and read it."

"The sad thing is it could be true. You *would* do something like that. Because of the aforementioned big ego."

"Ah, but you also admit that you think I'm charming and handsome enough to get the level of compliments required to keep a compliments journal."

"I admit nothing."

"Okay." He's laughing.

"I'm pressing play and I don't want you to say a single thing when the crow appears, or the mysterious fog," I say, leaning toward the laptop.

"Oh my God."

"Shhhhh." I hold up my hand.

"There's a *crow and fog*?"

"You are on very thin ice."

"Okay, okay. I promise. I won't say anything."

"No more chances."

"I don't need any more chances."

We smile at each other. I am trying not to smile, actually, but I can't help it.

We keep watching, and Jesse blessedly says nothing, sipping his tea, and after a while, I push a corner of my blanket over to him, in case his feet are cold.

FIFTEEN

Harper is trying to cook a recipe from my Ottolenghi cookbook, and she's near tears. Penny is coming over, and Harper made a big fuss about how she was going to cook a fancy meal for her.

"There are so many ingredients, Brooke, and I have no idea what I'm doing!" she wails down the hallway.

I am happy to be pulled away from my short story. Every time I write a sentence, I want to delete it two minutes later, because the thought of giving that sentence to other people in the class to read is too paralyzing. My story needs to be smart in a secret way, without looking like I'm *trying* to be smart. It needs to be funny without resorting to overt, embarrassing *comedy*. It needs to be sad without the clichés of death or abuse or anything *obviously* sad. It needs to be pithy and succinct but also filled with beautiful descriptions and layers of subtle meaning.

The first story we all read in class gave me confidence, because it wasn't good at all, and I was relieved—*thank God, I'm the best here just like at school*—but then the next story we read was great. It was surprising and dark and interesting and mature in a way I knew I could never write, and even though it was great, PJ still had a lot to critique about it, and all that confidence I had went slipping away. Then the next one was even better. How were my peers, half of them who looked like they had never grocery shopped for themselves or booked their own doctor appointments, writing these incisive, deep stories about the meaning of life? Ruby says her mum not only does all her washing but sometimes still lays an outfit for her out on her bed if she knows Ruby is going out, and then brings her breakfast in bed the next morning, and yet Ruby is confidently writing a gritty story filled with hard drugs and violence.

I walk into the kitchen to help Harper.

"I told you to pick something easy," I say to her.

"No one is impressed by easy." Harper sits on the kitchen floor and puts her head in her hands. "I thought I could just kind of wing it, but there are a *lot* of teaspoons of spices in the recipe and we have no baking equipment and I thought I could just shake it in there or use a regular spoon and estimate but maybe not. I'm spiraling, Brooke. I'm *spiraling*."

"Okay, let's just clean up a bit so we can see what we're doing here," I say gently, but secretly I'm excited. This is my moment to shine.

"I hate cooking."

"I know you do."

"I'll just order takeaway. I attempted to cook, that counts for something." Harper has a running list of reasons for ordering takeaway that she likes to say out loud to anyone in earshot, mostly as a way to justify it to herself, I think, which includes: had a bad day at uni and need to cheer up, had a good day at uni and need to celebrate, ate lunch at home, it's cold, it's hot, tired from cleaning up the kitchen, tired from going to the supermarket, hungover, got too stressed when reading the recipe, about to get period, has period, just had period.

"I'll cook it for you," I say.

"I can't let you do that," Harper says in the hopeful voice of someone who wants to let you do that, very badly.

"Yes you can." This is my friendship brand, my love language. Doing things for someone else, especially domestic things. I am the friend who will cook the dinner for you, who will show you how to get stains out of your top, who will proofread your assignment.

"But it's so much work," Harper says.

"I like work!" I say.

"What about your whole cyst situation?" she says, waving her hand in front of her pelvic area, then pausing. "Cyst situation. Cystuation?" She grins.

"My cystuation is fine," I say, smiling back. "Totally healed. And I'm cooking for you."

She gets up and hugs me. It makes my heart sing. We're at the hugging stage—we're definitely friends, or close to friends, it cannot be denied. I haven't been hugged in months.

"You're a lifesaver," she says. I turn away in case all that sudden emotion is showing on my face. I don't want to scare her off.

Harper opens the fridge and pulls out a yogurt that is two days past its use-by and I almost threw away.

"That's out of date." I don't want to sound like I monitor everything in the fridge for use-by dates, even though I do monitor everything in the fridge for use-by dates.

"It'll be fine," she says, opening it and smelling it and shrugging. The way she so casually takes her life in her hands is almost admirable.

"You can't smell bacteria," I can't stop myself from saying.

"Do you have an ex?" Harper asks suddenly, taking a big spoonful.

"Not really," I say, turning back to the recipe and the food laid out in front of me.

"She does, and his name is Tristan," Jesse says, at the same time, from the doorway. He works part-time at Bunnings and he's just finished his shift. He's still wearing the red polo shirt. I turn to glower at him.

"Don't be an asshole," I say, slicing into an eggplant. I don't think we have sharp enough knives for this. There's a lot of chopping involved.

"All I said was his name," Jesse says.

"You said it in an asshole way."

"Tell me about Tristan," Harper says, settling into a chair.

"There's nothing to tell," I say.

"They dated for years," Jesse says, leaning against the bench and getting in my way.

"Less than a year," I correct.

"He was her high school sweetheart," Jesse says.

"Hardly," I say, even though, I guess, technically it's true.

"He would always wait at the door of the classroom for her English class to finish, and then carry her things for her, and it confused me, like, how did he always manage to get out of his class early enough to be waiting at the door like that?" Jesse says.

"He was very considerate," I say.

"Was he getting special permission from his teacher? Did he have his schedule arranged so he had a free period every time you had English? Or was he a super-fast runner?" Jesse shakes his head like it's a fascinating unsolved mystery.

"He was the kind of guy who liked to open doors for you and carry things," I explain to Harper.

"An old-fashioned-gentleman type," she says, nodding.

"Yes," I say. I place the chopped eggplant into a dish and arrange the spice containers in a neat line on the bench, nudging Jesse out of my way.

"It was all a bit patronizing, though, wasn't it," Jesse says.

"No, it was nice," I say. "He was very sensitive actually. He liked to celebrate anniversaries."

"In a performative way," Jesse says.

"In a normal way," I say. I've found a proper measuring tea-spoon and I carefully shake the cumin onto it.

"I never trusted him," Jesse says to Harper.

"He's completely trustworthy," I say to Harper. "He mentored at-risk youth."

She's nodding seriously, like a detective on a case. "So was it a nice breakup, then?" she says to me.

"Oh no, it was kind of awful. He dumped me for someone else," I say, now measuring out the ground coriander.

"That sounds harsh," Harper says.

"It was not enjoyable," I say.

"See? Bad dude," Jesse says, looking triumphant.

I nudge him out of my way again to get to the olive oil.

"You seem very invested in this," Harper says to him.

Jesse pauses, picks up a tea towel for no reason, spins it around his hands. "No. I'm not *invested*. I just think, well, Tristan didn't suit Brooke."

"Everyone would always say how perfectly suited we were," I say.

"Well, they were wrong," Jesse says.

"This has been helpful," Harper says, looking thoughtful.

"Helpful?" I say, confused.

"I mean, you cooking has been helpful," she says, but she's a bad liar, and now I have a little hum of anxiety as to what Harper might have really meant.

SIXTEEN

Penny claps her hands with delight when she walks in and sees the food laid out on the table. I thought Harper wanted an intimate dinner between the two of them, but she tells Jesse and me to join them.

"Brooke, you did all the work—you need to eat the meal," she says.

"I only helped a little," I say.

"It's okay, Harps told me you did it all." Penny laughs.

We sit around the little table and it feels very adult and glamorous. I serve the meal, because I know Harper is stressed about lifting the eggplant out of the dish. Jesse offers to get Penny a glass of wine, then realizes we don't have wine or anything except water and the last pulpy dregs of a bottle of orange juice.

"Tell Brooke about your idea for a business," Harper says to Penny once we're all happily eating and chatting. There is an odd tone underlying her request. Harper is trying too hard to sound casual and offhand, which makes me think this is a conversation she and Penny have planned.

"Oh, I have this idea for running a bespoke dating agency for young people who are tired of bars and don't want to go on the usual dating apps. It's really selective; you only find out about it through word of mouth," Penny says, her eyes shining with excitement.

"That sounds great," I say, and Penny and Harper exchange a quick look.

"Yes, I'm developing it with Harper for our Entrepreneurship and Innovation class this semester. We had to come up with a business plan and prototype for a service or product," Penny says.

"And we need some real-life case studies," Harper adds, chin in hand, watching me.

They both fall silent. Everyone is looking at me now.

"Wait. Sorry? You want to use me?" I say.

"You're single, right?" Penny says.

"Well, yes, technically," I say. I don't know why I say "technically." There's nothing technical about it.

"Are you looking to meet someone but you're not into the club scene or dating apps?" Harper says, sounding as though she's reading off a questionnaire sheet at a doctor's office.

"Well, I guess so, kind of." I'm scrambling. I'm not into anything with the word "scene" involved, and dating apps scare the hell out of me, so she is right, but I also am very clearly falling into a trap. *Am* I looking to meet someone? Where does desperate-to-be-loved-but-terrified-of-intimacy fall on that scale? I kind of assumed, when I moved here, I would meet someone in one of three ways. Scenario one: While waiting for my coffee at a café, they would call out my order, and a cute guy would step forward because we have the same order, and we would smile at each other, and *just know*, and fall in love. Scenario two: I would be in a bookshop, looking for a certain book, and they only have one copy, and a cute guy and I reach for it at the same time, and we smile at each other, and *just know*, and fall in love. Scenario three, my most elaborate: A French exchange student would join my creative writing class and he would read my work and give me feedback in French and I would translate his note and realize it was actually him telling me how beautiful I am, and we would fall in love and he would make me croissants from scratch and show me how to wear little silk scarves.

None of these scenarios have come close to eventuating. I once saw a cute guy in a bookshop, but then I noticed he was buying a Jordan Peterson book and I lost interest.

"We've had some success setting up a few of our friends but we need some straight subjects too, to see how wide we can go with it," Penny is saying.

"Is this a real business or just a uni assignment?" Jesse says.

"It's just a uni assignment for now, but I think it could become a real business," Penny says. "Harper is a little more skeptical."

"It's a lot of work," Harper says. "Thinking of a cute business name has already taken us weeks, so we're behind on the actual assignment."

"We could be future billionaires—you never know," Penny says.

"We obviously hate billionaires, though," Harper says.

"The plan is to be like the queer, feminist version of Robin Hood, we're going to use love to make money and then use the money to give back to our community," Penny says, waving her fork around to emphasize her points.

"We still need to figure out how to make it profitable, though," Harper adds.

"Sorry, why aren't you asking Jesse? For this experiment?" I say.

"He already ruined things with Amber when he didn't message her after the housewarming, so he's had to be discounted from the options," Penny says.

"Wait, what!" Jesse says. "She was not interested in anything else happening! She was into some other guy she was already seeing. Brendan? Braydon? Bryon? Some guy with a B name. She kept talking about him. I shouldn't get blacklisted for that."

"I'm sorry. You're problematic," Harper says, offering him some bread.

"I was a perfect gentleman!" Jesse says.

"Still, the lack of attempted follow-up, letting her get traumatized by a mouse, it's not the upscale vibe we want for the agency. It doesn't look good on paper," Penny says.

"Don't put it on paper, then!" Jesse says, still looking outraged.

"Anyway, Brooke is perfect for us. You've got a relationship track record with Tristan, but you're over him and ready to move on," Harper says.

"Did I say that?" I say, thinking back to our conversation earlier. I definitely didn't say the words "ready to move on," but maybe I gave that impression.

"All we need is a nice photo of you," Penny says.

"For what?"

"To get you on our books."

"You have *books*?"

"Symbolically."

"What does that mean?" I say.

"I need a photo to send to my cousin Henry. He's the one we want to set you up with," Penny says.

Harper smiles at me in a don't-kill-me way.

"Henry is great. You'll love him," she says encouragingly. "Like a better version of Tristan."

"I'm not sure I *want* another version of Tristan," I say.

"He's twenty, a Pisces with Gemini rising, really cute, *loves* dogs. He's studying education, plays the flute, cheers for St. Kilda, if you care about football. He had a girlfriend in first-year uni, but they broke up and he's been single for a while, and my family all think it's time for him to meet someone new. Someone lovely and funny and kind. Like you!" Penny says.

"I'm not sure," I say, trying to process the wave of information I have just received about Henry.

"He's also an aspiring stand-up comedian," Harper says.

"Oh," I say. That is not the selling point she thinks it is.

"The good kind," she assures me.

I don't know what that means.

"Look at him," Penny says. She holds out her phone, and there is a picture of Henry, smiling. He *is* cute. Good hair, notable eyebrows.

A sudden, awful thought occurs to me. "Oh God," I say. "Have you already told him about me? What did you say?"

"No," Harper says.

"Yes," Penny says at the same time.

They glance at each other.

"We said you're brilliant, incredibly smart, very motivated, studying economics but also very creative, a talented runner, very organized, gorgeous, an amazing cook, a classic Virgo," Harper says.

"Oh God," I say. There is no way I can live up to all that. "And I don't have any nice photos," I add, panic rising.

"Let's just take one right now," Penny says soothingly.

Harper claps her hands together. "Photo shoot!" she says.

This is my hard line. I will not participate in a photo shoot. And I will not go on a date with flute-playing, stand-up comedian Henry.

Ten minutes later, though, I walk out into the lounge room in the first of multiple outfit options for the photo we are going to send Henry. I'm wearing the black dress I wore to the party.

"Okay, this could work. Oh! We could go for a kind of gothic, creative look. If we add plenty of eyeliner. And I have the perfect prop in my bag! It's a hardcover edition of the new Murakami novel that I bought for my dad," Penny says.

"I don't wear much eyeliner. Or read Murakami. Well, not yet anyway. I'm definitely going to."

"That doesn't matter."

"Aren't these photos supposed to represent reality, somewhat?"

"A version of reality," Harper says. "It's just about the first impression. A taster, to hook them in." She has gone to the bathroom and grabbed her makeup and she tells me to keep still and starts applying eyeliner to my eyes.

"Maybe we should take the photo in front of a bookshelf?" Penny muses, looking around the house like an art director.

"With the book and a cigarette." Harper nods.

"Oh perfect!" Penny says.

"I am not smoking. No one smokes anymore. Especially inside," I say.

"But you'd look so cool. Very old-school literary badass. Very I-don't-care-about-my-future-I-live-in-the-now. The photo could be in black and white," Harper says.

"But I do care about my future. Aren't you selling him on the idea that I'm someone who cares about their future?" I feel like we're getting too far away from the original purpose of the photo.

"Do you have a dramatic scarf?" Penny asks.

I'm not entirely sure what would constitute a dramatic scarf, but I know I don't have one.

"What about this?" I say, walking to the lounge room and sitting down on the couch with the Murakami book in my hands. I open it and hold my head slightly to the side, pretending to read.

"That looks extremely posed," Jesse says, shaking his head. He's apparently codirecting this photo shoot now.

"And why would someone take a photo of you on the couch reading?" Harper shakes her head.

"Why would they take a photo of me in front of a bookcase smoking and reading?" I say.

"Okay, we need to make it look like she's casually reading and has just looked up as someone says her name, and they unexpectedly take her picture," Penny says.

"Okay, Brooke, hold the book and then look up when I say your name, like you aren't expecting to have your photo taken."

I follow their orders.

"Give a kind of 'Don't take my picture, okay, fine, take my picture' sultry look," Penny says.

"That's exactly the face I am giving," I say.

"More . . . cheeky. Like a hint of a smile," Harper says. "Cute but coy, but also very confident in who you are, on the inside."

"Yes, like, you're tough but you're also a little soft, and you've got an edge of danger, and an edge of nerdiness, an edge of sweetness, and an edge of sexiness," Penny says.

"That's too many edges," I say. I can barely handle one edge.

"Try to be a cross between Sylvia Plath and Taylor Swift from her *Folklore* era," Harper suggests. "With a touch of Princess Diana."

I arrange my face in the best approximation of this I can manage, aiming for mysterious, pretending I have a scandalous secret that no one else knows. I can't look at Jesse, because I'm sure he's laughing at me. Well, laugh away, I'm the one deemed datable. Maybe. If they get a photo.

Harper is clicking her phone, endlessly, and saying, "Less, like, all those emotions, but more subtle. Smize, smize, *smize*. Do you know what smize means? Okay, let me review. Gorgeous, you look gorgeous. But, let's just take a few more."

"You'll need to take a minimum of fifty pictures of me to get one decent one," I say.

"They've got more than fifty here," Jesse says, peering over Harper's shoulder.

"Let me see," I say, grabbing the phone. I scroll through the photos. "No, no, no, no, no, no. NO, oh God, *no*." I look either in pain or scared or like I have just murdered someone and I'm pleased about it or my eyes are shut.

"Okay, new idea. Athletic, but sexy athletic," Harper says.

"Like, a sports bra and short-shorts?" Penny says, frowning.

"No, like, leggings and an oversize hoodie with a high ponytail," Harper says.

"That could work," Penny says. "She'll need one of your hoodies," she says to Jesse.

"We're going for adorable girl in an oversized guy's top," Harper says. "It's very 'look at me, I'm tiny and helpless and I need a man to protect me.' Gross, I know. The implications of it are deeply sexist and very gender essentialist, and, oh, I could write an essay on it for my class, but let's also see if we can get a cute photo first."

I dutifully put on leggings, and Jesse returns with a blue hoodie, and I really don't want to wear it, but I can't put into words why not. Jesse seems equally uncomfortable, which makes me even more so. It's too intimate. It's too much. I put it on, nervous that it's actually not going to look oversize on me at all. Jesse is taller than me, but I have boobs, and broad shoulders and a stomach and wide hips. I am not a cute or tiny person: there are a lot of bumps and lumps here.

The hoodie smells like Jesse, and I try to tell myself I don't like the smell but, unfortunately, I do.

I sit down in the hoodie and kind of slump forward, hoping that makes me look smaller and cuter.

"You look depressed," Penny says, frowning.

"You look like you're home sick from school," Harper says at the same time.

I sit up straight, very upright, and fold my hands in my lap.

"How about now?"

They both shake their heads.

"Can we lose the leggings?" Harper says.

"And put on what instead?" I say.

"Nothing. Just a peek of naked leg. Like you've just had sex and put on the hoodie—" Harper says.

"That could work! And rumple her hair," Penny says.

"No," I say. "Absolutely not."

"What about," Jesse says. "What about if you sit over here by the window, with the lamplight? Just wearing a normal top. And no props."

Harper looks unconvinced.

I take off the hoodie and sit in leggings and a plain white T-shirt.

"Can I?" Jesse says, holding out a tissue.

"I can wipe my own nose." I lean away from him.

"No, I was going to wipe off a bit of the eyeliner."

"No! That's my gothic masterpiece!" Harper says.

"Just a little. Just so she looks a bit more . . ."

"A bit more what?"

"A bit more like herself."

"Fine."

Jesse gets close to me with the tissue and I look up at him. My heart is suddenly racing, and I feel a little breathless.

"Do you know what you're doing?" I say. I am trying to stall him from getting any closer. I need my heart to slow down first. I need to regroup.

"I've put makeup on and off my little sisters lots of times," he says.

"Okay," I say.

"Close your eyes," he says softly.

I hesitate and then close my eyes.

He gently touches the tissue to the sides of my eyelids and softly dabs. His knuckles brush my skin. I swallow. I'm scared I'm blushing. What is wrong with me?

"Okay," he says.

I open my eyes. He's still very close to me.

"Wait, let me . . . Look up," he says. His voice, quiet and close to me like this, makes goose bumps appear on my neck. I hope no one notices.

He dabs under my eyes too, so gently the tissue barely seems to be touching my skin.

"Done," he says, and picks up a phone and takes a few photos.

"Should I smile, or what?" I say.

"Wait. One more second." Jesse steps forward again and moves a piece of my hair, pushing it back off my forehead. I don't like the way his hands on my forehead make me feel. No. That's not right. I very much like the way it makes me feel but I also don't like that it makes me feel that. I'm flustered now. I just need him to stay a good meter away from me.

Clearly I need this date. My hormones have gone awry.

"Look over there and think about Damon Salvatore," Jesse says.

His casual little *Vampire Diaries* reference makes me smile against my will.

"Got it!" Harper says, looking over Jesse's shoulder.

And sure enough, there's a picture of me, my face thoughtful and smiling, looking not at the camera but somewhere near it. Candid and relaxed. A portrait but not a portrait.

"Jesse, you did it!" Harper says. "Stunning! I'm sending it to you, Brooke. And you, Pen."

"Perfect," says Penny, receiving the picture on her phone. "I'm sending it to Henry right now."

Later, in bed, I look at the photo. I do look good. I look like me, in a way that feels personal, vulnerable, honest.

I think about how it felt when Jesse touched my face, the smell of his hoodie, his voice when it was quiet and low, and then I push those thoughts away.

SEVENTEEN

I've agreed to go on a date with Henry.

Penny passed along my phone number and he and I texted back and forth a little. This is the part I am actually good at, I realize. I can be funny and flirty in words. Impressing someone new via text is a bit like an assignment (*in five hundred words or less, show how you are perfectly likable and datable, using short sentences and answering prompts*), and I can rise to the challenge with ease. My body doesn't matter, what I'm wearing doesn't matter, the pimple on my forehead doesn't matter, I can just lie in bed with unwashed hair and no bra and a baggy old top and think up smart and funny things to say. I am so enamored with how well I'm doing, I forget to pay much attention to his responses. He seems nice. Not funny haha, but amusing. Droll, which is a word I've always wanted to use about someone. I expected more from someone who wants to be a comedian but I am also deeply relieved he didn't make any actual jokes.

We decided to meet for coffee on Saturday, which feels very fast to me. I would prefer a monthslong virtual courtship with plenty of time for me to imagine various possible futures for us before I am inevitably disappointed, but Harper and Penny need data for their assignment, so our relationship is on a timeline.

I chatted with Lauren, Mum, and Nanna the night before, and I told them I was going on a date.

"Who with?" Lauren shrieked with delight. There was far too much surprise in her voice.

"A blind date? Oh, be careful, honey," Mum said. "Tell us the address of where you'll be and turn on your phone locator so I can track you."

The difference in the way Mum treats me when I am going to a café in the middle of the day for an hour, compared with how she treats Lauren, who will casually announce she is going to a rave party on a remote farm that belongs to a friend of a friend of a friend and she's not sure what day she might be home or how she's getting there, needs to be studied by parenting experts for research papers. Why is she so much stricter and more protective of the responsible child? Is it that, after all we've been through, she's just given up on Lauren and channels all her stress and worry and neurosis into me, the child who can be controlled?

"If you'd given me more notice, I would have express-posted you my good boots, they're only a size too small for you, you could have squeezed into them. Now we're stuck with only your shoes to choose from," Lauren said.

"Remember, whatever happens, you are a beautiful, strong, independent, smart young woman who doesn't need a man to validate you," Mum said.

"If he asks you to get into a car or go back to his house, say no. It could be an abduction attempt," Nanna said.

None of this was helpful.

Now I'm about to leave and Harper is hovering around me.

"You look great," she says for the tenth time, which makes me think I don't look great. Once, it is believable, twice, I'm still with you, but this many times and I assume you are telling me the opposite, that there is some obvious thing wrong with my outfit that I've missed. I am tempted to run to my bedroom and change again but there's no time.

Jesse is lying on the couch, typing on his laptop, glasses on. I noticed he's started wearing them around the house during the day now.

"I don't trust guys named Henry," he says suddenly, without looking up from the screen.

"Why?" Harper says, hands on hips.

"It's the kind of name a serial killer would pick if they were trying to sound respectable," Jesse says, looking up.

"You sound like my nanna," I say, turning away from him. I need positive energy.

"Henry is not a serial killer, he's Penny's cousin, he plays the *flute*, and his name has always been Henry," Harper says to me.

"He could be a future serial killer. Brooke could be his first victim," Jesse says.

I am actually more worried about the fact he might use the date as future stand-up comedy material.

"Are you trying to sabotage this date?" Harper says, and Jesse's face goes a little bit red.

"Of course not," he says, looking back at his screen and adjusting his glasses.

"Then stop talking about serial killers." Harper shakes her head and turns to me. "You look great," she says. Again.

"It's going to be fine," I say to the room at large. "I'm good at dating." I don't know why I add this last bit. I'm trying to convince myself. I've never been on a date before, not like this, not a date *date*, where you meet someone you don't know at a predetermined location. Tristan and I got together at a party with all our school friends around, and most of our time together was either hanging out at home, studying, being on school committees together, or seeing each other at school. We didn't have a *dating* period. We were separate and then we were together.

"I mean, he might be awful," Harper says. "I can't know for sure, I've only met him at Penny's family stuff. Staking your reputation on a guy who you don't know very well is risky, it's risky, but I *think* it will be fine." This makes me lose a bit of confidence.

"He's very nice over text," I say.

"Nice guys are the worst," Jesse says. His negativity is starting to piss me off now.

"So we can't trust assholes but we can't trust nice guys either? Who do I trust then?" I say.

"Women," Harper says, then pauses. "Some women. About sixty percent."

"You can trust about thirty percent of men," Jesse says.

"Stop it," I say to him.

"Henry's in that thirty percent," Harper says. "He's related to Penny, so he has to be."

"We're not getting married. It's just a very low-key coffee date," I say. I am proud of the confidence I'm projecting. I look in the mirror one last time. I look fine. I want to look like the me of the photo or, even better, look like Lauren or Harper or Penny, all of whom have beautiful faces and their own distinctive styles, but I'm stuck being a deeply ordinary, mostly unremarkable person to look at.

"You could fall in love today," Harper says, clasping her hands together. Jesse's head snaps up from his computer, eyebrows raised.

That is somehow more stressful to hear than the possibility of death by serial killer. Fall in *love*? No. Horrible. I don't want love.

"Don't say that," I say.

I head toward the door.

"Brooke," Jesse says.

"I don't want to hear it," I say, turning around with my hands on my hips.

"I was just going to say. You do, um. You do look good," he says, and then clears his throat and coughs and looks back down at his computer screen.

"Oh. Thank you," I say, quickly turning away because now my face feels hot.

"Good luck!" Harper says. "Text us the minute it's over!" She's so stressed about this. She wants it to go well so badly, and I want to please her so badly, that I'm already digging in, telling myself, *Be open to love, be open to love, be open to love*, as I walk to the café.

EIGHTEEN

Now that I'm sitting in a busy café on a Saturday afternoon waiting for Henry to arrive, I understand that dating is hell and I want to die. I see why people date at night. If you're in a busy bar, there is darkness and crowds and noise, or in a restaurant there is a whole meal to be discussed and then ordered and then eaten and focused on and, if you're lucky, the lights are dim. And then there is the best option of all, the one I should have chosen, which is to see a movie together. True darkness and sitting facing forward and no possibility of talking and something to entertain you and snacks and maybe a recliner chair.

I can't remember what Henry looks like. I only ever saw that one quick photo on Penny's phone. Calm down. Yes I can. Brown hair, notable eyebrows. Brown hair, notable eyebrows.

I text him to say I'm at a corner table.

A few minutes later, a brown-haired guy with thick eyebrows approaches the table. He's in jeans and a black T-shirt, and maybe it's Henry. He's walking toward me with confidence and looking friendly, looking like a guy who plays the flute, and so I smile, and he smiles back. Yes, it's Henry, it's definitely Henry.

"Hi," I say brightly, and then I stand up, I'm not sure why, because I think maybe we're going to hug, although I have no idea why I think that, but now the thought is in my head. I'm going to hug him hello.

"Hi," he says, looking at me.

"How are you?" I say in my warmest voice, leaning forward a little, hoping he'll go in for a hug first.

"Good?" he says, looking hesitant and confused. Maybe he's wondering why I'm standing up or if we're going to hug. Be confident, be the one in charge. I'm already standing, I need to follow through. I reach forward and give him a quick "nice to meet you" hug and a cheek kiss. It feels very Melbourne, very adult, very "I'm experienced at dating," very "my life is sexy and interesting and I am too." I have transcended my small-town self.

He hugs me back, kind of, but he still seems hesitant.

I sit down, and he remains standing. Oh God, he's going to leave. The photo Penny sent was too nice, and in the light of day, the reality is starkly different. I should have sat somewhere with more flattering light. God, he's not even going to give me a chance to impress him with my personality. My pithy texts—do they count for *nothing*?

"So, um, can I get you anything?" he asks.

"Oh, I think they do table service here," I say.

"Yes we do," he says, nodding at me, and then I see he has pulled out a notepad and pen. The reality of what is happening is dawning on me, at first slowly, then all at once, like a bucket of icy water, a few drops, then the whole thing poured straight over my head.

That's not Henry. That is the waiter.

I hugged the waiter.

I *hugged* and *cheek kissed* the waiter.

I grip the edge of the table and try to stay calm.

"Um, just, I, I'm waiting for someone?" My voice is so high

that it's almost not discernible. I'm talking at a pitch maybe only dogs can hear.

"Right," he says. "I'll come back."

As soon as he leaves, I sit for three seconds, face burning. *This is okay, this is recoverable, this is a minor event in the course of a whole lifetime, think of the bigger picture, this is a funny story I can tell Henry when he gets here, we can make a joke with the waiter about it, if we get married they'll tell the story at our wedding ceremony, hilarious, hilarious, hilarious.*

And then the adrenaline of my fight-or-flight response kicks in.

I need to leave right now.

I grab my bag, get up, and run out the door.

NINETEEN

I have to walk around the streets and deep breathe for ten minutes until my heart slows down enough for me to think.

Henry has sent me a "Hey, I can't find you" text. And an "Are you definitely here?" And another one checking he has the right café. And then one saying, "The waiter thinks you might have been here and then left?"

That fucking waiter.

What a betrayal. He sits only slightly behind Jesse for deep, life-changing betrayals now.

Poor Henry. Poor lovely flute-playing, stand-up-comedian Henry with notable eyebrows who drove to the other side of the city to meet me.

What if someone saw the whole thing and filmed it and it's going viral right now? I resist the urge to go on every social media platform and start randomly scouring.

Okay, how do I recover this. I could just ghost him, never respond to his texts, block him, pretend it never happened. Except he's Penny's cousin, and everyone will know. Also that makes me an awful person. Henry deserves better.

I could tell him the truth. No, I can't type that story out. I just can't. And how do I explain the leaving, the failing to text him immediately and request a rain check? I just left him sitting there, stood-up, how bloody horrible.

How to say, I had to walk around the streets until the ringing in my ears stopped and my heart slowed and my face was no longer burning like the fire of a thousand suns. That I was in a state of such acute embarrassment, I was unable to communicate, that I briefly transcended the earth. But I'm completely normal and very datable. Please give me another chance.

What if Henry is my soulmate, my one true love, and I've blown it? He was so cute. Well, okay, I don't know this for sure, since I can't remember what he looks like, but the waiter was cute, and I have to imagine Henry looked somewhat similar to him.

Oh, God. And now I have to tell Harper.

And Penny.

And Lauren.

And my mother.

And Nanna.

Worst of all, somehow, Jesse.

Why do so many people know about this date?

I have to text Henry back something. I can't just leave those texts unanswered.

I write:

I'm so so sorry, I wasn't feeling well, I had to leave

I feel like I owe him more than that, he drove here and found a car park in a busy area, that's a lot of effort, so I need to add another line, a bit more detail, to make it more believable, something drawn from real life, maybe.

I ate a yogurt past its use-by date yesterday

Well. That's certainly something. If standing him up didn't

put him off, the implication I have explosive diarrhea certainly will have.

I stop in a bookshop on my walk home, to calm myself, taking long, shaking breaths at the nonfiction table, holding a Jane Austen to my heart, rereading a passage from my favorite YA novel until I am no longer on the edge of hysteria, and then I go home, trying to walk in the door as quietly as possible.

"Brooke! You're home already? Oh my God, how did it go!" Harper shouts, rushing out of her room. She must have been watching from the window.

"Um, not super well," I say.

Jesse puts his head out of his room. "What did he do? Did he have serial killer vibes?" he asks.

"He didn't do anything," I say.

"So. Tell us," Harper says, following me into the lounge room.

"I can't. It's too embarrassing." I have a feeling brewing in my chest and I honestly can't tell if it's laughter or tears.

Harper looks at my face, and she sits next to me and takes my hand in hers.

"I promise I won't laugh," she says, and her face is gentle, and I've never felt more like we're friends than right now.

"Or get mad?" I ask.

"Why would I get mad?"

"I might have mucked up your assignment."

"You won't have. All data is usable data. Also, who cares about the assignment."

"Okay."

Jesse is watching me, and his eyes are worried. I don't want to see them turn to amusement, or derision.

"I need Jesse to face the wall. I can't do it looking at his face."

"Come on, Brooke," he says. But there are only so many humiliations I can handle him witnessing.

"If you want the story, those are my terms," I say.

Harper makes a "do it" face at Jesse, who sighs and turns around to look at the wall.

"Happy?" he says.

"All right," I say. "I will tell you."

"Good," says Harper.

Deep breath. I can do this. Like ripping a Band-Aid off.

"I hugged the waiter."

"What does that mean?" Harper says.

"A man approached the table. I thought it was Henry. I hugged him. And kissed his cheek. It was the waiter."

"Oh my God!" Harper puts her hand to her mouth. She looks like she's not sure how to react yet and she's holding it in until she's heard all the details. I can see Jesse's shoulders shake a little. He's laughing, but silently, swallowing it down, at least.

"And then I just left, before Henry even arrived."

"Oh my God," Harper says again.

"There you go. Make fun of me," I say, throwing myself back on the couch and covering my face with a cushion.

"What did you tell Henry?" Harper asks.

"That I was sick. From eating bad yogurt."

"Oh my God," Harper says for a third time. Now she definitely wants to laugh.

"Stop saying that!" I wail.

"Okay, we can fix this," she says.

"I don't want to fix it. I want to pretend it never happened. I am never dating again. Never, never, never."

"This is totally recoverable," Harper says. "Don't you think, Jesse?"

"Ummmm," he says, sounding uncertain.

"Don't you think, Jesse?" Harper says again, emphasizing each word.

"Yes, yes, totally recoverable. Being stood up wouldn't put me off at all."

"I know it's not recoverable," I groan. "Henry was the perfect guy for me and I've ruined it."

"What can we do, to make you feel better?" Harper asks, kneeling beside the couch and speaking into the space between couch and cushion, where she can kind of see a bit of my face.

"Leave me alone to wallow in my pain," I say.

"What if we put *The Vampire Diaries* on?" Jesse asks, also bending down to peer in the crack. He and I have been watching it, late at night, together. It has become sort of a ritual. One I look forward to more than I want to admit.

I think about this for a second.

"Okay. But no one is allowed to look at me for two hours. In fact, I need a towel or something to put over my face." It feels very important to me that I can't see them and they can't see me until the humiliation passes.

"Here," Jesse says, pressing something into my hands. "Wear my blue hoodie again."

So I put on his hoodie, with the hood up, and it still smells like him, which I try not to notice, and we all watch *The Vampire Diaries* together, and Harper has no idea what is going on in the show, and Jesse earnestly tries to answer all her questions about vampire lore and love triangles. And it doesn't feel like the worst day ever anymore.

TWENTY

It's Harper's birthday, but she says she doesn't believe in celebrating birthdays or buying presents because it's childish, it's attention seeking, it's stressful, it's capitalism run amok. I accepted this and swallowed my urge to make a fuss, lecturing myself internally about respecting Harper's wishes and not buying her a gift even though I am exceptionally good at gift giving and already had three options planned. Then Jesse suggested we go to the pub for a few drinks as a household just to mark the occasion in some way, and Harper agreed, and she invited Penny, then some of her friends, and Penny invited more people, and suddenly it's a whole party, and I had to buy a present in a rush and ran out of time to wash my hair.

Now I'm sitting at the pub holding a soda water, which is my default drink when I'm out, even though I don't like it. I wish I had ordered a Coke, but somehow I am less embarrassed ordering a soda water than a Coke. I don't know why—there is just a random hierarchy of nonalcoholic drinks in my head and how ashamed of each one I should be, and Coke is at the bottom, the most shameful, because someone from school once rolled their eyes at me when I pulled a can of it out of my bag to drink at a party. The always hovering psychologist in my brain says, *Let's analyze why you attach shame to soft drinks at all.* But no, that is a thought for when I am lying in bed or sitting in an Introductory Microeconomics lecture, not now.

We have commandeered a bunch of couches in the corner of the pub, and Penny is sitting across from me. She's wearing a slinky satin dress she found in a thrift store, and her hair is in a long ponytail, trailing over one shoulder. Her skin looks like she has somehow applied a flattering photo filter to real life.

She leans over, suddenly.

"Okay, I have a surprise for you, Brooke." Her face makes me nervous.

"What is it?" I say, trying to look like I'm open to surprises, like I'm a perfectly normal person who enjoys unexpected things.

"It's a good surprise," Penny says. But if someone has to clarify the surprise is good, that means they think it might not be good.

I falter a little. "What is it, Penny?" I say.

"Henry is here!" Penny opens her arms wide.

"What, here *here*? Now?" I stand up, then quickly sit down. Jesse is looking all around, in a very unsubtle way. I want to yell at him to stop it.

"Yes!" Penny says. "He just walked in." She starts waving someone over.

Oh God, oh God. We've had no interaction since I told him I ate bad yogurt exactly one week ago. He never replied to that message and I don't even know if that counts as ghosting, since I was the one who stood him up, and it wasn't even the kind of message you can respond to. I sit up straight. I wish I could check my face, my breath, my armpits, maybe just run to a private bathroom and strip totally naked and examine every flaw, spray myself down, get dressed again and double-check nothing is tucked where it should be out or out where it should be tucked, but there's no time. He has walked over, and he's sitting down right in front of me on the couch opposite.

The eyebrows really aren't as notable as I thought they'd be. He's cute, but a bit less cute than the waiter was, maybe. He has heavy stubble, almost a beard, which he didn't have in the photo that Harper and Penny showed me, so I was never going to recognize him. They really set me up to fail. He's also shorter and more muscular than I'd expected.

"Hi!" I say way too brightly.

"Hi." He smiles with an equal amount of false cheer.

"Great to finally meet you," I say. *I did not have diarrhea.* How do I quietly slip that into the conversation?

"You too," he says, nodding. Oh God. This is awkward, it's terribly awkward. We have nothing to say and everyone is watching and I can't bring up the failed-date elephant in the room. My stomach is cramping like I actually have eaten bad yogurt.

Penny introduces him to everyone else, and she starts telling a story about her family, and Henry looks relieved, because he can chime in. They laugh together about an argument between his mother and Penny's mother, and everything is going well, except Henry and I haven't exchanged a word since he arrived. Maybe I need to move closer to him. Would sitting beside him be easier? No, opposite each other is best.

There is a break in the conversation, and Henry politely leans toward me.

"How's uni going?" he says.

"Good! How about for you?" I say.

"Yeah, good." He nods.

"That's good." I nod as well. There are too many "goods" and too much nodding. But my mind is completely blank, totally void of all conversation topics. I need to say something. Anything. What do I know about him? Dogs, St. Kilda Football Club, comedy, flute. Knowing he likes dogs doesn't really help with conversation. What am I going to say, "Have you seen any great dogs lately?" "What's your favorite breed?" They are not starter questions. The football team would help if I knew anything about football, but I don't. Comedy? Ask him to tell a joke? God, no. The flute. That's the best option.

"So you play the flute?" I say.

"Yes I do," he says. More nodding.

"For how long?"

"About ten years," he says. He looks incredibly nervous, and I can see him subtly wiping his sweaty palms on his jeans, which softens my heart a little.

"Amazing," I say. Is it amazing? Only by fairly low standards of what one might consider amazing, but I am reaching for any word that might help liven things up.

"What are your hobbies?" he asks me.

"Um," I say. Hobbies, hobbies. Watching cleaning videos. Browsing fancy furniture websites for things I can never afford to fit out a house I will never own. Watching YouTube compilations of couples from TV shows I've never even seen, because I like to know the whole relationship story before starting the show. No, no, no. These are not hobbies you talk about.

"I like reading," I say weakly.

"Cool, cool," Henry says, nodding with great enthusiasm and clearly not listening but instead preparing the next question he's going to ask. "And what are you studying? Oh wait, you already told me that when we were texting, I remember." He laughs, rubs his hands on his jeans again. He's so nervous, it feels contagious.

The funny sparkly person I was when we first texted is gone.

Maybe she only existed in my mind. I shouldn't ever read back over those texts, just in case.

Harper nudges me, and I look at her with relief. *Save me.* "There's a guy that keeps looking over here," she says after a minute. "At you," she adds.

"Who?" I say. Probably someone looking on in sympathy as I struggle through my Henry flirting.

"He's turned his back on us now, but that guy in the corner."

I look where Harper is pointing.

It can't be. Surely not. I have enough to deal with tonight.

My stomach is already sinking and clenching when he half turns and I confirm who it is.

Tristan.

Tristan is here, in *my* local pub, in *my* city, in *my* line of sight.

Fuck.

Fuck.

"Fuck!" I say.

"What?" Harper's concerned.

"That's Tristan," Jesse says in a voice that's way too loud. "Brooke's ex," he explains to Penny and Henry.

I watch as Tristan puts his hand on the back of a girl. It's Kendra. I know her mostly from my social media stalking of them, which I still do, almost subconsciously, as part of my weekend wind-down bedtime routine. Just checking in on the ten or twenty accounts of people, some of whom I know and some I don't, to see what they've been doing with their week. Kendra looks better in person. That almost never happens. Oh God, oh God.

"Tristan *and* his girlfriend," I add.

Penny puts her hand over her mouth and looks suitably horrified.

"What do you want us to do," Harper asks. She's fake smiling, turning to me, talking through gritted teeth. I appreciate she immediately knows that this is a crisis and that we need to pretend outwardly that it is not.

"Act normal," I say, also speaking through a gritted-teeth fake smile.

"Why wouldn't we act normal?" Jesse says.

"Because *Tristan* is here with his *girlfriend*," I say. I almost say "who he dumped me for," but I would rather Henry didn't know that fact, because even though I am already certain that Henry and I have no future, I still want him to have a sliver of respect for me as a person.

My palms are sweaty now. I am trying to see Tristan while not obviously looking. If you'd asked me this morning, "Do you care what Tristan thinks of you?" I would have said, "Of course not," and I would have meant it, one hundred percent. And now I see him here, in the flesh, I feel the complete opposite. It's not so much I care what he thinks, it's that I need him to have very specific thoughts about me at the end of the night when he's lying in bed, thoughts that include the words "God, she looked *great*" and "She's even smarter than I remember" and "She really *was* too good for me." Nothing I currently have at my disposal will make him think those thoughts. I need to quickly think of at least three impressive things I've done since we broke up to drop into conversation and also turn back time so I can change my decision to not wash my hair this afternoon.

"I'm freaking out. I can't just sit here and let him see me, here, like . . . like . . . this." I sound near hysterical.

"Like what?" Jesse says.

Henry is looking at me like I might be losing my mind. Clearly neither of them has the emotional capacity to understand how everything in my life now hinges on a possible interaction with Tristan.

"Like *this*." Exposed, unprepared, with no achievements, no secret weapons, at hand. Tristan will look at me, and he'll somehow know about everything: Dad standing me up, me hugging the waiter, the exploding cyst, the ingrown hair I currently have on my bikini line, that I haven't kissed anyone since him.

Harper puts her hand on my arm. She understands. Or maybe she's just learning how to read my anxiety spirals.

"Do you want to hide from him?" Harper says.

"Yes, I should hide. In the bathrooms? Maybe I'll just go home?" I say.

"No. No. Don't leave," Penny says. She's looking thoughtful.

"We can just ignore him," Jesse says.

"I can't ignore him," I say. Tristan and I are friends. Friendly. We said we would stay friends. We haven't actually spoken all year, but the *spirit* of friendship exists between us. Tristan is the kind of guy who likes to say, "I'm still friends with all of my exes." Whatever we are, I know he will come over and talk to me. I know it. And to ignore him, to act like we're not friends, to cause a scene, it would make me the loser in this scenario, because he and Kendra would assume I was still upset over the breakup.

"Okay," Penny says. "And just hear me out on this." She's smiling in an I've-had-a-wild-idea-that-just-might-work way, which makes me nervous. Even more nervous than when she told me she had a surprise. Still, any idea is better than no idea.

"I'm listening," I say.

"He comes over for a chat, and Henry pretends to be your boyfriend."

Henry looks startled and then terrified by this idea. Penny is looking pleased with herself, obviously thinking she can still make this match happen.

"I don't know," I say, looking at Harper. I need a voice of reason.

"It could work," Harper says to me, nodding vigorously.

"Um, I'm not sure," Henry says, also desperately looking for a voice of reason.

Penny turns to me, gripping both my arms, eyes wide with the excitement of hatching a scheme. She is not going to be a voice of reason for anyone.

"This is not a reflection on your life, Brooke. It's just sometimes, when it comes to running into your ex, even if your life is going perfectly, and you look hot—which you do, you look extremely hot tonight, doesn't she, Henry?—even if you love being single, even if everything is perfect, in this brief moment you just want that added element of having shown them you have moved on to a new relationship. It's not sensible, it's not healthy, it's not smart, but sometimes you have to do it."

I take a deep breath. Am I that insecure? That desperate? No! I'm here in Melbourne, with actual *friends*, wearing a (fake, cheap) leather jacket, my hair might be unwashed but it has dry shampoo in it so it's not *terrible*, and as much as I don't feel it, I'm living my best life. I am, or at least I'm living a good one. I'm fine, I'm fine, I'm *fine*. I don't need to step off the cliff into chaos.

"No, I think it's okay. I don't need a fake boyfriend. That's too much. That's going too far," I say. I smile reassuringly at Henry, so he knows I can recognize a bad idea when I hear it.

Henry looks relieved. Penny is disappointed.

"I think he's coming over," Jesse announces.

"Shit," I say.

I sneak a look. I can see Tristan kissing Kendra on the cheek, whispering something in her ear, and then walking in this direction. I look away before he can make eye contact. He's going to say, "How are you?" and, "What have you been up to?" and, "Are you seeing anyone?" and I don't know how to answer any of those questions. They feel impossible. Look at the failure of a conversation I've just had with Henry. I'm boring, and I have no news and nothing to say. Panic is rising in my chest. Penny's words echo in my head.

It's not sensible, it's not healthy, it's not smart, but sometimes you have to do it.

"I've changed my mind, I've changed my mind, I do need a fake boyfriend, just for the next ten minutes," I say. I need *something*, some kind of armor. Penny claps her hands with excitement, like a villain when their dastardly plan comes together, and she nudges Henry.

"Do it!" she says, nodding at him enthusiastically.

Henry looks like a man being dragged to his death.

"I don't . . . I don't think I can. I hate public speaking."

"How is this public speaking?" Penny says.

"I don't know, it's just giving me the same feeling. I'm not very good at on-the-spot stuff, I . . . ," he says, shaking his head.

"What about your stand-up?" Penny says. "This will be exactly like performing onstage."

"Not *exactly*," I say quickly. I don't want him doing comedy. "But similar."

"I haven't had a lot of stage experience yet," Henry says.

There is a beat of silence. Tristan will be here any second. I can almost see a droplet of sweat forming on Henry's forehead. I need to put the poor boy out of his misery.

"Henry, I swear to God, I'll message your mum and sisters right now," Penny says, holding up her phone threateningly.

"Penny, no," Henry says.

"I'm opening the family group chat," Penny says.

"Stop! It's okay, it's fine, don't worry about it, Henry does not need to do anything," I say, shaking my head at Penny.

"I'll do it," Jesse says, raising his hand like we're in class. "I'll be your fake boyfriend."

"Um," I say. "Really?"

"Sure," he says, shrugging and smiling. "Why not?"

I'm about to say, "Actually, it's a bad idea, a very, very bad idea, I can think of many reasons why not," but before I can, before I can think any of this through, Tristan is in front of me.

TWENTY-ONE

"Brooke!! And . . . Jesse!" Tristan is looking fake surprised, as if he hasn't been spying on me for the last twenty minutes. He holds his arms wide for a hug. I vowed never to hug anyone again after the waiter-hug situation, but, okay, we're doing this, we're going to hug. Tristan is historically a good hugger. I stand up, maneuver around the table between us. He pulls me close, a full-body deep embrace, because it's Tristan. Of course he does, of course he goes for a deep, meaningful hug. I bet his eyes are shut.

We pull apart.

"I'm here with Kendra," Tristan says, pointing to her chatting to a small group of people. She looks over and waves. Why is this the first thing he says? He's letting me know he's not available. He thinks he needs to say this up front in case I get any ideas. A ripple of anger goes through me.

"I'm here with my housemate Harper, it's her birthday, and this is Harper's girlfriend, Penny, and Penny's cousin Henry . . . and you know Jesse, of course." I falter. Am I really going to do this? Jesse stands up and walks over to us. He gives me a we've-got-this smile.

"Hey man," Jesse says to Tristan.

"Hey. How are you?"

"Good, good," Jesse says. He's using a slightly weird voice. I don't know if he's getting into character for our fake relationship, or if he is just slipping into a high school version of himself around Tristan.

"What are you doing here?" Tristan asks him.

"I'm here with Brooke. We're housemates and, um—" Jesse says, pausing, glancing at me, a final check-in, an are-we-really-doing-this? Now we're on the edge of it, it feels reckless, impulsive, unplanned. Not me.

But, screw it.

"And Jesse is also my boyfriend," I say.

There. I've done it. Look at me go!

I regret it immediately, of course. How absurd. The word "boyfriend" spluttered out of my mouth like it was something I swallowed and then coughed up.

Tristan laughs, then stops.

"Wait. You're serious?" he says.

"Yes," Jesse says, moving slightly closer to me.

"You two? Together? Together, like a *couple*?" Tristan says. He looks completely shocked and not at all happy with this news. I toss my hair a little. Maybe I don't regret it. Maybe Penny is a genius.

"Yes," Jesse says again, and to his credit, his voice has not wavered. He is steady. He is committed to the lie. He is enjoying Tristan's outrage as much as I am.

"Oh my God," Tristan says.

I can see Henry, Penny, and Harper watching us in fascination. Now that he's not involved, Henry looks like he's happily settling in for the show. He gives me a little thumbs-up. Harper stands up and joins us.

"Hi, Tristan, I'm Harper," she says. "How do you know Brooke?" she adds, which I appreciate. Setting the groundwork of making sure he knows I have never spoken of him or thought of him again and certainly didn't discuss him tonight or any night previously.

"Brooke was my high school girlfriend," Tristan says, all nostalgic sounding, as if we are at our school's twenty-year reunion not barely six months into our postschool lives.

Before Harper can say anything else, Tristan turns back to me. "So. Wait. I'm sorry. How did you two get together? Because this is *wild*," he says.

I need an amazing getting-together story. No, wait, I don't. Keep it simple. Simple is believable. But I could add some fun, romantic details. He can't prove me wrong. I'll say I fell off a boat and Jesse dived in to save me, no, maybe Jesse fell off the boat and *I* saved him, or probably neither of us should fall off a boat but I feel attached to the admittedly very improbable boat idea now.

"We moved into the same share house, and started spending a lot of time together, and it just happened one night," Jesse says.

Fine. That sounds normal and believable. It doesn't sound romantic, though. I need Jesse to be a little more "head over heels in love" and less "her room is near the kitchen and it's convenient to stop there after I get a snack."

"Wow. Wow. I just can't get over this. Brooke used to, I mean, she really didn't—" Tristan stops himself from outright saying that I hated Jesse. I am starting to remember that I did complain to Tristan about Jesse on occasion. Multiple occasions. Tristan wasn't at Gretel's party, and I never told him about what happened there, although he may have heard it from others. But I did tell him Jesse and I had once had a fight that ended our friendship.

"Well, you know, people change, feelings change," I say quickly, to head off anything further Tristan might say on that topic.

"So you're *living* together? This is really serious then?" Tristan says.

"We're not living together in the sense of living together as a couple. I mean, we live together, and we're together, but we're not *living together*. We just happen to be a couple who live in a house together. Harper lives there too," I say, descending into babble and making big hand gestures.

"It's very casual," Harper says, then pauses. "I mean, the living situation. Their relationship is serious, or semi-serious. Well, no, it's serious, but our house is casual, it all has a casual feel." She's worse than I am. She looks at me, helpless and apologetic.

My scalp feels itchy and sweaty. Is that normal, when you lie, for your head to sweat? And itch? I know I have lied many times before, I must have, but not like this, a whole big *scenario*.

"I just can't get over this," Tristan says, and he turns and sits down on the couch next to Henry, as though he's settling in for a long conversation. "I have so many questions," he adds.

This might have been a huge mistake.

"I mean, there's not much to tell," I say, sitting down too. Jesse sits next to me, and I am acutely aware of the amount of space between us. At a glance, about fifteen centimeters. That's too much. That's platonic space. We need to reduce it to a couple of centimeters at most. I shuffle a bit closer, in the most subtle way I can, until our legs are near touching.

"Let's go back to the beginning. How long *exactly* have you two been together?" Tristan asks.

"About a month," Jesse says without hesitation. A month. Okay, yes. That's a believable amount of time. I just need to very quickly think of a potential month's worth of fake memories and lies.

I lean back against the couch and Jesse does too, and his shoulder touches mine and his whole body is very close. We've never sat this close before. On the nights we've been sitting up watching TV together, we stay on opposite ends of the couch, a blanket sometimes stretching the distance between us, our feet bumping one another occasionally. To be this close, gently touching from shoulder down to our knees, feels good. No, more than good. It's almost thrilling. It's probably just the adrenaline from the lying, or maybe my body has developed an involuntary physiological reaction to Jesse's body, a deep, automatic, biological response that is completely separate from my actual feelings.

"So, I'm sorry, I know I'm dwelling on this, but how did you two get past all your issues?" Tristan is asking.

"All their issues?" Harper says.

"Jesse and Brooke really did not get along in high school," Tristan says.

I can see Harper absorbing this information, tucking it away to discuss later. She and Penny exchange a look.

"It's all ancient history," I say airily, waving my hand. "Now tell us about *you*."

"Who made the first move?" Tristan says, ignoring my desperate attempt to turn the conversation back on him. He has always been a good listener, a good asker of questions. Too many questions. He likes to analyze. His parents are psychologists, after all. He loved saying, "Tell me what you're thinking about right now," or, "Tell me what you think about this," and would hand me his phone open to a five-thousand-word article I didn't have time to read on a topic I knew nothing about, but I would stop everything and skim-read it, determined to say something intelligent, because I never wanted him to think he was smarter or knew more than me, because I suspected he thought he was. It was exhausting. He's a deep diver, a person who needs to *understand* something intimately.

He also loves gossip.

"Well, I mean, that's kind of private," I say, and at the same time Jesse says:

"Brooke did."

"Brooke did?" Tristan says. His eyes are wide.

Damn him. *Him* being both Jesse and Tristan.

"Yes, I did," I say, because I have no other option and this whole situation is basically an improv sketch now.

"She held my hand during an episode of *The Vampire Diaries*," Jesse says. It takes all of my power to stop my face from reacting with anything other than what I hope looks like a glow of happiness. On the inside, I am a desperate churn of emotions. Anxiety, as always, front and center, the star performer.

"Since when do you watch *The Vampire Diaries*?" Tristan says to me, and it occurs to me how many bits and pieces of myself I hid from him to make sure he considered me an intellectual equal.

"Oh, I made her watch it," Jesse says.

"So how does it work? Getting together while living together?" Tristan asks. He's leaning forward, sleeves rolled up, ready to dissect our life. He's holding a beer, thank God, because I need him to lose some of his sharpness. Tristan doesn't handle his alcohol well. He'll turn from sober and thoughtful to a gluggy mess very quickly, and the faster he gets there right now the better.

"Well, we have a lot of rules," I say. Rules seem the obvious solution. If you were to date a housemate, it could work, with the right structure, the right boundaries, the right system. A contract even.

"What kind of rules?" Tristan asks.

"We really limit any displays of affection around Harper. No kissing unless it's a peck hello or goodbye. Small amounts of couch snuggling," I say.

"Except when I have Penny over, and then it's, like, we're on more equal ground," Harper interjects.

"And we have set nights that we spend in each other's rooms, and set nights we spend on our own. And we still go on dates outside of the house, every Thursday night. And we have an agreed-upon code word we use, when we want or need space from each other, and you can use that word up to three times a week, without the other person getting offended."

"The code word is wackadoo," Henry blurts out, apparently also wanting to be included now. He smiles nervously at me, and I look at him in slight horror. Why would he say *that*? Why would he even pretend to know our code word? And why would it be *wackadoo*?

There are too many people trying to help and get involved now.

"Wackadoo. Okay, sure," Tristan says. "That's a lot of rules," he adds, but without judgment. Tristan knows me. This all seems normal to him. He helped me color-code my study schedule six months in advance, blocking in time for "intense study," time for "light study," and time for "productive rest" to absorb everything I had learned.

"I have the rules all typed up, and spiral bound. They have

a table of contents and everything," I say, because I can see it in my mind's eye, a lovely black folder of rules that keep a relationship on track, contained, safe.

I feel Jesse's shoulder press into mine ever so slightly, a warning, perhaps, that I am taking it too far.

"Huh," Tristan says, and shakes his head. "Brooke and Jesse. Jesse and Brooke. I just never would have picked it." That's the part bothering him most, I can tell. That he can't understand it, that he doesn't see how it could have happened. Maybe he's not convinced. I feel acutely aware of him watching us closely. We're still sitting up against each other, but it might have been long enough that we should have touched in some other way by now.

I try to think of a natural way to touch Jesse. How did I use to touch Tristan? He was very touchy-feely. I don't remember ever thinking about it, other than wishing he weren't touching me so much. He would come up behind me and rub my shoulders, which should have been a lovely gesture, and it was, but it always got on my nerves. It made me feel like I was wearing a heavy, oversize, itchy jumper that I just wanted to pull off. It was suffocating. It's things like that that make me think I'm not cut out for intimacy.

I glance at Jesse, and he looks back at me, and there's a lot we are both trying to communicate in a two-second exchange of facial expressions, and I don't think either of us successfully gets anything across.

I go to touch his knee and then I chicken out and kind of oddly brush my hand across his thigh, and then to cover that up, I pretend there is something on his leg that really does need wiping off and I swipe a few more times. I can see an amused what-the-hell-are-you-doing look in his eyes.

A waitress brings over a platter of food Harper ordered and puts it on the small table between our couches. I lean forward and pick up a warm olive. As I sit back, Jesse reaches out and tucks my hair behind my ear, like he did when we took the photo. It's a very quick, soft movement, his hands brush against my neck with the lightest touch, and suddenly I have goose bumps all over my arms.

Why did he have to do that? Why did he have to be *tender*? It's becoming very clear to me this isn't a good idea, emotionally. Seeing Tristan, meeting Henry, pretending with Jesse. My heart and my head are getting all mixed up.

Tristan, Jesse, and Henry are making cheerful small talk, and I keep eating, because if my mouth is full, Tristan might not ask me any more questions. Then Henry suggests a game of pool, and suddenly it's Tristan and Henry pairing up against Jesse and me.

I follow Jesse over to the pool table. Tristan was supposed to have returned to Kendra by now.

"You're up first," Jesse says, handing me the pool cue.

I have only the vaguest idea of how to play. I hold the cue loosely in my hands and then try to copy what I've seen other people do. It feels very unwieldy.

Jesse watches me for a second. "Can I show you how to use it?" he says.

"Are you going to mansplain pool to me?" I say.

"I think it's only mansplaining if you already know something. If you don't, then it's just regular explaining," he says, smiling.

"Now you're mansplaining what mansplaining is." I smile back.

"I'm honestly just trying to stop you tearing up the felt," he says, gently nudging me with his shoulder.

"Okay, fine, show me." I put my hands on my hips and watch him demonstrate proper technique.

I try to copy him, but the cue feels big and cumbersome in my hands. I really do hate being bad at things. Jesse walks behind me. "I know it's a cliché, but I have to do it like this," he whispers in my ear, leaning his body over mine and adjusting my grip. We are pressed entirely against each other, my back to his chest, his hands over mine as he shows me how to hold the cue. Goddamn it. Why are my hormones so weak, why is my body so weak, why does he smell so good? This is about me. It's only because I am sex starved, attention starved, touch starved. I would react this way to anyone right now—it's not Jesse-specific. Well, except I was just thinking about how I didn't like Tristan to touch me. But that's different, that was last year. If it were Henry pressed against me right now, my body would react in the same way. Probably. Maybe. I look at Henry, earnestly chatting to Tristan, nodding enthusiastically about something, foam from his beer on his top lip, and my certainty falters.

I pretend to adjust my grip, but really it's an excuse to step back into Jesse's body a little more. I accidentally step on his foot.

"Ow," he breathes into my ear.

Why is that so sexy, damn it?

"Sorry," I say.

He gives me instructions, and I nod, then I tap the ball with my pool cue, and it's a surprisingly good shot. I turn and hug him in celebration, which feels like what a couple would do. But it also feels natural.

Jesse lifts me up off the floor with the hug, and my face is right at the part where his neck meets his shoulder, and I have a particular weakness for where a neck meets a shoulder, so it's only natural my heart flutters. My cheek presses against his bare skin, and I resist the urge to keep it there, to burrow in, to just stay put.

He puts me down, and I turn away, because I'm scared of what my face might be revealing.

We keep playing, laughing, high-fiving when I hit a good shot, teasing each other, and I forget we are only pretending to be a couple. I forget that this is Jesse. I forget *Do I like Brooke? No. No. Fuck, no.*

We beat Tristan and Henry. Twice. Mostly because Henry is quite bad at pool and obviously doesn't care about losing. He cheerfully clapped and cheered whenever Jesse or I made a good shot. Tristan pretends like he doesn't care, but I know he loves to win a game, any game. There's nothing less appealing than someone who really, really loves to win but pretends they don't, and then makes excuses as to why they're annoyed when they lose. "Just admit it," I want to say to him. "I can admit it."

"I guess Jesse and I are just a really good partnership," I say, mostly because I want to see Tristan's reaction. He'll dwell on this, the idea that I might be in a more successful partnership of any kind.

"How many times have you played together before?" Tristan asks suspiciously. He's been drinking beers throughout the game, and I can see he's almost drunk.

"Never, she's just naturally talented," Jesse says, standing behind me, and then he puts his arms around me in a hug, his arms meeting across my chest and his head resting on the top of my head, and my face feels burning hot, like a full-body blush, my skin tingly from my toes to my head.

Brooke, this is fake.

Fake. Pretend. Not real. A fiction.

Do I actually like Jesse in some way, or do I just like having a pretend boyfriend, or maybe it's because Tristan is here stirring up things, combined with the failure of Henry, or maybe it's just my loneliness sparking a fire inside me, or maybe it's some kind of psychological reaction to my history with Jesse. I need someone to analyze me, slap my face, pull me together, tell me what the hell is going on.

TWENTY-TWO

Tristan is definitely getting drunk and sloppy now. So is Henry. Kendra is still with her group of friends, but she keeps looking over at Tristan and making faces. I can't tell if she's unhappy that he hasn't rejoined her or if she wants to escape and join him. Tristan and Henry are busy bonding over a comedy show they both love, quoting it at each other and collapsing in laughter.

"You've seen it, haven't you, Tooky?" Tristan says to me. Tooky was the nickname he called me when we were together. I tense at his use of it.

"Yes, I watched a bit of it," I say.

"Sorry. Did you say *Tooky*?" Jesse says to Tristan.

"Tooky was her nickname," Tristan says, smiling sadly and shaking his head like I'm dead and he's reflecting back over my life. He's way drunker than I'd realized. Classic Tristan. He does this, seems fine, and then, bam, he's very drunk, and there's no time to adjust between the two states.

"Interesting," Jesse says, looking at me with wide eyes, and I know he's going to tease me about it later.

"Tooky," Henry says, and laughs. He seems to have crossed

the line into drunk at the same time as Tristan. Jesse, thankfully, hasn't been drinking at all.

Jesse and I sit, pressed close on the couch, and listen to Henry and Tristan happily chatting, moving on from the show they both like to a podcast they both love, talking over each other. We occasionally try to join in the conversation, but they're not really listening to us. Henry and I might have failed but I'm happy he's at least getting a good friendship date right now. It's only when I see Harper and Penny chatting to a big group of Harper's friends that I realize Jesse probably wants to escape this and go and join them. Amber might even be here somewhere.

"I'm sorry. This was supposed to be a five-minute thing. And it's ruined your whole night," I say to him.

"It hasn't ruined my night. I'm having fun," he says.

"Really?" I'm not sure if I believe him. This is the problem with pretending to be in a relationship. Where does the sham stop and the truth start. Also, I'm never sure other people are having the same amount of fun as I am.

"Well, we won pool." He ticks it off on his fingers.

"That's true."

"And Tristan is clearly pissed off on some level that we're together." Another finger tick.

"Also true."

"And these two are very entertaining together." Tick. "Plus I found out Tristan's pet name for you was Tooky." He holds up four fingers. "Are four reasons enough evidence?"

"You need a fifth one before I can officially accept you might be having fun," I say.

He drops his hand and lets it rest near mine. "Number five. Pretending to be your boyfriend isn't the worst thing in the world," he says. He's looking at me like he's trying to gauge my reaction to that comment, and it makes me swallow nervously. I glance away.

"Okay, good, five solid reasons," I say, still not looking at him.

Across from us, Tristan gestures wildly and his beer sloshes onto my shoe.

"Tooky, I'm sorry!" he yells. Henry kneels down to wipe it with a clean tissue he pulls out of his pocket, despite my protests that he really doesn't need to do that.

"I can fix this for you," Henry mumbles, looking up at me with big drunk eyes as he runs the tissue over my shoe. I resist the urge to pat his head like he's a sweet-tempered dog, and I help him get up again because he seems a little unsteady.

"How much time have you spent in your life managing other people's drunkenness?" Jesse asks when I settle back against the couch beside him.

"A fair bit."

He doesn't know about Lauren, not really, or Dad, so he doesn't know the true extent of it.

"Were you happy, at school?" he asks. His eyes are so serious.

"I was. Sometimes." I pause and look at him. "I think I was pretty lonely at school but I didn't realize the feeling was loneliness because I was surrounded by people all the time." The confession slips out, like water through the cracks in a dam. He's causing cracks in me.

"Yeah. I know that feeling," he says.

"You do?"

"I felt like that at home."

"Oh," I say. "I'm sorry." There's a beat, where we just look at each other. Jesse looks away first this time.

Henry suddenly leans toward us.

"Do you want to hear my comedy set?" he asks.

"Yes," says Tristan emphatically.

"Oh, we definitely do." Jesse grins.

"Okay. It's not, like, edgy or anything," Henry says, pressing his hands together anxiously.

"We don't need edgy," I assure him. I almost want to hug him. I suspect he and I operate with similar levels of anxiety humming through our brains.

Jesse reaches out and holds my hand while we listen, sliding his fingers between mine. It really feels like we're a couple, that we've been a couple for a long time, while also feeling like the most new, exciting, delicious secret in the world.

I lean into him a little more. The feel of his hand against mine is irresistible. I look at him at the same time he looks at me. Henry is talking, doing a sort-of-funny bit about the self-checkout at supermarkets, but I can barely hear him over the roaring, pounding of my heart in my ears. We're so close, it's almost unbearable. I'm worried I'm going to just pour myself on top of him, like a glass of water. I need to get myself under control but I don't know how.

"I'm just going to get a drink," I say, letting go of his hand and standing up.

Jesse's eyes follow me.

"Brooke, you're going to miss Henry's punch line!" Tristan yells.

"I'll be back," I say, hurrying away from them. I lean on the bar, ask the bartender for water, and then sit on a barstool sipping it, trying to get my bearings, trying to dampen all the nerve endings that have come alive inside me, trying to convince myself I am not really feeling what I'm feeling right now. I need to cool down, in every sense of the word. I take off my jacket and run a droplet of water up and down my arms.

"Hey," says Jesse, at my shoulder.

"Hey."

"Kendra came over to talk with Tristan and I think she's unhappy about all the time he's been spending catching up with you," Jesse says. He slides onto the barstool next to me, and I sneak a look over my shoulder at Tristan and Kendra. Things do seem a little heated between them.

"But he dumped me for her. There's nothing for her to feel insecure about," I say.

I turn sideways on the stool so I can keep subtly watching them. They have the distinct look of a couple who are tearfully arguing in public but desperately trying to hide the fact they are tearfully arguing in public. Kendra points at me, and Tristan shakes his head.

"I feel bad," I say.

Jesse turns on his stool too, so he's facing me. Our knees bump together. "We could help them," he says.

"Help them how?"

"Well, we could show them how into each other we are, so Kendra can see that your focus is on me, not Tristan," Jesse says. His tone is light, carefree, but his knee is pressing against mine and my mouth is suddenly very dry. I take another sip of my water.

"Oh," I say, struggling to think of words because my cheeks feel very warm and I want to appear as calm and unruffled as Jesse seems right now. Nothing to see here, just two people talking about ways to demonstrate how deeply into each other they are, if they were, in fact, deeply into each other, which they are not. Probably. Possibly. My hands are trembling. I put my glass down on the bar and square my shoulders.

"So, how do we show them that?" I say. "They've already seen us looking fairly couple-y."

"Well, to start, you could look at me adoringly," he says, smiling.

I frown. "Or you could look at *me* adoringly," I say.

"I am," he says, and the way he says it makes my heart speed up.

"All right. Adoring looks. And then?" I say.

"Then you could move a bit closer to me," he says. "If you want to," he adds.

"Okay," I say. I can't say, "I want to," because I can't say the word "want." It's too revealing. I slip off my stool and stand between his legs. I'm hovering, not sure what to do, how close to get, until he puts his arms around my waist and draws me to him. The stool is tall, and so is he, so even though I'm standing and he is seated, our eyes are level.

"What else?" I say.

"You could put your hands like this," he says. He gently takes my hands in his hands, lifts them up, and puts them around his neck. It feels a bit like we're actors in a play, following directions—at least, that's what I tell myself, until our eyes meet, and then everything inside me is aflame.

"Is it working?" I say, willing myself back into a cold and clinical state. I need to become a statue—unmoving, emotionless, safe. "Are they looking at us?"

Jesse glances to his left and then back at me.

"They're looking," he says.

"Okay. What next?" I am trying to sound casual. Bored, even. To show him this is nothing to me. Standing here, with my hands around his neck, inches from his face, his arms around my waist, my breathing rapid, this is *nothing*. It has to be nothing.

"We could . . ." He pauses. "I could . . ." He trails off again. His composure has slipped, and he's lost his nerve. He seems almost shy.

"You could . . . ?" I prompt him. My heart is racing.

He clears his throat. "I could kiss you," he says quietly, looking at me intently, waiting for my reaction.

I wonder if he is thinking of what I am thinking of—when he kissed me at Gretel's party, and what happened after. He must be. It's unavoidable. My mind touches on the memory and skitters away, the jab of pain it brings still there, bright and sharp as ever. But I don't want to think of it, not right now. I don't have the capacity to think of it. I can't hold that alongside everything else going on in my mind and body. I just want to be in *this* moment, for once.

"You could kiss me," I say back to him, nodding. My tone is light, but my voice hitches a little.

"Just to help Tristan and Kendra," he says. "So there's no confusion. Or doubts. Kendra probably needs that certainty."

He runs his fingertips up and down my back, very gently, almost absentmindedly, and I have to close my eyes for a second, to catch my breath. I'm wearing only a thin top, and my skin is alive to every part of his touch.

"She does, she does need that certainty, I think," I say, desperately trying to make my voice sound normal, natural, unaffected by his hands on me, unaffected by what he is proposing. "And Tristan needs the closure of seeing me kiss someone else," I add.

"He definitely does," Jesse says, nodding.

I nod back. "Good. We're agreed. On kissing."

"Yes," he says.

Jesse moves, and I think he's going to kiss me, but instead he stands up from the stool, which means our faces are farther apart, but our bodies are suddenly pressed closer. I rest my head against his chest. I can feel his heart beating through his T-shirt. It's going as fast as mine.

I look up at him.

"So," I say. I'm nervous. I'm so nervous, I almost want to run away and hide. It's too much, everything I am feeling, everything I don't want to be feeling.

"How about I just lean down, like this?" Jesse says, kind of murmuring, our faces almost touching. He seems to understand that I need to feel in control. That he needs to move slowly.

"Okay," I say.

"And then I put my hand on your cheek, like this," he says.

"Mmm-hmmm," I say.

"I'll push back this bit of hair," he says, tucking it behind my ear.

"Okay," I say, closing my eyes because looking at him feels unbearable.

"And then I'll kiss you very, very slowly," he says, his words barely words, barely a whisper, and then his lips touch mine as he finishes the sentence.

He kisses me as slowly as he said he would, and I kiss him back. It's soft and careful and lovely. He starts to draw away, but then changes his mind, and he leans back in and kisses me again, but with more urgency this time. I kiss him back.

We kiss like we're in private, like we're not standing in the middle of a pub. I push my hands into his hair. He has his hands on my back, pulling me in closer. I didn't know kissing could feel like this. I didn't know *I* could feel like this.

Then I realize what we're doing, and where we are, and I pull away, almost panting. I'm scared he's going to find me out, that he'll be able to easily see how much I wanted it. I kissed him back with too much hunger, too much care, too much naked desire. And I did it in front of everyone.

But, God, he's a good kisser.

"That was good, I mean, that was good as in believable," I say, my face burning hot.

"Yes, it was. That'll do it, I think," he says. His hair is mussed and he looks slightly shell-shocked.

We make quick, anxious, what-the-fuck-have-we-done eye contact, and I turn and rush away.

TWENTY-THREE

I hurry to the bathroom and it's blissfully empty. I stand at the sink. My cheeks are pink and flushed in a way that makes me look better than usual. I glare at myself in the mirror. *Stop it. Stop looking pretty and pink cheeked and giggly, you pathetic fool.*

We kissed.

We kissed and it was *so good.*

I allow myself one very quick, excited smile.

I splash water on my face and take a few deep breaths, and check my teeth, just in case, just in case there is going to be more kissing. Probably not. But maybe. Tristan and Kendra could still be fighting. Who knows? *Who knows anything right now?*

I walk back out and I can see Jesse and Harper sitting together, on the couch, talking. Henry and Tristan and Kendra are all nowhere to be seen. I walk up behind Jesse, and I don't mean to eavesdrop, I plan on saying something and moving into their eyeline, but before I can, I hear their conversation.

"But you two just kissed," Harper says.

"Yeah," Jesse says with a little laugh.

I don't know how to interpret that laugh.

"It looked intense. It looked *real*. Are you actually, you know, starting something?" Harper says.

"With Brooke? No! No," he says. "It's just for the fake boyfriend thing."

There it is.

Do I like Brooke? No. No. Fuck, no.

A cold, slow prickle is unfurling itself down my back, my arms, my scalp. What the hell am I doing, exactly? This isn't real. I *know* it's not real, and the bit before this, helping me at the hospital, watching TV together, hanging out at home, all the little steps we've taken toward—what—friendship? That's probably not real either. Jesse is the same guy he was six months ago, the same guy he was five years ago, the same guy who casually humiliated me, who broke my heart, and I'm the same girl I was then too, and I don't know why I thought anything had changed. I let my guard down, for what? For *nothing*.

Forget the house rules. I need to remember *my* rules. My rules have always been, don't let your guard down, and don't expect anything. He'll let you down (the original *he* being Dad, but it has expanded to everyone very nicely).

And I'm right. I'm right.

I turn around, feeling suddenly dizzy.

Henry is standing behind me.

"Brooke," he says. "Are you okay?"

"Yes, I'm fine."

"I just wanted to say, I'm sorry. I should have done the fake boyfriend thing with you. I was really nervous, meeting you in person, and I'm not good under pressure."

"Hey, it's okay. It all worked out," I say. I'm trying to be warm and cheerful, but he's standing too close to me, and my stomach is hurting and I'm worried I'm going to cry.

"I was thinking. Well, it's just an idea. If you want to—" He stops, takes a breath. "We could try a do-over on our date?"

"Um," I say. "I, ah . . ." I can't process this request. I should be ecstatic that he's giving me a second chance. And he seems really sweet, someone I want to get to know. But my emotional nerve endings are fried. My brain is soggy. I can't deal with this right now.

"Brooke . . ." Someone touches my arm. I spin around and it's Tristan. He looks upset.

"Can I talk to you?" His eyes are shiny with emotion and he holds his hand on my arm for longer than is probably necessary.

"Ah," I say. Words are really letting me down right now.

Tristan is a good excuse to get away from Henry, but the downside is then I'm stuck with Tristan. I look between them. I'm not sure which option is more stressful or which I am less capable of dealing with. I need to be alone to process *my* feelings.

"I'm sorry," I say to them both. "I'm really sorry. I have a bad headache. I have to go home."

"Home?" Harper says, joining the group.

"Yes," I say. "I'm sorry. I'm really tired. Do you mind?"

"Of course not," she says. I say quick goodbyes to Tristan and Henry, both of whom say they'll text me, and then I head to the door. Harper walks with me.

"Are you okay?" she says.

"I'm fine, I just have a headache. And I feel bad, you know, lying to Tristan." I realize that Jesse is behind me.

"Wait, Brooke," he says. "Where are you going?"

"Home."

"I'll walk you," he says.

"It's okay, it's only a five-minute walk," I say.

"Exactly. It's only five minutes and it's dark, I can walk you home and come back here in no time."

"Fine," I say, because I don't want to fight with him in front of Harper, or Tristan or Henry. I need to get into the cool air of outside.

I walk out the door as quickly as possible, hoping I can somehow lose Jesse.

"What's going on?" he says, a step behind me. "One minute you're smiling, and now you look upset and you were going to leave without telling me? Did Henry say something? Or Tristan?"

"No. They're fine. Everything's fine. I'm not upset."

"Yes you are."

"I just feel bad, lying to Tristan."

"Since when?"

"Since I thought about it in the bathroom."

"Well, it was Penny's idea, let's blame her," Jesse says. "Anyway, Tristan probably won't even remember this night at all—if he keeps drinking."

"He will. And he'll tell other people from school about it. This is going to become a whole thing, people thinking we're together."

"It's fine," Jesse says. "My school friends aren't in touch with Tristan."

"Well, some of mine are."

"Okay. So we'll say we broke up, if anyone asks. Or we pretend to be together for a while. Or we tell them it was a joke. Or whatever you want! Who cares what they all think," Jesse says.

It really doesn't matter to him. The tangled web of lies and rumors and people asking questions and our reputations and some people never knowing the truth, because the original gossip headline travels faster and further than the correction, everyone knows that, and so most people will just hear that Jesse and I are together, and why does the thought of that hurt me so much, and why didn't I consider all of this before I agreed to the plan.

"I do. I *care*," I say. I can feel anger bubbling.

"Okay, fine, you care," Jesse says. He sounds confused. "Did I do something wrong?"

"You just don't seem to care about much," I say.

"I did you a favor tonight, and you're mad at me for not caring that it might be a big mistake?" Jesse says, half-angry now too.

"I'm not *mad* at you."

"It sounds like you are."

"Well, I'm not."

"Can you slow down for a second?"

"No."

"Is this about what just happened, with the kiss?" he says after a beat of silence.

"*No.*"

"Are you sure?"

God, his tone is so patronizing, I could scream.

"I don't care about the kiss," I say, walking faster.

"Ten seconds ago you're telling me you do care, now you're telling me you don't care."

"I was talking about different things."

"Okay. Well, what if *I* care about the kiss?"

"You don't." I stop, swing around, and look at him. "I know you don't."

God, I'm so angry. With him, yes. But with myself too, because I swore I wouldn't let myself be humiliated again, and now here I am, humiliated and heartbroken and crushed again. And worst of all—it's by the same person, in the same situation.

"How do you know?" he says.

"I heard you, talking to Harper."

"What did you hear?"

"You said something like, 'Do I like Brooke? No. *No*. Fuck, no.'"

There's a pause.

"I didn't say that to Harper," he says quietly. "I didn't say it like that."

"Whatever."

I turn onto our street. I just want to get through the door and away from him, get into the shower and cry, then put my head under a pillow, maybe two pillows, really burrow down. Then I need to take every emotion I have felt tonight and squash them, one by one, like a line of poor, sad little ants.

"Brooke! I didn't say it like that," he says, jogging up beside me.

"You did," I say. "You said it to Gretel. And you said it again tonight."

"Tonight is nothing like that," he says.

"Yes, it is," I say. "What? You thought I'd forgotten what you said?"

"No, I—"

"You thought the memory of that night had just faded away?"

"No, I—"

"Do you know what it's like to be a fourteen-year-old girl? To be *me*, specifically, at fourteen, with a hot older sister like Lauren, with every insecurity you can possibly think of, and then to have you do that to me, you who I thought was my friend? Like I was nothing, like I was a piece of garbage. Do you know what that's like? To have the first boy who ever kissed me do that? Do you have any idea what that was like?"

I'm starting to cry now, angry tears blurring my vision, and I wipe them quickly away.

"Brooke," he says, sounding agonized. "I'm sorry."

I need him to stop saying my name.

"Don't. I don't want to talk anymore." I fiddle with the front door. The key always sticks unless you hold it at just the correct angle, and my hands are shaking. I can't get it quite right.

"Can I, can you just let me explain?" he says, close behind me now. "About then, and about tonight."

I'm scared he'll reach out and touch me. I'm scared I'll still feel it when he does, that my body will still jump to his touch, and I can't risk that.

"No," I say. "Becoming friends or whatever it was we were doing was a mistake."

My key finally works, it turns, and I go inside and close the door behind me.

TWENTY-FOUR

Jesse and I are officially not speaking. Not even "hi" and "hello."
He tried to talk to me a couple of times but I shut him down.
He even knocked on my bedroom door and said, "Do you want
to watch *The Vampire Diaries* with me?" late one night, but I
didn't answer. He's given up and I'm back to hiding in my bedroom, like when I first moved in, except so much worse.

At least I still have Harper, but I also feel like I need to avoid
her, because she can tell something is off, and I don't want her
to kick us out for breaking the rules. Technically, maybe, the
romance rule, definitely the unnecessary drama one.

I don't think she would kick us out, not now, because we're
friends, but maybe I am wrong about that. Maybe I can't trust
any feeling I have. Maybe every relationship is up for debate.

It's Friday, and I am having a very bad day. It was my deadline to email my story to PJ, so she could check it over and print
it out and give it to everyone in class on Monday, to be taken
away and read ahead of Thursday's class, when it will be discussed and critiqued.

I emailed her my story, feeling sick but hopeful, whispering,
"Go safe, little Word doc."

She wrote back an hour later and said, "Brooke, you should take the weekend to think about whether this is the version of the story you want to submit." Apparently, it feels not quite right, not my voice, not the voice she read in the first piece of mine, and she'll give me until Monday morning if I want to submit a reworked version.

I don't even know what to say to that. I sat through my Principles of Management lecture in a daze, thinking of nothing but that email. My only distraction was when Jesse's face slipped into my mind, and I pushed it out so violently that I almost physically jolted. Ruby, Justin, and Sophie message me, asking if PJ said anything when I sent her my work, and I am too ashamed to tell them the truth, so I just write, "No response yet!"

I am walking home from the train station, planning how I will be going straight from the front door to the bathroom for a very long hot shower and then I will take all my snacks into my room and lie in bed and google "how to write." Then I'll drink two coffees—no, three—in a row and I'll sit up till four a.m. rewriting my story, just forcing myself to stare at the screen until I figure it out.

I open the front door and Harper is hovering in the hallway. She must have been watching from her bedroom window.

"I have a surprise for you," she says. Her voice is heavy with a tone, but I'm not sure what kind of tone exactly.

"Can we skip it? I'm not really in the mood for surprises. I've had a crappy day."

"Well, too late, because the surprise is here and there's no escaping it," she says.

I follow her to the lounge room and see Jesse first, talking to someone who has their back to me, but I know that hair anywhere, the long, luscious, ashy-blond ponytail.

Lauren is here.

She hears my footsteps and turns around.

"Surprise!" she yells, leaping up and hugging me. She smells like home.

"What are you doing here?" I say. I hug her again, because that smell, the feel of her body against mine, the sudden hit of *family*, is like a drug I thought I was over but now I've got a taste, I need it more than ever.

"I thought I'd come and crash here for a few days."

"A few days!" A few days could mean a week, it could mean longer. My heart is hammering. I needed notice, I needed to plan, I needed to clean, shop, clear my schedule, buy new clothes and more towels, tell everyone, adjust my uni schedule, get ahead with my work. Doesn't she know this about me after all these years? She does know, but she thinks it's just my neurosis, just me being controlling, just me being anxious, resisting spontaneity and fun, rather than crucial to my actual emotional well-being.

But, she's here. She's here. I'm trying to keep my reaction under control.

"What brought this visit on?" I say. I am barely listening, scrolling ahead in my mind to what it means, to have Lauren stay, to have Lauren here in my world, my fragile and recently imploded little world.

"I thought you might need cheering up. The cyst, the bad date, goddamn *Dad*, all that crap."

"Right," I say. A nice list of my humiliations. I didn't even tell her the truth about the date, I just said it hadn't gone well, we didn't click, which is technically not a lie. "Does Mum know you're here?"

"Not yet. She would have called to warn you and then it would have turned into a whole thing. I wanted to keep it low-key. And to give you a surprise!"

"I am definitely surprised," I say. Lauren follows me down the hall to my room, where she lies on my bed and watches me fuss around.

"Also, Mum and I are fighting," she says.

Of course they are.

"What about?"

"The usual, you know."

That could be one of a hundred things, really. I don't have time to dig into that because my mind is still racing.

"I'm starving," Lauren says.

"I'll get you something to eat," I say, defaulting straight to mothering mode. "Where did you park your car? It's a permit zone all round here."

"It'll be fine," Lauren says, waving her hand.

"No it won't be, you'll get a ticket—"

"Are you okay?" Lauren says, looking at me.

The thing is, Lauren knows me. She *knows* me, knows me. She knows the difference between grumpy me, regular me, sad me, and something-is-really-wrong me.

"Yes, I'm fine," I say, avoiding her eyes.

"You're giving off a very dark energy."

"I'm fine. Just a bad day at uni."

"Okay," she says, looking like she doesn't believe me. She gets up and walks back out.

"We're all going out, by the way," she yells from the lounge room. "Jesse and I have decided."

I sit on my bed and push my face into my hands. Of course they did. She knows Jesse, a little, from our town, but I'm not sure she's ever spoken to him before now. She used to dislike him in support of me, not that she ever actually knew why I didn't like him, until I told her earlier this year we didn't need to do that anymore. Now she's been here for fifteen minutes and she will have charmed him and made him feel like they're best friends. That's one of Lauren's superpowers. She can get you to skip levels, to make you feel like you're better friends than you are. People have said to me, "I'm friends with Lauren," and when I mention their name to her, she will say, "Who?" with genuine puzzlement.

I decide I am going to force myself into a more positive frame of mind. This is good, this is going to be fun. Forget rewriting my story, forget Jesse, put on a happy face.

"We're going on a pub crawl," Lauren says, appearing in my doorway.

"Great!" I say in my most upbeat voice. She opens her bag and starts pulling clothes out and throwing them on the floor. I pick up each thing she tosses and fold it neatly in a pile, almost without noticing.

"You don't want to go, I can tell," she says, putting her hands on her hips.

"I do. Sort of. I just wish you'd told me you were coming, because I have so much uni work to do over the next few days," I say.

"For which subject?" Lauren asks.

"All of them."

"Come on, Brooke. Just do what I used to do when writing essays."

Lauren used to google phrases she could use instead of a single word, to pad out her word count, and she would write "as noted in my previous paragraph" in every paragraph. I would then go through and cut it all when I proofread her essays and she would yell, "If you're deleting things, you better think of some new words to add," and then we would argue and I would stop helping her until she cried and Mum told me if I helped her write the essay just this one time, then Lauren would clean up the kitchen the next day when it was my turn, but she never did.

"I need to rewrite my *entire* short story," I say.

Lauren does not gasp or look at all concerned by this momentous news. To be fair, she's studying nursing, so the plight of a short story is hard to empathize with. I shouldn't have said "short," for a start. That gives the wrong impression. The shorter the story, the harder it is to write, I want to explain (which is something someone in class said, and it sounded smart and impressive, so I'm going to pretend it's something I know to be true). I'm making art, I want to tell her, I'm trying to create something from *nothing*, I'm trying to make people *feel* something, I'm doing the hardest thing of all, I'm trying to make them chuckle to themselves and then feel a little bit sad, all in the space of three thousand words. None of these arguments will mean anything to Lauren, who goes to uni to learn things like how to save someone who is choking, administer lifesaving medications, and insert a catheter. I sag in defeat.

"What about this top?" she says, holding up something sheer and black.

"It's see-through," I say before I can stop myself. God, I sound so prim and proper. Let her be as naked as she wants. "But you'll look hot," I say.

"Thank you, I will," Lauren says, smiling at me.

I watch her shake out her toiletry bag and start doing her makeup in front of my dresser mirror. I have watched Lauren do her makeup so many times. I find the process incredibly soothing. I sit cross-legged and tell myself, *Do not lecture Lauren. Do not give her rules. Do not give her ideas. Don't do it. Don't do it.*

But I can't help myself.

"You know you can't bring anyone back here, right?" I say. I'm light, I'm breezy, I'm relaxed, I just refuse to sleep on the couch while she has sex with some random in my clean, white sheets. Sheets that I just washed and dried and put on the bed this morning. That's all. I am not a prude. I care about my sheets.

"I won't." She makes circles with her makeup sponge, blending the foundation and not really listening to me.

"I'm serious." My voice is at least an octave higher than I would like. I clear my throat, try to get back down to *relaxed* levels.

"I *know*, Brooke. Calm down." She walks over and smooshes my face with her hands as she says it, and I close my eyes. "Let me do your makeup," she says.

The thing is, Lauren won't *plan* to meet someone or to go clubbing or run screaming through a dodgy park with bare feet or sit in a shopping cart with a wobbly wheel as a drunk guy she's just met pushes her at high speed down a busy street, but that doesn't mean it won't happen. We'll go out for a quiet drink, and somehow she'll end up at a club with four people she didn't know two hours earlier, texting me something like "Whats your address again and is there a spare mattress in case I bring people with me xxxxxx." She once brought a random home from a party and they peed all over our air mattress. Another time, we found two girls asleep, entwined, in the bathtub, using a loofah as a headrest.

Lauren is chaos. I don't have the capacity for chaos right now. I am deeply embroiled in a very quiet, private, inner turmoil.

TWENTY-FIVE

We're at the first bar of the night, the first of several Lauren wants to check out, and I am trying to hide the fact that Jesse and I are not talking to each other by keeping the conversation a group conversation and setting Lauren up with easy entry points to her best stories ("Loz, remember that time you got drunk and fell asleep in the children's maze and your friends called the police when they couldn't find you?"), and I laugh at everyone's jokes and try my very, very best to project a *fun* energy.

Jesse goes to the bar and Lauren watches him walk away.

"Is he single?" Lauren asks.

"I'm not sure," I lie.

"Interesting," Lauren says, and my stomach drops.

"Don't," I say, and my voice is pathetically desperate.

"You told me not to bring anyone new back to the house, and Harper's taken, so that narrows my options," she says, smiling at me. "Plus, he's hot."

"I mean it. Please don't." I feel like a guitar string that's been twisted too tight, I'll snap at the slightest pressure.

"*What* is going on? You're tense, even for you," Lauren says, peering at me with concern in her eyes. "I'm only kidding about Jesse."

Maybe she is just kidding, for now. But Lauren is going to sleep with Jesse. I can see it in her eyes. I can feel it in my bones. She'll keep her options open, but lightly flirt with him all night, keep him in the mix, then turn on the charm on the walk home if she's bored and in the mood. I know her moves. I know how long it takes her to turn from light flirtation into real seduction. (Less than a minute.)

My palms are sticky with sweat.

I want to stop anything happening between them. I want to stop it so badly that I will do anything to keep them apart (tell Lauren he doesn't shower, that he's a climate change denier, that he kicks puppies?), but I also don't want to want that. *I don't want to be that person and I don't want to feel like this.* My heart should be closed to Jesse. I vowed to myself that it was closed. I want to be fine with them hooking up, I want to get rid of anything that might resemble a dramatic feeling about the prospect of it. How do you cleanse yourself of feelings? There must be a proper scientific process.

Jesse returns with drinks for everyone and a Coke for me, which we didn't discuss and I take with a curt "Thank you," but I am actually grateful. Lauren says something that makes him laugh, and she laughs too, with a little toss of her hair, and I feel a bit like I want to die.

The more space Lauren takes up, the more she shines, the more her hair gently waves down her back like a silky blond waterfall, the more I feel myself becoming silent and dull and closed up and limp haired.

And Jesse. He's warming to her. Is he? Yes, for sure. When Lauren turns her charm on, and adds in the frisson of sexual possibility, it's irresistible.

I channel my anxiety into food and order three bowls of hot chips for everyone to eat to soak up the alcohol. Penny arrives at some point, and we head to another bar. I am already tired of switching venues, of finding a new spot to sit and making sure Lauren and Jesse don't sit next to each other, but also that I don't sit next to Jesse either, and making upbeat remarks about the decor and the atmosphere even though both are usually tired and downbeat, and I hope that the next one will be the last for the night, that we'll stay put.

As we walk in the door to an upscale-looking pub, we realize it's hosting a trivia night.

"I hate trivia," Lauren says, scrunching her face.

"Me too," Jesse says.

Oh great. They're bonding.

"Well, I like it," I say. I don't, not in a big rowdy group like this with no one to take it seriously, but if I have to play trivia to ruin Jesse and Lauren's night, I will. And there's nothing that dampens sexual tension like demanding someone tells you the capital of Bulgaria. "Let's get a table!"

"Brooke! Jesse!" a voice yells. I know who it is from the first syllable.

"God. No." I turn away. Maybe if we pretend we haven't heard him, we can just leave. We could just leave anyway, but I can't quite bring myself to be that rude.

"Is that *Tristan*?" Lauren says, her voice filled with delight.

Jesse and I look at each other, properly, for the first time tonight. He looks as stressed as I feel. I have no idea what to do. Should we pretend as if we've broken up? No, that would be too sad for me—"Dumped again, and so soon," I can imagine Tristan and Kendra whispering. But we can't do another night of fake dating. Not now, not like this.

"No one look at him," I say. "Huddle together, we're deep in conversation, we can't hear him."

"Brooke!!" His voice is louder and more insistent. He sounds so excited to see me. That's a win for me, surely. He texted me earlier in the week, telling me how good it was to see me.

"We can still pretend we haven't seen him and leave, as long as no one turns around," I continue, even though I know we can't.

"Harper!" Tristan says, and Harper turns her head. She makes eye contact with Tristan and waves, and then turns back to us. "Look, everyone, it's Tristan," she says weakly.

"Harper!" I say, outraged.

"I'm sorry, it's a natural instinct to turn your head when someone says your name!"

We all look at Tristan and wave. He's with Kendra and another guy.

"Wait. That's *Henry*," Penny says.

I can't believe it, or maybe I can. Tristan and Henry had hit it off the other night.

"You're hanging out with Tristan again?" Lauren says to me. "Things are worse than I thought."

"We are not hanging out again. He lives in the area, we bumped into him last week."

"Well, he sure seems excited to see you."

Tristan is already on his way over to us.

"Join our team, we need some more people!" he says.

All the other teams are at least ten or twenty years older. This is how Tristan and I were compatible. We are the kind of insufferable teenagers who derive great pleasure from trying to prove we are intellectually superior to a bunch of adult strangers.

"Oh, we were just leaving," I say.

"You just walked in. Hi, Lauren!" He pivots to shake Lauren's hand. God, why does he have to be so polite, so people-pleasing, so inviting? I admire it and I can't stand it.

"Hi, Tristan," she says. "I haven't seen you since you broke up with my sister." She's using her don't-mess-with-me tone.

I give her a warning look, but I'm also secretly glad she said it. Everything else aside, Lauren always has my back.

"Breaking up with Brooke was one of the hardest things I ever had to do," Tristan says earnestly.

For God's sake. He always sounds like he's a celebrity on a talk show, carefully revealing some pre-agreed private detail of his personal life.

"We really don't need to get into all that," I say, waving my hand cheerily, because I can see Lauren opening her mouth to say something in response.

"And anyway, we've both moved on with other people, so it's fine," he says to Lauren.

"Both?" Lauren says, tilting her head to the side.

"Me with Kendra, and Brooke with Jesse," Tristan says.

There's a pause. I look at Lauren. Not just look at her, but *look* at her. Sister look. The thing about having almost nineteen years of knowing each other is that we communicate very quickly and easily, in ways I can't with other people. I give her fleeting intense eye contact, and I know she knows what it means—I can see things shifting in her brain, I can see her understanding she needs to accept this statement about me being with Jesse. Not just accept it, but embrace it. She's a very good liar, so this won't be a problem.

"I'm glad you guys are mature enough to be friends," she says.

"Well, we're not in high school anymore," Tristan says. "So you'll join our team? Just for a round?"

"Sure," Lauren says. "That would be fun." She turns and gives me an evil grin, then, when Tristan has moved away, she grabs my arm and Jesse's arm. "The happy couple, huh! What's the deal?"

"It was just a spur-of-the-moment kind of joke we did the other night that has got a little out of control now we're apparently seeing Tristan everywhere," I say.

"Oh, this will be fun," Lauren says. "I love movies with fake-dating plotlines." She does a little jump of excitement as she heads to the bar.

"This is not a movie," I call after her.

Jesse and I are left standing awkwardly next to each other.

"We don't need to do it again," I say. I am torn between making sure he knows I'm still angry at him and making sure he knows that I have no emotions about him whatsoever.

"You want to pretend to be broken up?" he says. "That feels more complicated."

"Well, no, we can just . . ." I hesitate. "I guess we can pretend to be together but just not be really *together*. We don't need to put on a whole performance like last time."

"Right. Okay." He looks uncertain.

"Or we can tell Tristan the truth! I don't care." I shrug my shoulders, even though I think I have developed a tremble in my right leg from the layers of stress I am internalizing right now.

"Is that what you want? To tell him the truth?" Jesse says.

"Not really. I don't know," I say. I feel desperate and pathetic. My head is aching now.

"It's fine, Brooke. We can be a fake couple again, if it doesn't mean anything to you, then it doesn't mean anything to me," he says, jamming his hands into his pockets.

"It doesn't mean anything to me," I say with more aggression than I really planned.

"Great. Fake couple it is, then," he says. We walk over to the table, where Tristan is beaming at us, and Henry is explaining that he and Tristan decided last weekend to start their own trivia team after they realized they have perfectly complementary interests: Tristan can do science, geography, and celebrity, and Henry can do history, music, and sports.

"Shots! I bought shots!" Lauren yells, and several of the trivia teams around us turn and frown at her like she's a hooligan interrupting everyone's pleasant evening, which I guess she is.

She carries the tray over to the table, and everyone but me downs a shot. I watch Jesse knock it back with ease, and Lauren smile and elbow him and say something, and, oh God, he's definitely going to sleep with her. He looks so happy, laughing with her. Harper and Penny do too. Henry, who initially seemed excited to see me even though I have avoided a do-over first date, seems enchanted by her. *Fine, Lauren, take everything then!* The thing is, she doesn't even want it. My friends, my housemates, my sad little life, this is just another night out for her—she can't help being a force of nature. The more fun she is, the sterner and more sober I feel.

I've missed my calling. I needed to be born in a time when people used to have chaperones on dates. I am the perfect chaperone, I just need a few crisp shirts to button up tight and put my hair in a bun, and voilà, I could grimly oversee any kind of shenanigans.

Get a grip.

I take charge of the pen and paper, since everyone else is getting steadily drunker, and if we're going to play, I want to at least *try*. Lauren shouts the wrong answer every time, and Henry and Jesse laugh. God, they are both so *transparent*. I'm not even sure which one I dislike more right now. Tristan takes it seriously, as I knew he would, but I can feel Kendra monitoring how many times Tristan and I interact, so I am trying to avoid talking to him. I am also busy monitoring how much Lauren is drinking, because I know the exact number of shots it takes before she attempts to do a handstand (she cannot do a handstand), and I'll need to step in in case she hurts herself. I write down answers on the sheet as best as I can, but at some point, the pen is grabbed from my hand so Lauren can draw "an anatomically correct shark penis."

The mood of the pub is turning on us. We're ruining trivia, and I'm thinking we should go when Lauren yells, "Karaoke!" and Penny shouts, "Yes!" and I mentally delete another $50 out of my account, which I can't afford, but I would rather be in serious debt than go home and lie in bed imagining them having fun without me. Better for me to go along and watch them have fun without me.

"Yay, karaoke," I add to the general excitement, but my acting skills are slipping away.

Tristan walks over and says, "Are you okay?"

"Fine," I say.

"You and Jesse aren't talking to each other," Tristan says.

Why does he need to notice this? And worse, comment on it. *Mind your own business.*

"We had a fight before we came, but we're over it now," I say.

"As long as you're sure you're okay," he says.

"I'm fine."

"You can talk to me, you know."

"Well, you didn't say a word to me for months after you brutally dumped me right before exams, so excuse me if I don't feel like confiding in you," I snap. Tristan hates conflict, so starting fights with him is a pointless exercise. He'll grovel and backpedal, but it does feel cathartic. He'll take my guilt-tripping tactics and my anger and swallow them down hungrily.

"I'm so sorry, Brooke. I wanted to reach out to you so many times," he says.

"It's fine," I say.

"It's not. I know it's not. I wrote so many texts and then deleted them. I even wrote you a letter. Well, it was actually kind of a poem, about our relationship, a kind of follow-up to the other one, but Kendra and my mum both said not to send it."

Another poem! I could have had a matching pair.

"Well, it doesn't matter now," I say.

"It does matter. You still matter to me," he says, putting one hand over mine and squeezing it, before letting go and looking into my eyes. I feel my face burning a little, because Tristan is over the top and the touch of his hand makes me want to run, but something about his earnest intensity is still appealing. At one point in time, we really liked each other. Maybe he's still a little bit in love with me or, even better, in *lust* with me. Would that be so bad? He's the only person here tonight who I am confident is more interested in me than in Lauren. I refuse to analyze how pitiful that thought is.

Jesse is suddenly by my side.

"Hey," he says.

"Hey," I say.

Jesse hesitates for a second before reaching out and taking my hand in his. I expect him to hold it limply, perfunctorily, but he holds it tightly and rubs his thumb over the top of my knuckles gently, and it feels so nice I could almost cry.

Jesse and Tristan chat, and then Tristan moves away, and I immediately take my hand from Jesse's, and we don't speak or even make eye contact. But I keep thinking of his thumb rubbing over my hand.

Damn it.

All those movies, all those books, they made fake dating look fun. Doing this in real life feels awful, because I'm just lying to people, for no reason other than I'm insecure, and I'm lying to my body and maybe my heart, and I don't know how to make myself numb again.

We find a newly opened karaoke bar and, fifteen minutes later, we're all in a booth, and Lauren and Penny have their heads bent together, poring over the options for songs and shrieking with laughter.

Penny and Harper decide to sing an old Lady Gaga song together, alternating lines, and then a Beyoncé song after that. Harper has a lovely voice, good enough to be in a band. Everything about her, really, screams that she should be in a band. She and Penny look at each other with such joy while they are singing that watching them makes me feel better about the world.

Lauren goes next, singing by herself, then a duet with Henry, who is so nervous he drops the mic three times but actually has a nice voice when he gets going. Lauren is not a good singer, and she misses all the notes, but she has the confidence that gets her through any kind of performance, and she wiggles and shimmies around, throwing her head back, hamming it up.

I keep sneaking glances at Jesse, who is definitely watching Lauren, possibly because she's onstage singing but possibly because he finds her irresistibly attractive. The thought of him and Lauren in his bedroom at the end of the night is looming over me like a specter, and I feel it, how much I don't want it to happen, rolling through me like waves of nausea.

Tristan and Kendra do multiple duets next, and then they call Jesse and me up.

"No thanks. I don't sing," I say. My voice isn't as bad as Lauren's, but I have never enjoyed karaoke.

"Me neither," says Jesse.

Tristan shakes his head. "I'm not taking no for an answer!" he says.

Jesse and I stand up, and I feel everyone's eyes on us. The pressure to perform both being in a relationship and singing at the same time is a lot. Lauren starts heckling, and I determinedly ignore her, but I can feel my face getting hotter and hotter. Jesse points to song after song, but I keep shaking my head. *No, I can't sing that.* I can feel aggravation rising inside me.

"Just pick one," Jesse says, and he's clearly frustrated with me, and I can see Tristan's eyes widen with concern.

Lauren stands up and grabs the mic off me.

"You're taking too long," she says. "I'll duet with Jesse."

I grab the microphone back.

"Actually, we've already heard two songs from you tonight and it's two too many," I say.

Lauren makes a face at me.

"So start singing," she says. She's looking at me like I'm the one behaving terribly, which makes me want to cry with frustration, because, yes, I am behaving terribly but also no one understands how misunderstood and alone I am in this horrible world.

"I will if you give me a chance, but we know how much you need all the attention, all the time," I snap. All my emotions have merged into a kind of red haze of anger and Lauren is the easiest target here. A nice, familiar target.

"What the hell is wrong with you?" She grabs at the microphone again, and I wrap my hands tightly around it and push her away. She doesn't let go, and we wrestle with the mic. I feel like we've stepped back in time and we're seven and nine years old, wrestling over the TV remote or a hair tie or a piece of clothing or the last packet of Tiny Teddies in the box, or any of the many items we have fought over in our life.

Jesse jumps back to get away from us, and he trips over the microphone stand and falls onto the floor, and I turn to grab him and trip on his leg and fall as well, and Lauren comes crashing down on top of us both.

TWENTY-SIX

Everyone rushes over to help. Lauren and I are absurdly both still gripping the microphone, and Jesse is trying to wriggle out from underneath me, and Harper is saying, "Here, let me help," but not actually doing anything to help. Tristan says, "We need to separate them," like we're toddlers, and there's a lot of stumbling around, and Kendra falls over and her knee squishes my boob, briefly, and it hurts enough to send a jolt of rage through me and suddenly I can't stand any of it anymore.

I haul myself out and stand up, and shove the microphone at Lauren.

"Here, it's all yours. I'm done."

"*What* is going on with you?"

"Nothing."

"You're acting so weird. What is your problem?"

"You! You're my problem! You showed up here with no notice. You've hijacked my whole night. You've ruined every-thing!"

"Ruined *what* exactly?"

"Everything!"

"Fine, I'll just drive home right now if that's how you feel."

"Good! Go!" I yell.

"I will!"

We pause, breathing hard, glaring. I am acutely aware of everyone watching us with interest.

"Don't go," I say, suddenly worried she'll drink and drive.

"Obviously I'm not driving home right now." She rolls her eyes and then turns back to the song list, shrugging off the fight with ease.

That's it, that tips me over the edge.

"You know what? *I'm* going home!" I shout. I turn to the room at large. "And Tristan, I'm going on my own because, surprise, Jesse and I aren't really together! We lied about it so I would look less pathetic in front of you, and yes, now, ironically, I look more pathetic than ever! So you win. I hope you're happy. I hope everyone is happy. Jesse, you're free. Lauren, you're free too. You can hook up with Jesse tonight, no worries. Do it now! Right here onstage!"

I have lost control. I, the queen of control, am now yelling wildly at people. I have stepped into total meltdown territory. I'm ready to be cast on a reality TV show. Tristan and Kendra are staring at me, mouths agape. Jesse is still on the floor and he's wincing, either at what I said or because he's hurt himself, or maybe both. Penny and Harper exchange a she's-lost-it look. Henry looks incredibly anxious at the whole situation. Lauren lets out a laugh.

I turn and storm out. My outburst might be mortifying, but I'm hoping my exit looks good. I don't even look back. If it were set to music in a TV show, put into slo-mo, I'm confident I would look great, but in real life, it's hard to tell what the effect is.

But by the time I have stepped onto the street, I've lost all my anger and I am deeply embarrassed and I need to escape.

I am not a maker of scenes. I hate making scenes. My role is to smooth things over when someone else makes a scene. The streets are busy, filled with drunk people and happy people, the worst combination for a recently humiliated sober person. I want to put my hands over my face and sob. I want to scream. God. Why do I feel so *unhinged*. It's like I'm thirteen again.

I am due to get my period this week, so that probably explains some of it. A lot of it. But not *all* of it. This feeling is something else, an unhappy, impatient beast inside me, roaring and clawing, pacing the corners of its cage, wanting to spill out and cry and wail and hurt everyone around me, and I don't understand it or know what to do with it.

The thought of going home and sitting in the empty house depresses me.

I sit down on a bench and wait to see if I will cry. I blink a bunch of times, to hurry the process along, but nothing. There's still too much adrenaline coursing through me. Plus I left my jacket when I stormed out and now I'm cold and getting colder the more I think about it. I want to go back and get it. I'm worried they'll leave the room and not pick my jacket up and I'll have to call the bar and ask them to look through lost and found, and it will be a whole annoying thing. They've probably gone right back to singing and have forgotten I've even left.

Lauren and Jesse are probably hooking up right now. Probably on the stage as I suggested. *Why* did I give them permission? I practically spoke the situation into existence, I've pushed them together—I have no one to blame but myself.

The bench is close enough that they'll be able to find me if they come looking. I need someone, anyone, to come and look for me. I'm getting colder and colder now, so I walk back to the karaoke bar, trying to decide on my approach. Options are: slink in the back of the room, grab my jacket, and rush out and hope they don't notice, or throw open the door dramatically and storm back in and make another scene and have another speech ready to go and pretend it was my plan all along, then quickly grab the jacket as I leave.

I briefly fantasize about walking into the room with a cute guy and letting them think I've just met him, or, no, that we know each other from uni maybe, and I'm taking him back to the house to hook up—there's a cute guy standing in the doorway of the 7-Eleven up ahead and he looks like he's up for an adventure, he might agree to come with me for ten minutes—but then I realize that would be trying to play a fake hookup scenario over the top of a fake boyfriend scenario. How many layers of fake can you really have? I need to draw the line.

Stop making plans that hinge on people pretending to like you.

If any of them had stormed off into the night, alone, I would have chased after them. I would have been worried they were upset and worried they were unsafe. I would have noticed they didn't have a jacket and would get cold. I would have cared! I always care.

No one came chasing after me. Not my sister, not my housemate, not even my ex who claims he still cares about me.

Not Jesse.

I walk back to the karaoke bar, and I have a new speech ready to go in my head.

You're all selfish and you should all be ashamed of your-selves.

No, I need something less obvious. I can't tell them to be ashamed of themselves, I need them to come to that conclusion on their own.

I storm into the room, head held high, ready to make at

least two of them feel intensely guilty, but it's empty. They've all gone.

Somehow this is more upsetting to me than if they'd carried on singing.

My jacket is gone too. Now I really do have to walk home, cold and alone.

I go as slow as possible, hoping they've gone home and found me missing and they're worried as hell.

TWENTY-SEVEN

I open the front door of our house and there is music pounding, and shrieking, and Harper saying, "Let me just get something to wipe that up," in a stressed tone. If Harper is stressed about a spill, I am worried about what my reaction might be. I could legitimately have a heart attack. I vow not to even look at it.

I walk down the hallway and into the lounge room, and I can see Lauren and Kendra jumping on the couch in time to the music, and Penny and Henry doing some kind of complicated dance that Penny is explaining they choreographed in their childhood as part of a family talent show. Tristan is lying on a beanbag, and Jesse is nowhere to be seen.

"Brooke!" Lauren screams. "You're okay!"

"We were so worried," Tristan says, taking a long drink of whatever is in his glass, leaning farther back in his beanbag, kicking off his shoes.

"Yes. You seem very concerned," I say.

"We are! We were!" Lauren says, breathless from jumping around.

"Brooke, you're okay, thank God," Harper says, appearing behind me with a roll of toilet paper that she starts tearing pieces from and dabbing on the carpet. She actually sounds sincere.

"Not that anyone here actually cares," I say, because apparently I'm not quite ready to give up my moment to be dramatic.

"Brooke, I swear to God, life is so much easier when you stop feeling sorry for yourself," Lauren yells from the couch.

I am overcome with the urge to wrestle her again but I settle for giving her a nasty look. I want to ask where Jesse is but I'm scared to reveal I care.

"Jesse is out looking for you. We were going to join him if you didn't turn up in the next five minutes," Harper says from where she is on the floor, holding a wad of scrunched-up toilet paper. "Do you think this will come out?" she says, gesturing to the carpet. "Am I cleaning it right?"

I look at the red-wine stain. Who is even drinking red wine? I can answer that without looking. It will be Tristan. He always boasts of his parents training him to have a sophisticated palate from a very young age. He was eating Brie and olives by age three apparently.

"Put baking soda on it for now. I'll clean it in a minute," I say. I can't watch what she's doing to the carpet right now. Little bits of toilet paper are sticking to it. She may as well be putting pins in my heart.

"Can you call Jesse and tell him you are okay and to come back here, because I've made him a delicious cocktail?" Harper says, looking up at me. Penny dances by and grabs the toilet roll and throws it, the paper streaming out behind it like a comet. Lauren and Kendra fall about laughing like this is the funniest thing they've ever seen.

"Sure, I'll let him know." I don't want to but I can't think of a good reason to say no.

I pull out my phone and see a bunch of missed calls. I forgot to actually check my phone—I was too distracted by my own outrage. Lauren, then Harper, then Jesse. At least Lauren called, I guess. That's something. And Jesse. Well, so they all should. They pushed me into acting terribly, if you look at the situation through a very narrow lens, a narrow lens that is basically my brain saying, *It's all their fault.*

I send Jesse a curt text saying, "I'm home," and then I go and sit on my bed to quickly wallow a bit more. If I process these feelings, then I can go back out and have fun, maybe. I do want to see Penny and Henry's choreographed family dance. I lie back on my bed, hugging the toy dog that Jesse bought me. Lauren is wrong. Feeling sorry for yourself feels really good sometimes.

The door cracks open and Penny pokes her head in.

"Hey," she says.

"Hi," I say, quickly pushing the toy dog under my pillow.

She walks in, sits on the bed beside me. "So. You're having a night."

"I am."

Penny is the one person I really wish hadn't seen my outburst earlier. She doesn't know me as well as Harper and Lauren do, and I still want her to think the best of me.

"We've all been there," she says. "I once had a meltdown and cried in front of everyone before we'd even left the house, because I couldn't get my hair to curl right."

"That makes me feel a bit better," I say.

Penny looks at me closely. "You're not into Henry at all, are you?"

I wasn't expecting this question.

"Oh. No. I don't think I am. I'm sorry," I say. "I mean, I like him as a friend, obviously. Besides, I'm pretty sure he likes Lauren."

"He likes Lauren paying attention to him, because he's a

straight guy and she's hot. But he's interested in you," Penny says. "But that doesn't matter. Your feelings matter. What you want matters. Or should I say, *who* you want matters."

"I don't want anybody."

"I think maybe you do," she says, smiling at me. I'm scared she's going to say more, but she doesn't.

"I wish I had what you and Harper have," I say.

Penny laughs. "We're not perfect," she says.

"You're not?"

"Well, okay, maybe we are. But we have our challenges. Like, for example, Harper's family is very overprotective, and they worry we've gotten too serious too quickly. Harper's older sister moved in with her girlfriend straight out of high school, and it went badly, she had a really traumatic breakup. Her older brother got married young and then divorced before he was twenty-three. And Harper is the baby of the family. They want her to travel, be single and unencumbered, date around, meet lots of people, and not make the mistakes they did."

"What does Harper think?"

"She's pretends not to care, but it gets to her, a bit. Sometimes it feels like they're just waiting for us to break up so they can say I told you so."

"What do you think?"

"I think . . ." Penny pauses. "Maybe, they're right. Life might be easier if we were single now and met later. But, I love who Harper is *now*. I don't want to meet her at twenty-nine and miss ten years of knowing her."

"That's very romantic," I say.

"I know." Penny smiles.

"What are you going to do?" I ask. I see, suddenly, why Penny's dating agency would work. She exudes relationship wisdom. I want her to run my whole life, not just my love life.

"I'm going to keep loving her and see what happens," Penny says. "Anyway, my point is, there is no perfect relationship. The timing might be wrong, people might be trying to set you up with someone else, everyone might be telling you it's a bad idea, but if the person is right, it can be worth the risk."

"Thank you," I say. There's another knock on the door then, and Jesse's face appears.

"Oh sorry, I'll go," he says.

"No, I'm just going," Penny says, and she slips out of the room.

Jesse hovers in the doorway.

"I was out looking for you," he says accusingly.

"Thank you," I say. "But I was fine," I add.

"Right," he says, and turns to go. "Oh, here's your jacket," he says, and throws it on the end of my bed.

"Thank you," I say, and this time, I do mean it.

He walks out, shuts the door, and then almost immediately opens it again, poking his head in.

"I'm not going to have sex with your sister," he says.

"Oh. Okay. Good."

"In case you think that's happening."

"I don't think that's happening," I say.

"You said you did before."

"I was maybe being a bit dramatic." I almost add, "I'm about to get my period," but I stop myself.

"Well, it's not happening. She's not my type," he says.

"Excuse me, why not?" I say, sitting up.

"I don't know. She's just not," he says, looking surprised at my reaction.

"That's rude."

"You're mad I won't sleep with your sister, after being mad that I would?"

"They're different kinds of mad. I don't want you to sleep with her, but I don't want you to be rude about her either."

"Was that rude? Saying she's not my type?"

"How could you not find her attractive?" *How dare he turn down Lauren. Who does he think he is?*

"She's attractive, yes. Absolutely. I'm just not . . . into her that way."

"Why aren't you into her?" I ask. I don't know why I'm pushing this. I have to know, though.

"I don't know. Because." He drums his fingers on the door-frame.

"Because why?"

"Because, she's not my type! I already said that. She's really nice, but I'm not interested. And even if I was, which I'm not, I wouldn't do anything because it would . . . muck everything up." He looks like he regrets saying that last bit.

"Oh. Okay."

I pause, in case he wants to tell me muck up *what*, specifically. That's a statement that needs clarification, it needs fleshing out. I am waiting for him to elaborate but he doesn't say anything else. Then he sighs and steps into the room.

"Look. Can we talk for a minute?" he says.

"Yes. We're talking right now," I say, folding my legs under me.

"Okay. Well. Back when we were in high school—"

"No. I don't want to talk about that," I say quickly, shaking my head.

"Brooke, if you never let me bring it up then we can never get over it."

"We're over it. It's fine."

"Okay, let's talk about what happened last week, then."

"I'm over that too."

"You were really upset. And we haven't spoken since!"

"Well, I'm fine now. I've had my outburst. We can move on."

"Okay," he says. "So . . ."

"So we're friends. We're back to being friends," I say. Being friends, I have decided, is the best and safest way forward. As long as I don't think about any of our history, the kiss, the way I feel, as long as all of that is safely bottled up, being friends will be easy.

"Good," Jesse says, nodding. "Good."

I see his eyes land on the legs of the dog that are sticking out from under my pillow, wearing the telltale green dogtor scrubs. I can tell from his expression he knows what it is. Great. Now he'll think I sleep with it. Which I do sometimes. But I never want him to know that.

He looks like he's working himself up to say something else, but suddenly there's a scream, followed by another, and a smash, and someone yells, "Brooke!"

TWENTY-EIGHT

Lauren is sitting on the couch, clutching her hand, which is bleeding.

"There was a mouse!" she shrieks. "It ran that way." She points down the hallway and blood drips from her hand, adding a new shade of red to the wine stain on the carpet.

"What happened?" I say.

Everyone starts yelling at once. Apparently, Lauren was going to attempt a handstand with Henry and Kendra holding her legs and Penny supporting her butt and Tristan filming, when mid-maneuver they all saw the mouse and everyone freaked out. In the chaos, someone smashed a tray of glasses and Lauren rolled *into* the smashed glass.

"It touched my foot!" Kendra is yelling about the mouse.

"Babe, no it didn't. That was me," Tristan is saying.

"Get me a bandage, and we can still do the handstand. Quick, before I lose momentum," Lauren says.

"Show me your hand," I say.

This isn't my first rodeo. Lauren was once drunk and walked on broken glass and I had to pick the shards out of her feet. I feel a sense of almost calm settle over me. I knew something was going to happen to Lauren, because something always happens to Lauren, it's just a matter of what it is and how bad it is. And now it has happened, and it is this—a small, manageable thing—and I can deal with it.

"It'll be fine," she says.

"It looks deep," I say, grabbing the roll of toilet paper and tearing off sheets to hold against it.

"Brooke—"

I interrupt her. "Just let me handle it, okay?" I say, and she shakes her head and flops back against the couch.

"My parents are doctors. I can help," Tristan says.

"Your parents are psychologists," I reply.

"I have first-aid training," Henry says.

"That's more helpful," I say, making room for him on the couch.

"Well, I mean, I did the course online, and they sent me a PDF afterward. Let me just find it in my emails. I might need a quick refresher," Henry says, a lot less sure when he sees the blood.

"It's barely a scratch," Lauren says, but I shush her and look at Jesse. "Can you get the first-aid kit?"

"We have a first-aid kit?" he says.

"Yes, in the kitchen. In the medicine cabinet."

"We have a medicine cabinet?"

"Jesse, *please*."

"I'm sorry, this is all news to me!" He throws his hands in the air.

"Harper, can you help him find it?" I say.

"I didn't know we had a first-aid kit either," she says, giving me an apologetic look. She and Jesse hurry off together to investigate.

"Oh my God, oh my God," Kendra says with a mixture of horror and excitement. "I feel faint. That's a lot of blood."

"Stop looking at it," I tell her. "Tristan, can you please get a towel?"

"Should we call someone?" Penny says.

"Who?" I ask.

"An ambulance?" she says.

"No," I say.

"Nurse-on-Call?" Penny says. "What does your PDF say, Henry?"

"I'm only on page four of twenty-six," he says. "It's really hard to read on my phone."

"Calm down, everyone. We don't need Nurse-on-Call, because *I'm* a nurse, almost," Lauren says. "I can assess it." She peers at her hand. "I pronounce it . . . totally fine! Let's go out," she shouts, standing up.

"No. Stop. You're drunk and losing blood and you might need stitches," I say, pulling her back down.

I am suddenly very aware that I'm the only sober person in the room.

"Here's a towel," Tristan says, breathless, hurrying back into the room.

"It's wet," I say.

"It was the one hanging on the towel rack."

"It's not clean. I need a clean one. From the cupboard near the sink."

"Okay, okay, cupboard." He hurries off.

"We found it," Jesse says, appearing with the first-aid kit.

"Okay, open it," I say. "Where's that towel?" I yell to Tristan.

"Blue or red?"

"*What?*"

"Blue or red towel?" he asks.

"It doesn't matter!" I yell at the same time as Harper yells, "Red! Red!" The blue ones are hers.

"Bandages? Antiseptic cream? Tweezers?" Jesse is holding things up from the first-aid kit one at a time.

Tristan appears with a clean towel, and I hold a ball of wadded-up bloody paper towels toward him. He steps backward and gags, and Kendra shrieks.

"Brooke, Mum's calling. I'm going to put her on speaker," Lauren says. "And give me the tweezers, I need to get some glass out."

"Why is she calling us so late?" I know why, though. She knows Lauren is here and she's checking in. Mum has a sixth sense about this stuff.

"Hi, Mum!" Lauren calls. "You're on speaker. Don't worry, my hand is fine."

"Why wouldn't your hand be fine?"

"Oh, I thought Brooke must have texted you."

"I did not text her," I say.

"Brooke, what's happened to her hand?" She sounds disappointed in me, like I'm the friend's parent who let her daughter get out of control. This annoys me more than anything else about the situation.

"Nothing, a little cut," I say, pulling the tweezers out of Lauren's hand. She cannot operate on herself while drunk.

"Hi, Michelle," Tristan calls out. I glare at him and shake my head.

"Who's that?" Mum says.

"No one," I say.

"It's Tristan," Tristan says.

"Brooke is hanging out with Tristan again, Mum," Lauren says, her voice emphasizing the words "hanging out" so it sounds like Tristan and I are embroiled in some kind of casual-sex scenario.

"We're just friends. Tristan is here with his girlfriend," I say, still trying to wipe blood from Lauren's hand.

"Hi, I'm Kendra, nice to meet you," Kendra calls.

"Hello, dear," Mum says. "Is this the Kendra that Tristan left you for, Brooke?"

"Yes, Mum, yep, she's the one," I say as upbeat as possible.

I look around, desperate to steer the conversation in a new direction.

"We need to stop the bleeding and then irrigate the wound," Henry says, looking up from his phone.

"Oh my God," Mum says. "What's happening? How *bad* is your hand, Lauren?"

"Mum, it's fine," I say.

"Who was that talking about irrigating Lauren's hand?" Mum says.

"It was me. Hi, hello, this is Henry?" Henry says, looking nervous and waving at the phone for some reason.

"Mum, I'm hanging up," I say.

"Call me back when you have things under control," she says.

"Everything is under control!" I yell as I hang up. "Okay, let me think," I say, looking at Lauren's hand. I actually have no idea how to tell if a cut is deep enough to need stitches.

The music is still going, and everyone is talking over each other, and Penny and Harper are laughing helplessly about something, and Harper is trying to explain to me what's so funny while still reassuring me that she's taking the medical crisis seriously, and Jesse has dropped the first-aid kit on the floor and is trying to pick it all up before he thinks I'll notice.

Lauren touches my arm.

"I know you don't trust me, ever, with anything, but I promise, I do know what I'm talking about when I say this cut will be fine if we clean it and then bandage it, and I don't need stitches. It barely even hurts! You don't need to look after me."

"It doesn't hurt because you're drunk," I say.

"Brooke," she says. "Just. Trust me."

I stare into her drunk, mascara-smudged blue eyes.

"Okay." I sigh. "But if you bleed to death overnight, you are not allowed to come back and haunt me."

"Don't worry, you are way too boring for me to even consider it," she says, poking my cheek with her finger.

I start to bandage her hand when she stops me.

"Wait! We need to get some photos first, with all the blood."

"Do we, though?" I say.

"Photo shoot!" Penny yells, overhearing her.

"No, no, no more photo shoots," I say, but it's too late. They're getting props.

TWENTY-NINE

Hours later, I walk into my room and find Lauren asleep, lying diagonally across my bed. I slip under the covers, gently pushing her. She opens her eyes, snuggles closer to me.

"Your breath is in my face," I say.

"If I turn the other way, my hair will be in your face."

"I would rather hair than breath," I say. Lauren sighs and rolls over. Her long hair is in my face, it's all over me, and it's incredibly annoying, but I don't say anything. It smells nice, fruity and floral and musky all at once.

"Thank you," she says after a minute.

"What for?"

"For looking after me."

"It's my job." I don't know why I say this. If I were the older sister, it might make more sense to say it and pretend I mean that society has decreed it my job, but no one expects anything of the younger sister, not really.

"Wow, do you put me on your résumé?"

I can hear the edge in Lauren's voice. "Not like that. You know what I mean."

"Is that how you think of me? As a job, an obligation?"

"No. I think of you as my sister. We're family. We look after each other."

"I would do the same for you."

I could let the words sit. I could just say good night and be done with it. But Lauren triggers my need to pick, to scratch, to push, to not let things go.

"Except you've never had to," I say.

"What does that mean?"

"It just means I'm always the one looking after you, not vice versa." I need her to acknowledge it. I need her to *know*. What's the point of worrying about someone, looking after them, making all these sacrifices, if they don't even realize, if they don't even give it a second thought? God, is this how parents feel every day of their lives? But I'm not a parent.

Now Lauren rolls back over to face me.

"You think I've never looked out for you?"

"I think our roles in the family are you, the wild reckless fun one, and me, the boring, responsible protector."

Lauren snorts.

"Do you remember, in primary school, when Luke Taylor stayed after school and hid in the bushes and threw water bombs filled with his piss at you?"

"No. That never happened."

"Exactly. Because I heard about what he and his friends were planning and I scared the shit out of him."

"Really?"

"Yes. And do you remember how you were never bullied on the bus to and from school? You got to sit there and read your book and talk to your friends and not be harassed by fucking Josh Kelly and his mates, who would go up and down the aisle making other kids give them food."

"That was you?" All this time, I had imagined I was invisible, that I was safe because I read books and worked hard at school and did the right thing and was responsible and the universe was rewarding me.

"On your first day, I told Josh if he ever so much as spoke to you, I would ruin his life. He was a creep who harassed the younger girls."

"He was a creep. I had no idea you did that." I wish she had told me.

"Well, now you know."

She rolls back over.

"I worry about you, Brooke. I do. It's just different from the ways you worry about me. I wanted to make sure no one bullied you, I wanted to make sure your life was easier when I could make it easier, that no one preyed on you like they did on me."

I look at her back and listen to her breathe.

"Thank you," I say.

"You expect so much of people, sometimes you can't see the good parts because you're dwelling on the ways they don't live up to who you want them to be."

"I don't . . . I mean. Yeah. I guess I'm too judgmental."

"Of me, for sure."

"You make it hard sometimes."

"I know."

"I worry about the way you drink." I've never said this out loud before, but it's not a surprise, of course—it's there in the subtext of our entire relationship.

"I'm fine."

"Not always, though."

"No. Not always. But you can't live your life being careful about every single thing and taking no risks."

"There's a difference between taking no risks and living the way you do, and you know it. Sometimes, you remind me of—"

"No. Don't go there." Lauren's voice is sharp. She knows I'm going to say Dad. We have an unofficial rule that we can talk about Dad only in certain ways, and this—talking about the dark parts of him and which of those parts might be inside of us—is not on the table for discussion. She never lets me talk about the things that would make her uncomfortable.

"You keep throwing yourself off cliffs and hoping someone is there to catch you, and I've been doing it for a long time but I'm not there anymore. I can't catch you anymore, and it keeps me awake at night."

"Just let me fall off the cliff," she says, yawning.

"I don't want to."

I don't know where we go from here. She's not going to stop drinking. She loves drinking in ways I will never understand. And I know I won't stop worrying. How do you change who someone is, fundamentally, in their bones? I'm a worrier. She's a drinker. This is going to be it, for our whole lives, maybe.

"My hand hurts," she says.

"Do you want me to get you some painkillers?"

"No. But remember when we were little, and we would get into the same bed and Mum would stroke our hair until we fell asleep?"

"Yeah."

"Can you stroke my hair like that?"

"Okay."

I stroke her hair, over and over, until I hear her breathing deepen and she falls asleep.

THIRTY

I wake up to the smell of pancakes. I roll away from Lauren, my arm dead from lying in a pretzel shape all night while she stretched out. I pull on my dressing gown and head out to the lounge room. Tristan and Kendra are asleep on the couch, Kendra tucked under his arm, with several towels draped over them in lieu of blankets. Two weeks ago, I thought he was gone from my life forever and now he's spending the night on my couch, snuggled cozily under my towels, with my saucepan next to him in case he needed to puke, and I haven't fully examined how I feel about this, but I think I might be okay with it.

Henry is in the kitchen, making pancakes.

"Oh my God, they look delicious," I say. He's wiping down benches and cleaning as he goes, and I feel instantly relaxed.

"I'm an average cook, but I make really, really good pancakes," he says, smiling at me.

We talk and laugh while he makes them, and I appreciate how careful he is, pouring exactly the right amount of batter in the pan, lifting the side gently to see if it's done, and turning it over with an expert flip. And once you get past his shyness, he's funny and smart. Penny was right to set us up. He's perfect for me. I stare at him and will myself to like him romantically, to find a spark. I *want* to want him. To bundle up all the desire inside me and redirect it toward this lovely guy.

"Sorry?" I say when I realize I missed the last thing he said.

"I said, we could get tickets to see something at the Melbourne International Film Festival later this year," he says. We've been talking about documentaries.

"I'd like that," I say, then stop. Have I committed to a date? No, because we're talking about an event that is months away. But I probably need to clarify. But maybe I will fall in love with him sometime between now and then.

He's watching me and I feel like he can tell what I'm thinking, and my cheeks get warm.

He puts a plate of pancakes in front of me.

"As friends," he adds.

"Right," I say. I hope my face isn't revealing too much relief.

"I know we met through a setup, but I think we could be good friends. I mean, good *as* friends. But also maybe good friends," he says, and then laughs nervously.

"Me too," I say. This, this right here, is more evidence that I should be falling in love with him. Maybe I can see a hypnotist, or a love chiropractor, and get my feelings realigned.

"Morning," Jesse says, walking into the kitchen, yawning and rubbing his hand through his hair so it sits up at a weird angle. He pours himself a glass of water, drinks it, and leaves the glass on the bench. This should be deeply unattractive to me. And yet . . .

Damn it.

I like him.

I like him so much.

I need a feelings exorcist.

Everyone else eventually wakes up and joins us, and Henry

makes another round of pancakes, and Tristan puts on *Lord of the Rings* for "background ambience" and then nearly faints when Harper says she's never seen it and doesn't know what a hobbit is. Lauren complains she can't drive home because her hand is too sore to hold the steering wheel, and even though she said she wanted to stay a few days, she wants to go home today because she's heard a rumor that some of her friends might be sending flowers for said cut hand (in response to some dramatic bloodied photos she posted to her social media late last night after the photo shoot).

I tell her I will drive her home in her car and get Mum to drive me back into Geelong tomorrow morning and I'll get the train back, but then Harper says, "Why doesn't Jesse go and visit his family too and then he can give you a lift home tomorrow?"

Jesse looks immediately stressed with this idea, but Lauren says, "Yes, perfect," and Tristan says, "Sounds like the best solution," and Henry agrees, and the decision is made.

Lauren puts the radio on loud on the highway home, and we sing together and laugh. Why couldn't I have been like this at karaoke last night? Thankfully, Lauren doesn't bring up my outburst.

Mum and Nanna are waiting for us as we pull up, watching at the window. Mum rushes outside.

"Brooke honey," she says, coming to me first, and I am secretly relieved, because I was worried she would go and check Lauren's hand first, but she hasn't seen me in months and I needed to be first. I probably need therapy for even having this thought, but I don't care. I bury myself in her arms when she hugs me, and I almost cry. I haven't let myself go home much since I moved to Melbourne, because I was afraid I would burrow back into their love and safety and I wouldn't want to leave.

I needed to build up a life that was good enough to make sure I would go back to first.

"You look pale," Nanna says, bundling me into a hug.

"I'm always pale," I say.

"Michelle, she needs more sun!" Nanna says to Mum.

"Is anybody going to ask about my hand?" Lauren says.

"Go straight down to the beach and get some salt water on it," Nanna says.

"Do not do that," Mum says. "Keep it bandaged." She kisses Lauren's forehead and links one arm through mine and the other through Lauren's.

"Both my girls are home. We're going to celebrate," she says.

"Champagne?" Lauren asks hopefully.

"Scones," Nanna says. "And a pot of strong tea."

"God, please don't let them be date scones, the only thing worse than a scone is a date scone," Lauren moans theatrically.

"They are date scones," Nanna says.

We walk inside, and it feels like layers of me are falling away. Like I'm putting down my sword and taking off my armor, until I'm stripped back to family Brooke, old Brooke, home Brooke.

THIRTY-ONE

I'm the only one awake. Lauren went to a friend's house, Mum went to bed early because she is trying to reset her sleep schedule after a few weeks of night shift, and Nanna went to bed early because that's what you have to do when you get up at five a.m. every day for no reason. I'm still up, with only Minty the Siamese cat for company, staring at my laptop and a blank Word document, trying to rewrite my story from scratch. I need the perfect opening line, I decide, and then the rest will just flow.

She used to be such a nice girl. Delete.

Jane wasn't a dog person. Delete.

She hadn't spoken to him in a year. Delete.

I like all of these first lines. They are all perfectly good first lines. But the weight of expectation, of finding an equally good or better second line, and third line, and fourth line, and then building a whole story around it, is too much. It's too hard. I'm not cut out for this. With all of my other subjects, I can just study harder, learn more, and be confident in getting better. But writing is slippery—I could do it every day of my life and never be any good and, even worse, not realize I'm not good. And what is *good*? Who decides? So much of who I am and how

I want to see myself—on the inside, the real me—is tied up in the idea of being a creative person, a Writer. I sit and stare at the blank page and will myself to be braver.

There's a quiet knock at the front door. The barest rap of knuckles, like the person knocking is regretting the knock even while they do it. I should be scared, it's way too late for anyone to be knocking, but I feel safe here, at home.

I can see a familiar tall silhouette through the glass.

I open the door, and Jesse is standing there. I'm wearing my old fluffy bathrobe, the one I deemed too ugly for me to even consider taking when I moved to Melbourne. Even though we live together in the same house, I feel exposed by him seeing me like this. This is home Brooke, truly at home Brooke, in a way I never am in our share house.

He's standing there in my doorway, one hand loosely on the frame, wearing his glasses, and looking cuter than I want to admit. Why does he look so good in doorways? Does he know this and deliberately position himself in them? Does he *practice*? Or do I just have a thing for men standing in doorways?

It takes me a second to notice the expression on his face. He looks sad, and vulnerable, in a way I've never seen before.

"Hi," I say.

"Hi," he says.

I smile and wait for him to tell me why he's here.

"I had a fight with my dad," he says in a tone that he's trying to make sound normal, a bit cheerful even, a joke. But his voice trembles the tiniest, tiniest bit at the end.

"Come in," I say.

He follows me in.

"Is this okay? That I came here?"

"Yes. We're friends."

"I know you said that, but—"

"We're friends, Jesse," I say firmly.

"Where's Lauren?"

"Out."

"What about your mum and nanna?"

"Asleep."

Jesse follows me into the lounge room and sits next to me on the couch.

"Hello, buddy," he says, leaning down to pat Minty. She yowls.

"That's Minty. She's technically Nanna's cat, but she kind of owns all of us a bit."

"Nice to meet you, Minty. I'm Jesse." He touches the top of her paw with his finger, like a little cat version of a handshake.

"Do you want to talk about the fight?" I say.

"What are you doing?" Jesse says, ignoring my question.

"Trying to write a new story for my class. My teacher said the one I submitted wasn't good enough."

"Why not?"

"Because I'm a bad writer who handed in a pile of shit and I shouldn't even be taking the class."

"She really said that?" he says.

"I'm paraphrasing the general vibe of her email," I say, pulling my hair out of its messy bun and then changing my mind and twisting it back up. I shrug out of the ugly dressing gown and try to subtly discard it over the side of the couch.

"Can I read it? The story she didn't like?"

"No," I say. I almost laugh at the absurdity of the request. I was just considering dramatically deleting the file off my computer altogether, except I already backed it up to the cloud and also an external hard drive and emailed myself a copy, so it would be a fairly meaningless act.

"Come on. I need a distraction," he says, and his cajoling face, his glasses—it all weakens my resolve a little.

"No," I say, but with a bit less conviction.

"Please, Brooke." He smiles at me.

As the story goes in my family, Mum chose Lauren's name, and Dad chose mine, and I always hated that, because it feels like I am tied to Dad in some symbolic way I don't want. I already have his surname, and having him linked to my first name as well feels too much. Maybe because of this, the word "Brooke" has always sounded rough and unpleasant to me, a one-syllable punch of a word that lands like a thud. *Brooke.* But the way Jesse just said it, he made it sound soft and lyrical, he made it sound like it belonged to no one but me.

Minty has crawled onto Jesse's lap and is purring away. Minty doesn't normally like men; she once perched on Tristan's lap, and we all exclaimed and thought she was finally accepting him, and he leaned his face down near her, and she took the opportunity to bite his nose so hard it bled. He always stood a good meter away from her after that, and if she leaped up on the couch, he would stand up and pretend he needed to get a drink of water or go to the bathroom. But, now, seeing Minty happily kneading her claws into Jesse's leg and curling up in a ball pushes me over the edge.

"Fine," I say, and I click the file open and slide the laptop toward him. I feel sick immediately. Letting him read my story—my bad story, my rejected pile-of-shit story—is somehow more emotionally exposing than kissing him.

I go into the kitchen and then quickly run back.

"It's just a messy first draft."

"I know." He nods.

"I want complete honesty," I say, pointing at him aggressively.

"I will give you complete honesty," he says.

I walk out of the room and then straight back in again.

"But don't be *mean*, though. Nothing too critical. I'm too creatively fragile."

"Total honesty, but nothing critical. Got it," he says, smiling. Is this a *joke* to him? He has to walk a line so fine that the slightest misstep could ruin my entire future career and deprive a whole generation of my brilliant novels, if I ever write one.

"This is a bad idea," I say, gripping the top of the laptop and thinking about pulling it away from him.

"It's not," he says, putting his hand over mine and looking up at me. "Go and make some cups of tea or something."

I swallow and slip my hand out from under his.

I fuss in the kitchen, looking for Nanna's stash of biscuits. She always has the old-school Arnott's family assorted pack, and I open it and lay a selection of biscuits on a plate. This is kind of a psychological challenge. Whichever biscuit he chooses will reveal something about him.

I carry in cups of tea and the plate of biscuits.

"Well?" I say, looking at his face.

He's frowning slightly. Maybe in concentration. Maybe in horror at the awfulness of my writing.

"I haven't finished yet," he says, reaching for the teddy bear biscuit. An acceptable choice. Teddy bear biscuit eaters are usually laid-back outdoorsy types. I pick up a Scotch finger and dunk it in my tea, still watching him, waiting for the slightest microchange in expression.

"Okay," he says, sitting back. "I'm done."

"Well?" I say.

"You're a really good writer." He smiles at me. "*Really*, really good. Professional good. A natural. But you already knew I thought that."

I feel a warm little glow in my chest when he says this, an

instant, involuntary reaction to any kind of praise, but especially that kind, the words "you're a writer" said in any context. But I don't really believe it. I don't believe he's being sincere, I'm not sure he has the level of expertise required to make this pronouncement anyway, and the whole situation is giving me flashbacks to the last time he said this and how I can't truly trust him.

"But?" I press.

"But nothing."

"Come on. There's a reason why my teacher wants me to write something else."

"Well, it's about a married couple in their thirties, right?"

"Yeah."

"And you're eighteen."

"Almost nineteen."

"So, could you, like, take most of that plot, the essence of the story and characters and the relationship stuff, but make them younger? Maybe draw on your own experiences?"

"Maybe," I say. My brain instantly scoffs, *He's wrong. What does he know? That would never work. How many books has he even read this year?* But that's just my instinctive defensive reaction to any feedback, I need to let that chatter run its course and then dig down underneath it, where maybe, yes, he's a tiny bit right. I thought the story would matter more if the characters were older, with kids and houses and finances at stake, but maybe I'm wrong. Maybe it doesn't need any of that.

"And—" he starts to say.

I hold up my hand.

"Stop. I need to just sit and think about that. I need about ten minutes between every bit of feedback—to emotionally process."

"Okay, so we sit in silence?"

"No, it's your turn now. Tell me about your fight with your dad."

"Nah."

"You've read my story. You tell me a story now. A real one."

"It's not a good story."

"That's okay. Mine wasn't either."

"It's not even a story."

"Just talk," I say gently.

"You really want to hear about it?"

"I want you to tell me every detail."

"Okay," he says. "Well. Dad and Bree, my stepmum, had plans to go out to dinner, nothing special, just the local pizza place, and when I told them I was coming down, I thought they might change them or invite me or something, so we'd all have dinner together. But instead they canceled the babysitter and asked me to mind the kids, and I said fine, and then Dad and Bree came home from dinner and complained about the house being messy and Tilda wasn't in bed early enough and Toby had too much screen time and that I've let everyone down. And it's just like—it never feels like *my* house, you know? I'm always kind of this outsider who is on the edge of *their* family. I'm always doing the wrong thing. And when I go to my mum's place, it's the same. I just fit in around everyone else's schedule, tag along, join in on their stuff, their plans, try to fit with their rules, rules that are always changing, live with whoever they want me to live with at the time. They are two full-time families, and I'm part-time in both. Or something. I don't know. I don't even know what I'm saying, really." He looks away.

The words have poured out of him fast, so fast that it makes my heart hurt.

"I'm really sorry." I shuffle a little closer to him, moving the laptop out of the way. I want to hug him but I don't think he'd let me. "I mean, you saw what happened with my dad. He has never made me feel like I might be a priority to him. It hurts. I know how it hurts."

"My dad tries. So does my mum. It's not like with your dad, but they just . . . they're busy, and they don't see it. I don't know. I don't think my dad is very interested in my life. Or me." He pauses, and I wait for him to say more.

He looks at me, as if to check I'm still listening, and then looks down and pats Minty as he continues. "Anyway, I sort of tried to talk to him about it tonight, but it was a disaster."

"What happened?" I ask.

"Well, I said something like, 'Everything I do in this house is wrong,' and he said, 'That's a cop-out, you need to take responsibility for your actions,' and I said, 'Sorry I'm not perfect then,' and he said, 'No, you're most certainly not,' and then we just yelled at each other and I walked out."

"That sucks," I say.

"Yeah."

"He's the dad. *He's* the adult. Well, I guess technically you're an adult too, but he's been one for a really long time. We're still new at this. He's the one putting unfair pressure on you. It's his responsibility to fix your relationship, to ask about your feelings, to figure out a new approach. Not yours." I'm passing this off as my own wisdom, but really, Nanna told me this, when I was thirteen and told her my plan to help Dad navigate the school holidays with us. She said, "Oh honey, that's not your job."

"Yeah, I guess. It all feels a bit hopeless. It's pathetic, even talking about it," Jesse says.

"It's not pathetic," I say, putting my hand on his arm. I wish I had the superpower to transmit comfort and happiness through my touch right in this second, to inject him with every good feeling I can think of. "This stuff matters," I say. "You matter."

"You matter to *me*," I wish I had the courage to add.

"With your dad, how do you do it?" he asks.

"What do you mean?"

"How do you handle it? When he lets you down, or you get angry with him?" He's looking at me like I might have a magic answer. As if I haven't wasted countless hours of my life trying to figure it out.

"I don't, really. Or I guess I do. I just kind of try to accept how it is now and keep hoping we might figure it out one day. It's different with us, because there's not much there, really, to fight against anymore. Getting angry at him is like being angry at a void. He'll listen, or pretend to listen. He'll say sorry, send me a random gift I don't want, give me money, and then do it all again. It's okay, I don't need him to show up in that way, because I have Nanna and Mum and Lauren," I say. I have a home and Dad isn't part of it.

"I used to get so angry sometimes," says Jesse. "That's why I started running, you know? I didn't want to turn into an angry guy, it's such a cliché, and there are enough angry men out there. Running got rid of all that." He pauses. "I want . . . I guess I just want to find somewhere I feel like I belong."

"You belong with us. With me and Harper and our house," I say.

We look at each other, and then I look away, because it feels like the eye contact is taking us somewhere.

"I'm sorry," he says.

"What for?"

"For coming over here with no warning and turning your night into a fucking therapy session."

"I don't mind. I like talking to you."

We smile at each other.

"I also want to say sorry for—" he starts, then stops. "Can

we talk about this? About what happened back in school? Because you never want to talk about it."

I have a sudden flash of Lauren not wanting to talk about Dad with me. Am I being like her, avoiding the hard stuff? No, this is different. Or maybe it's not. I look at Jesse and say, "We can talk about it."

"Okay," he says. He seems nervous now. "Well, I'm sorry. I'm really, really sorry. I've felt bad about it ever since."

"I accept your apology," I say, careful not to say "I forgive you" because I don't know if I do, not yet. "But I want to know why you did it," I add.

"Oh. Well, it's complicated. Or I guess it's not. I was an immature dickhead."

He pauses, and I give him a keep-going look. We both have our heads leaning back against the couch, facing each other.

"Okay. Um," he says, and laughs, looking uncomfortable. "I liked you. I had a crush on you. I mean, obviously I did. I kissed you."

"And then you very publicly rejected me," I say.

"Yeah. That part was awful. I panicked. I thought . . . I thought you pulled back after the kiss, I thought you were rejecting me, that I'd put myself out there and been rejected. And the kiss was bad. I knew it was bad. It was all too fast because I had no idea what I was doing. The whole thing was so embarrassing. Then suddenly I had an opportunity to, I don't know, recover and look cool in front of other people, and I took it. It was a shitty thing to do."

"It *was* shitty. And then at school you told me our story was crap." I don't want him to forget that part.

"That was only because you ripped up my map," he says, smiling a little.

"And that was because of what you did!" I say. I am acutely

aware of how inconsequential it all sounds, what a tiny thing it is in the scheme of everything. There is war, disease, climate change, and I'm going on about hurt feelings from five years ago. I almost want to laugh. And yet—the pain of it was real then. It's still real to me now.

"I'd just moved to a new school and I wanted to fit in. But that's not an excuse. I was a terrible person."

"You weren't a terrible person. That's the thing. We were friends and you ruined it."

"I know." His voice is quiet and serious now. "I know I ruined it. I used to spend all day looking forward to seeing you on the bus. I would save up things to tell you. And then we didn't talk anymore. You hated me."

"I didn't hate you," I say quietly. "I never hated you."

We stare at each other in the dim light.

"You were wrong, you know," he says.

"When?" I say.

"When you were listing your worst qualities."

"I'm not controlling or anxious?"

"Oh, you're controlling and anxious. But you're also fun. I've had a lot of fun since we've been living together."

"Fun with me?"

He laughs.

"Yes," he says. "Why do you find this so hard to believe?"

"Name the most fun you've had with me."

"Well, you introduced me to the delights of *The Vampire Diaries*. That can't be underestimated. Just hanging out with you is fun. I feel like . . . I feel comfortable when we're together."

"Me too," I say.

"But the best time I had with you was the night of Harper's birthday," he says. "The part before the fight, obviously."

"That part was fun," I say carefully. This feels dangerous.

This is a pathway we don't need to go down. We've just made it back to our friendship, a nice, safe place where I can manage my feelings.

"It didn't feel like we were just pretending," he says.

"No, it didn't." My brain is buzzing, and my hands are sweaty.

I want to get up and run away. Minty must sense my nervousness. She opens her eyes and gets up, stretches, jumps onto the floor, and leaves the room. I want to scream after her, "Don't leave me! I need emotional support right now!"

"Would you ever want that?" he says, so quietly it's almost a whisper. A piece of his hair has fallen over his forehead, and it takes all my power to stop myself from pushing it back.

"A relationship like that? Sure," I say. I'm being deliberately obtuse.

"I mean, would you ever want that with me?" he says. His eyes are soft and he's looking at me in a way I don't think anyone has looked at me before.

"Would *you*?" I say, my voice rising a little, louder than I want to be, but I can't help it, because here we are again. "I heard you, remember. I heard you say no when Harper asked if anything was going on."

He shakes his head.

"That was because of the house rules, because I didn't want her to think anything was happening, and because nothing *was* happening, technically."

"But the way you said it," I say, closing my eyes. "You meant it."

We're talking in and around things. We're talking about being together without actually saying it. We're fighting about it without saying it. This is the worst possible way to go about things, because I won't even get a moment, a nice moment before we fought, before I shut things down, a nice, clear, definite romantic moment to hold on to.

"You're wrong." His arm is touching mine now, just a tiny bit.

My heart is racing, and I open my eyes.

"It doesn't matter anyway. We live together, it would be too hard. Too messy. There are *rules*. It wouldn't be like it was that night. It would be a mistake," I say firmly.

I wish he would kiss me. It's a thought that pops into my mind often these days, but it's never been stronger than now, and I need to Whac-A-Mole it down in case he can read it on my face, in case he can *feel* it in my skin.

He nods.

"You're right," he says. "It would be a mistake. But—"

"But what?" I say.

"What if we pretended again? Just one more time, just for one minute." Our arms are pressed together now, our faces close.

"For one minute?" I say.

"Just one minute." He gets out his phone, sets a timer for one minute, starts it, and puts the phone down. I almost laugh at the absurdity, but my heart is going too fast for the laugh to escape.

"Okay," I say.

It feels like we're playing a game, again, and it's not real, again. But I can't help myself. I'll take any scenario, any chance to kiss him again. I know this, but he can't be allowed to know this—no one can. I close my eyes, sensing him getting closer. I feel his hand on my cheek, and I open my eyes and look at him. He takes my face in both his hands and then he kisses me, and it's somehow even better than when we kissed at the bar.

I slowly move from sitting up to lying down, and Jesse follows, leaning over my body, kissing my neck. Then the one-minute alarm dings, and he stops kissing me, turns it off, takes off his glasses and puts them beside the phone, and comes right back to kissing me.

I don't want it to end. Kissing Tristan was always nice, but that's it. Just nice. Kissing Jesse isn't even in the same realm. They don't even seem like the same activity. Kissing Jesse is making me feel things I've never felt before. It's like someone has flipped a switch and turned on nerve endings I didn't even know existed.

I want to stay like this forever, but my brain starts interrupting me. With chatter, with anxiety, with warnings.

We live together.

It won't work.

You're going to get hurt. Again.

The house rules!

I pull back from him.

"This doesn't change anything," I say. "It was a moment of weakness. A minute of weakness. A few minutes. That's all."

"Okay," he says, and then kisses my neck again.

"We can't do it again." I extract myself from underneath him and stand up. I need him to agree, I need him to say it. I can't be the one making all the decisions.

"Okay," he says, nodding.

"So we're agreed," I say.

"Shake on it," he says, and when I put my hand in his to shake, he pulls me down toward him, and I let him, and then we're kissing again.

I'm lying on top of him on the couch, my legs between his, my hands in his hair, his hands sliding up underneath the back of my top, slipping around toward the front, when I hear a door open. My brain is slow in comprehending, because it was finally blissed-out and silent, so I don't react quickly enough.

Lauren flicks on the light as she walks in the room, and

shrieks. "Oh my God," she says. Then she bends over, laughing. "Oh my God, Brooke!" She is delighted.

Jesse and I have leaped apart, and now we're both standing up. His hair is askew, his T-shirt rumpled and hitched up oddly on one side.

"Lauren!" I say, as if she's done something wrong. "Shhhh! Don't wake up Mum."

"But Mum would love to know. Finally some gossip about little baby Brooke."

She's drunk, but only slightly. Enough to be annoying.

"What gossip?" Mum says, appearing in the doorway like a demon spirit. She's wearing a loose T-shirt and underwear almost big enough to be considered shorts but definitely still underwear.

"Mum! Pants!" I say, and Jesse quickly turns away. "And a bra, please!"

"Sorry, honey, but this is my house, and I don't normally expect to find strange men in it in the middle of the night," she says.

"It's Jesse, not a strange man. He was just helping me with my story," I say, glaring at Lauren.

She mimes locking her lips and throwing away the key, which is entirely unhelpful when Mum can see what she's doing.

"I should go," Jesse says. He still hasn't turned around. "Bye, everyone."

He brushes Minty's fur off his jeans, grabs his phone and glasses, and walks toward the front door. I go with him. We agree on a time he'll pick me up tomorrow morning to drive home, and there's a lull where it feels like we should hug, or say something significant, or kiss again, but instead he lightly touches my shoulder and turns and walks down the steps.

"Wait," I say. I can't leave it like this. I won't be able to sleep,

I won't be able to exist. I need to push it one direction or the other, to make it real or make it nothing, to feel like I have it safely in check and under control.

He looks back at me.

"It still doesn't change anything," I say. "Right? We agree that we can't be together."

He is silent for a beat.

"If that's what you want," he says.

"It's what we're *both* agreeing to."

"All right, Brooke. I agree," he says, and lightly jumps down the last few steps and walks away.

THIRTY-TWO

"I've been thinking about your story," Jesse says on the drive home.

"Oh yeah?" I say. I was worried things would be weird between us after last night, and they were, at first, when I got in the car and looked out the window, feeling shy. Then we got takeaway coffee at the little café on the way out of town and made the requisite jokes about how Melbourne coffee is better, which felt very adult, and that smoothed over the awkwardness. I stare straight ahead, sipping on my average coffee and hiding behind my sunglasses.

"Okay, so if you make them younger—"

"Which I have decided I will do," I say. I thought about it a lot in bed last night, in part as a way to stop myself replaying the real-life couch scene between Jesse and me over and over. I worried it would be like when I play a song I love over and over, or watch one scene of a show over and over, and I strip all the pleasure from it. I need to keep the pleasure of the couch memory because who knows how long it will be before I kiss anyone like that again. It might never feel that good again in my life. And thinking of our night on the couch was also getting my feelings all scrambled and making me deeply regret saying the words "we can't be together" even though we *obviously can't be together*. So I focused on my story, and as much as I resisted the idea of changing the characters' ages, it suddenly clicked into place and I saw he was right. Damn him.

"Ah, see. I am a genius," he says.

"Okay, calm down. It was one good suggestion."

"Genius. Say it. *Gee-nee-us*."

"Don't make me regret letting you read it," I say.

"I have plenty more ideas, so get ready for your mind to be blown," he says, grinning.

We talk about the story more, and laugh, and I start taking notes in my phone. Some of his ideas are terrible, some are just things he's saying to make me laugh, but some are pretty good. The most important thing is that I feel the spark, the very particular writing energy I need, and even though I have less than twenty-four hours to do it, I feel like there's a chance I can crack the story open and rewrite it into something to send to PJ by tomorrow morning.

We stop for petrol, and as we're pulling back onto the highway, he turns to me.

"I have something to show you," he says.

"What is it?" I say, wary. Surprises, especially the ones I've had lately, put me on edge.

"On the back seat, there's a bag." He sounds very ominous.

I turn around and see a big brown paper bag sitting there.

"Is it another stuffed toy dog?" I ask.

"Very funny, but no. It's actually sort of worse than that."

"I love that dog," I admit.

"Well, I need to give you context for this first, before you look at anything."

"Set the scene," I say, pushing my sunglasses up onto my head.

"So, after everything that happened back then, in school, the kiss attempt and me being awful and you ripping the map," he says.

"After all that, yes," I say.

"There's a bit more I never told you."

"Oh?" I say, my stomach suddenly bubbly with nerves.

"I was feeling guilty. I knew I'd fucked everything up. And I thought if I could just show you how sorry I was, we could be friends again."

"Okay," I say. I had no idea he felt this way back then.

"I thought I should get you a present. Well, first I thought about writing a letter, but every time I tried, it was really bad. I had no idea how to write a letter to a girl without sounding cheesy. I still don't. So I decided a gift was the best option," he says. He's watching the road as he says this, occasionally glancing at me. I don't know where this story is going, and I still have no clue what is in the bag.

"I wanted to give you something meaningful and heartfelt."

"What is it?" I say, reaching around and picking up the bag. It's heavy.

"Well, I took the ripped-up map home. At first, I thought I could tape it back together, smooth it out, but that didn't work, so I drew the whole thing all again. I re-created it and made it better, put in a few more of the details that you had written into the story, and then I got it framed."

I reach into the bag and pull it out, the map he drew of the world we made up together, in a lovely plain wooden frame, behind glass. I have to take a second, to swallow and make sure my voice won't wobble when I speak, that my eyes won't fill with tears. Because it's so lovely and sentimental and gorgeous.

"You really did this, back then?"

"I did. And I kept it all this time. I went looking for it in a box last night, after I got home."

"Why didn't you give it to me when you had it framed?"

"Well, I hesitated. You were so angry, and we weren't talking anymore. All of a sudden it seemed like a bad idea. Why would you want a bit of homework framed as a gift?"

"I mean, have you met me? Of course I want a piece of homework framed."

He laughs. "I know. My instinct was right, but I couldn't bring myself to actually give it to you. I was scared you'd laugh at me. Or yell at me. Or both. And it was so big. There was no easy way to give it to you without making a whole scene. So then I googled 'what do fourteen-year-old girls like.'"

"Oh my God. Then what?" I can't help smiling.

"It said jewelry. So I bought you a necklace."

"You bought me a *necklace*?"

"I did."

"What kind of necklace?"

"It's in there too. The square box."

I put my hand in the bag and pull out a square jewelry box and open it. There is a black leather choker-style necklace with a big plastic red heart charm on it.

It's hideously ugly and absolutely not my taste, but I am touched, and I was also brought up to be appreciative of any gift, whether you like it or not, or, I guess in this case, whether you were actually given it or not.

"It's cute," I say, in what I hope is a believable way.

"It was very expensive," he says.

"It was?"

He bursts out laughing.

"No! Look at it. It's very cheap."

I laugh too.

"I still like it."

"You do not. You couldn't. It's truly awful."

"So you chickened out of giving me this as well."

"It was a *heart*. A big red plastic heart. I realized after I bought it that I couldn't give you a goddamn heart necklace. And that I'd never even seen you wear a necklace anyway."

"Wow. You really went through a process."

"I haven't finished yet."

"There's *more*?"

"There's more," he says.

I am laughing now, I can't stop.

"Oh no," I say. I am picturing Jesse anguishing over these gifts and the thought of it, the thought of his uncertainty and clumsy desire to make things right, is filling me with tenderness.

"I thought maybe I could make you something," he says. "My stepmum had these paint-a-mug kits, so I decided to paint a mug for you."

"That sounds promising."

"It did not go well."

I pull out the mug. It has a face on it, a terrifying face that looks kind of distorted and almost clown-like.

"Who is that? Is that *me*?" I ask.

Jesse is laughing, almost too hard to answer.

"It was supposed to be, yeah. And then I smudged it, and tried to fix it, and it got worse. And then I thought, why would she even *want* a mug with her face on it? So I tried to make it look more generic, just an anonymous person on a mug, which seemed even weirder, so then I tried to make it look like Harry Styles because you loved his song, and that's when it started looking really bad."

I am laughing hard now too.

"So you painted the mug, and then what?"

"I gave up. I put it all in a box under my bed and told myself I would figure it out on the weekend, and then I kept putting off thinking about it because I was so anxious about it, until it was too late to give you anything, and then we just never spoke again."

A part of me wants to travel back in time and hug fourteen-year-old Jesse.

"So why did you dig it out now?" I say.

"Because I want you to know. I felt so bad back then, Brooke, for what I did and then losing you as a friend. I want you to know I didn't just move on with my life. I really wanted to fix things, I just didn't know how."

I smile at him.

"I'm glad you told me. It does make me feel better about everything. And I can't wait to use the mug."

"We don't need to actually use it."

"Are you kidding me? This is my number one mug from now on."

He smiles, and we drive in silence for a moment.

"You can trust me," he says suddenly. He says it so calmly, so matter-of-factly, that it gives me a little jolt in my chest.

"What do you mean?"

"You can trust me. With your writing. As a friend. With anything. With everything."

"I don't think I really trust anyone," I say with a small laugh, even though it's not funny. It feels like something I should be saying to a therapist, write in my journal, put in a dramatic letter to my father on his deathbed with the addendum "And it's all your fault!" It's a fundamental truth I don't want anyone else to know, but here I am, saying it out loud at nine a.m. on a Sunday morning in the car with the boy I have never trusted.

"You can trust me," he says again. "I know, with our history, you think you can't, but you can now, you can."

I want to believe him. Every time he says it, I feel it, in my chest, a rumbling. My heart, pricking up its little ears like a hopeful puppy.

"Okay," I say finally, because I want to, I really do want to.

THIRTY-THREE

Harper and I are making soup together in companionable silence, chopping and slicing vegetables for a giant pot that we're planning to eat for the next three days. She turns to me.

"I have something to tell you."

"Okay." Her tone is making me nervous. It's an I-have-bad-news tone.

"I'm setting Jesse up on a date," she says.

"Oh." I work very hard to keep my face still and unresponsive, which is hard because I'm chopping onions and my eyes are burning. "As part of your matchmaking strategy with Penny?"

"Yes, we need one more data set. And we want to give the straights one last chance before we deem them unworkable in our business model."

"Oh God. I feel like I've let the entire straight community down. And we already have a terrible reputation."

"We can apportion some of that blame to Henry."

"Let's give him a significant portion," I say.

"Anyway, I guess, I just wanted you to know, ahead of time. In case."

"In case what?"

"In case the idea of Jesse going on a date upsets you and you need to talk about it or stop it or something." She says this very quickly and then watches my face for a reaction.

I almost say, "Why would it upset me?" but I don't want to give her the opportunity to answer that. I don't want to know what she thinks the answer is.

"I'm fine. Completely and totally fine with it. One hundred percent fine. There's no reason not to be. And there's nothing to talk about. It's actually a great idea. Good for Jesse, you know." The more words I say, the faster I say them, and I'm chopping the vegetables faster too, wiping my streaming onion eyes with the back of my hand, and I can hear myself—I know I don't sound believable. I sound like someone who shouldn't be handling a knife right now.

"Okay." Harper is staring at me, her knife held poised.

"Don't say, 'The lady doth protest too much.'" I turn away from the onions, eyes burning.

"I have no idea what that means," she says.

"It's a line from *Hamlet*."

"Ugh, Shakespeare is a pig," Harper says.

"Oh God, is he?" I was in the Shakespeare Society at my school, but we just read his plays, and I don't know anything about the man.

"I actually don't know, I just assume he was." She laughs. "And if I say that, it distracts from the fact I never read any Shakespeare at school and I made my sister write my essay on *Macbeth*."

I need to learn how to deflect like Harper. Tomorrow is my creative writing class, when we'll be discussing my story—my rewritten story. I got home from the trip on Sunday morning, sat at my laptop, and wrote for almost twelve hours straight. I was buzzing. I think I had runner's high, but from writing. I went to bed at one a.m., woke up at six a.m., proofread it and shockingly still felt okay about it, and emailed it to PJ. She replied at eight thirty a.m. saying she was sending it to the class and looking forward to the discussion on Thursday. Nothing else. I don't know if that's a good sign or a bad sign or what. At least I can't fail, surely. I wrote *two* stories for her. That has to count for something.

I thought nothing could distract me from the stress of the impending class discussion, but Harper has managed to prove me wrong.

"So who is Jesse going on a date with?" I say, trying to sound casual.

"Amber. Remember, from the housewarming? With the nose ring? And the fear of mice?"

"Oh," I say, trying to keep my voice neutral. "I thought she wasn't interested in him?" My voice sounds way higher pitched and more desperate than I was aiming for.

"She's been kind of on and off with her ex, Brody, but now she's definitely, finally over him. Which is good, because he had this weird mustache that made me feel a bit sick when I looked at him."

"Oh. Well, good for her, good for her. And Jesse. Good for Jesse. Sounds like perfect timing for the two of them." I hate myself but I keep talking anyway. "When is the date?"

"Tomorrow night," Harper says.

Jesse walks in at that moment. "Whoa. I have never seen so many vegetables in my life," he says.

"Brooke is teaching me about cooking. And meal prepping. And budgeting," Harper says proudly.

"Sounds like a big day in life lessons for you," Jesse says, grinning.

Harper throws him a parsnip.

"Can you chop that up?" she asks.

"Sure. What are we making?" he says.

"Soup," she says.

"Soup!" he says with a level of enthusiasm that I try not to find adorable.

I have remained silent throughout this exchange because I don't trust myself not to bring up his date. But I'm mature. I can handle this. We're friends. It's fine. I am not going to say anything, I am going to be normal and chill and—

"So Harper tells me you're on her matchmaking books after all," I blurt out. It was there, sitting in my throat, busting to get out. I had to do it. I wipe my eyes with the back of my hand, then worry he's going to think I'm so upset about the date that I'm crying.

"My eyes are running from the onions," I add.

"I assumed," he says.

"Well, good luck for the big date," I say, because once you've started down the road of letting your brain make bad choices sometimes you have to just stay the course. My subtly snarky tone would be so much more effective without the weepy eyes and runny nose.

"Yes, let's hope it goes better than yours did," he says.

"Henry and I are friends now, so it *was* a success actually," I say. Henry and Tristan have asked me to join their trivia team.

Harper leaves the room to find her phone charger, and I narrow my eyes at Jesse.

"You didn't tell me you were going on a date," I say in my most accusing tone.

"We're just friends, aren't we? That's what you said, isn't it?" he says, his eyes flashing with an emotion I can't decipher.

"Yes."

"So why do you care if I'm going on a date?"

"I care as a friend, in a friendly way."

"Well, as a *friend*, I'm sorry." He pauses, halfway through chopping a potato. "And I was going to tell you, I just haven't had a chance."

I open my mouth to say something in return, but Harper comes back, and I decide it's better to stay quiet.

Jesse chats with Harper and looks so relaxed I am appalled. He should be tortured by what happened on the weekend. We kissed! Four days ago! He should not have the emotional capability to go on a date for at least a month, maybe two. I should be consuming his thoughts the way he is consuming mine. I have been secretly drinking my sleepytime tea out of the ugly mug and I hung the framed map on my wall, for God's sake. (I did draw the line at wearing the necklace, though.)

Harper is looking between us and pressing her lips together in a way I am trying not to take as disapproving.

"So where are you going? For the date?" I ask, because I'm a dog with a bone. Harper gives me a pitying look, which I ignore.

"We're getting a drink at a bar," Jesse says. A drink at a bar at night beats my coffee date during the day. Not that my coffee date even happened.

"Have you been texting with her?" I say. I sound like a jealous girlfriend, or a cop. *Calm down. Be a tiny bit normal.*

"A little bit." Jesse bites a bit of carrot and chews it noisily.

"I'm happy for you," I say. I have no idea why I add this. I'm in the hole and digging, I guess.

"You're *happy* for me?" he repeats.

"Yes," I say.

"Great. I guess we're all happy, then," he says. His eyes burn into mine.

"Extremely happy," I say.

"I'm glad we established that," Harper says, looking between us and sighing a little to herself. "Now Jesse, show me your clothes options. I know she's seen you before, but I pitched you as well-dressed."

THIRTY-FOUR

"What do we think of Brooke's story?" PJ asks.

She's holding the pages in her hand. I am trying to read her face. I am trying to be strong. I will not cry. I will not *react*. I will take what happens and become a better person. Failure leads to success.

Or, my backup plan. Revenge. One day in the future, I will write a novel about PJ and describe her in really harsh but recognizable ways, and she'll pick it up in a bookshop and read it, and feel the icy-cold recognition sliding down her spine, and she'll write me an email and say, "I was wrong, I was so wrong, Brooke, please forgive me . . ." and I'll write back and say, "Sorry, I don't remember being in your class," and then she'll sit there and think, *Maybe that character isn't me after all, but no, it's too coincidental*, and she'll need to examine her ego and her behavior and the whole thing will haunt her forever.

Okay, calm down, let's see what she has to say first.

Justin, Sophie, and Ruby all messaged me before the class.

It's so good!

I laughed but also the ending was really fucked up and sad!

It's really funny!

This means they hate it and they think it's not funny, obviously. If you truly think something is good, you tell the person, "I loved it so much, I practically cried laughing, holy shit." And you use lots of emojis or at least six exclamation marks or all caps. You have to overhype and exaggerate so they know you're being truthful. "It's so good" actually means "It's average at best," "I laughed" means "I know I was supposed to be laughing at something in there but I wasn't," and "It's really funny" means "I do not understand your humor."

Is it worse if people have something to say or nothing to say? From previous classes, if lots of hands go up, that's a bad sign, but if no hands go up, that's also a bad sign, because it means people were bored or didn't finish, and you'll find that out when PJ presses them to respond.

I want two or three people to put up their hands, say I'm brilliant and will probably get a book deal before I'm twenty, I'll blush, and then we move on. Those people *could* be Justin, Sophie, and Ruby, but they won't be. Sophie never talks unless she's encouraged to, Justin is deliberately withholding of praise because he thinks people take you more seriously if you never admit to enjoying anything, and Ruby doesn't like me enough to put herself out there, I don't think, although she's probably my best chance. And when we read her story, I said really positive things. I look at her. *Remember the nice things I said, Ruby. Remember.*

"I'll start," PJ says.

This startles me. She never starts. She likes to go last so she doesn't influence the discussion.

"Great," I say. My mouth is very, very dry. I grab my water bottle and chug down as much as I can. Which is a mistake, because I almost instantly need to pee and I'm giving my body more moisture—I'm basically forcing it to produce tears.

"What many of you don't know is that Brooke got some pretty harsh feedback from me when she first submitted her story. I told her I thought she could do better and gave her the weekend to rewrite it if she wanted to. This is not something I would say to everyone. It's not easy to hear that kind of feedback, but I thought Brooke could handle it, and I was right. She went away, she didn't have a tantrum, or maybe she did but she didn't tell me about it, she didn't email me and refute my criticism, she took on my feedback and she reworked her story, in two days, no less. And now it doesn't matter whether the story is good or not because Brooke, you've shown you can take feedback, you've shown you can work hard, you can start over, you've shown dedication and that you're not going to give up. These are very, very important skills for a writer. And you have them."

My face is burning. The one good thing about her email had been that it was private. Now everyone knows my humiliation. But I sit up straighter and take the praise. I try to rearrange my face into a humble expression. I actually drafted several emails to her and had a tantrum, but I was too cowardly to send them. No one needs to know this.

"Now let's talk about the actual story. Brooke, it's good. There's a lot to be fixed, some of the transitions are clumsy, and I'm not sure about the reveal at the end, but overall, it's good. You've nailed the voice, the dialogue is funny and authentic, and I believe in the characters."

"Yeah, I was going to say, the voice is there," someone says.

"I liked the bit where the car broke down."

"Me too."

"And the scene at the family dinner was funny."

"But I hated the guy."

"No, I like him!"

I thought I would be fixated on any criticism, and no amount of praise would feel enough, but, actually, listening to them talk about it, I feel detached in a pleasant way. It kind of feels like they're discussing a real story. By a real writer.

THIRTY-FIVE

I get home from writing class, high on happy feelings, and then I remember Jesse is going on a date with Amber tonight. The thought makes me irritable and itchy. Not itchy in a way I can scratch, but itchy in my brain, itchy deep under my skin, itchy in my soul. I can't sit still. I pace around my room. I decide to clean the bathroom. I need to put my energy somewhere, and getting the bathroom really clean always makes me feel calm. The shine of a white bathtub! The gleam of clean tiles! But no matter how hard I scrub, it doesn't give me the satisfaction I am looking for.

I want to tell Jesse about the class, the story, the fact that I'm not going to give up on writing, that I don't need to dedicate my creative life to revenge on PJ Mayfield. He is the first person I want to tell, but I wish he weren't.

I decide to go for a run. An exhausted body simply can't feel as many feelings—it's practically a scientific fact—plus, despite everything that happened on my first run, I still have a vision of myself as a person who runs.

I start jogging very, very slowly. I have my pump-up-feel-good-you-can-do-this playlist on, and the sun is shining, and I have some of the skills it takes to be a writer. This is as good as it gets. And yet . . .

Jesse is going on a date with Amber.

I picture them. Staying up all night talking and then they'll go out again and suddenly they'll be in a relationship, and things will get serious quickly, and she'll be at the house all the time, and she and I will pretend to be friends but we absolutely won't be, and she'll make comments like, "Wow, those earrings are eye-catching," or, "Oh, you got a haircut," observations that might sound like compliments but are actually criticisms, and she and Jesse will double-date with Harper and Penny and I'll be a fifth wheel all the time, and I'll end up joining Amber's mother's book club and showing them how I do my fruit platter.

I drop to a walk, gasping for breath.

Why is this bothering me so much?

I don't want him to go on a date with her.

Or anyone.

I like him. I know that. I have kissed him multiple times now. I find him attractive—no, more than attractive; lately it's been hard to even be in a room with him without wanting to get closer, without daydreaming about something happening, without thinking of us kissing on the couch. But I thought it was the kind of crush that could be overcome. I'm good at compartmentalizing. I'm good at boxing away feelings.

But this time, this feeling, doesn't feel like it can be boxed away.

I look at my phone. Lauren has sent me a photo of her hand, unbandaged. There's no caption or further info. This is standard for her. She'll say she's busy, she doesn't have time to write words or record a voice message to provide context, and yet, I know right now she'll be reclining on the couch with a hydrating face mask on, gently pushing a jade roller over her cheeks, scrolling on her phone.

I call her.

I never call Lauren to chat, ever. I've called her to find out where she is, to make sure she's okay, to see if she's dead, to help find her lost phone. But to talk? To ask for *advice*? Never. Never, never, never. I haven't had to. People who live together and have had easy access to each other for their whole lives don't have a phone relationship and you can't just suddenly develop one out of nowhere, after eighteen years of yelling at each other from different rooms and talking in shorthand. But this is a crisis. And maybe Lauren has more wisdom than I give her credit for.

"What's wrong? Is Mum okay?" she says as soon as she picks up.

"You live with Mum. Not me. How would I know?" I say.

"Mum!" Lauren shouts. "Where are you?"

"On the toilet," Mum shouts back. "I'll be a while."

"Mum's okay," Lauren says.

"That's not why I called. I called to talk to you."

"You never call to talk to me."

"I need . . . advice."

"What kind of advice?"

"Romantic advice."

"Oh my God. Yes. I've been waiting for this day. Wait, let me get comfortable."

"If you make this weird or into a big deal, I'm hanging up," I say.

"No you won't, because *you* need *my* advice."

She cackles and I almost do hang up, but she's right. I'm desperate.

"So," I say, not really sure where to start.

"So after witnessing the two of you dry-humping on the couch, I'm assuming this is about Jesse."

"Can you not make it sound disgusting and immature?"

"Fine. After witnessing the comingling of two precious souls—"

"I will hang up."

"Okay, okay. So you hooked up with him and now you have feelings and—what?"

"What do I do?"

"How does he feel about it?"

"I don't know. I told him we can't ever be together because we live together, and now he's going on a date with someone else."

"And how do you feel about that?" Lauren sounds like she's impersonating a therapist.

"Panicked! Sick to my stomach! Like I might die!" I am shouting, and a woman nearby turns to look at me with concern.

"*Ohhhhhh.* I see what's happened. You've fully fallen in love with him."

I give a yelp that is half laugh, half expression of horror. Am I *in love* with Jesse? No. Surely not. For God's sake. Love is for when you're thirty-three and ready for marriage, or it's for people like Lauren who have the confidence to throw the idea of love around casually and recklessly, knowing there are many people out there who will say it back, or it's for soulmates like Penny and Harper. It's not for me. Not yet.

I don't believe in loving someone until you've been in a

romantic relationship with them for at least a year. Until you know everything about them and their life and all their secrets. Until you've seen them at their very, very worst, until everything has been dug through and examined, until you have all the facts and you're sure about everything and there's a plan in place for your future, until you are very, very sure they will not leave or hurt you. Love comes after all that, it's the very, very last thing. It doesn't just arrive in your brain suddenly like this. It has to build slowly and carefully, over a lot of time, with a lot of thought and planning and a lot, *a lot*, of hard work. Love that slips in, sudden and unexpected and easy, love that turns up on your doorstep like a surprise package—that's not to be trusted.

"So what are you going to do about it?" Lauren says.

"Nothing! We live together." I'm sort of shouting and pacing in circles.

"Well, shit happens."

"What does that mean?"

"It will make things convenient. You won't have to argue over whose house to stay at."

"You're jumping ahead. I need to sit down and think about this for a few weeks."

"No, you need to go and tell him how you feel! Wait for him in his bedroom in sexy lingerie or something."

My head is spinning. Is a plain black bralette with no underwire sexy? I picture myself hiding in his bedroom wearing this, and Jesse and Amber come home from the date, and I crawl under the bed in a panic and cower beside the mouse while they kiss and moan above me. No. This whole scenario must be stopped.

"Do you have time to buy a dozen red roses, crotchless underwear, and a tub of thickened cream?" Lauren is saying. "If so, I can direct you on what to do from there."

"*Lauren!* This is serious. He's going on a date with someone else *tonight*." I am still walking in circles, and I almost bump into a man running past.

"So tell him before he goes," Lauren says.

"I can't. I can't just *say it*."

"Write a letter and put it in his wallet, but loose, so it falls out during the date."

"Your ideas are so bad." I sit down on a nearby bench before I get in the way of any more runners.

"Repurpose that poem Tristan wrote for you."

"I'm really hanging up now."

"This isn't an assignment, Brooke. There's no perfect way to do it. Just tell him, for fuck's sake."

"I can't."

"You can."

"I *can't*."

"He's into you. It's very obvious. It's going to be fine."

"If he has feelings for me, then he should tell me first."

"Has he tried to, but you shut him down?"

God, she knows me too well. I look up at the sky. "I don't know. No. Maybe. I can't be sure."

"Brooke."

"Yeah?"

"Just, relax. This is the kind of cliff it's okay to jump off. This is a good risk to take."

"A good risk. Okay. Okay." She's convincing me. Sort of. A little.

"You can do this," she says.

"I can do it," I repeat, sounding anything but sure.

We say goodbye and hang up, and then she sends me a text saying, "YOU CAN DO THIS, I LOVE YOU," in all caps.

I read her message three times, and I tell myself it's true. I can do this.

THIRTY-SIX

By the time I get home, I'm hot and sweaty and still full of feelings.

I can hear Harper chatting to Jesse.

I imagine bursting into the kitchen, and saying . . . what? "I have an announcement to make." How do people tell other people important things? It would be much easier if we were standing in the rain, and I was dramatically shouting to be heard over the howling wind, maybe wearing a cape. Anything but this, an ordinary afternoon.

I look at myself in the mirror. I can't make a love declaration with slicked, sweaty hair.

I shower, wash my hair, and am staring at myself in the mirror, wet haired and towel clad, when Jesse calls out, "Bye."

I rush to the door and lean out into the hallway. "You're going?" I say. "I thought your date wasn't for ages."

"We decided to meet early," he says.

Oh God, their text banter got so hot, they couldn't wait any longer. They're already in love. I'm too late.

"Have fun!" I'm too high-pitched.

"Thanks," he says, and he moves toward the front door, then stops and turns back to me. His brow is furrowed. "I—"

"Yes?" My wet hair slips over my shoulder, and I stand there, too eager. Let him say he's changed his mind and he's not going. If there's no date, then I'll have time to breathe, very slowly analyze my feelings from every angle, and squash them all back down.

"Never mind. I'll see you later." His expression is unreadable.

And then he's gone, and I walk to my room and lie on my bed, defeated. I expect to feel a release, with the giving up, but I don't. The urge to do something about it, to do the very thing I know is stupid and messy and will very likely make my life harder—is stronger than ever. I never have urges like this.

I sit up.

I have to do something. I have to do something right now or I might explode.

I'm going to crash his date and tell him.

I get dressed before I can talk myself out of it. This is the kind of wild and terrible idea you really need to be riding on adrenaline to follow to completion, because any kind of close examination will derail you into rationality.

I dry my hair and put on the lipstick Lauren accidentally left here that she said is practically magic and can change your life if you layer it just right, and I walk down the hallway with purpose. Harper sees me and comes out of her bedroom.

"Where are you going?"

"Nowhere," I say, trying to sound casual as I slip past her, reaching for the door.

Harper looks at me closely. "Oh no," she says.

"What?"

"You're wearing lipstick. Are you doing what I think you're doing?"

"No! It's just lip gloss. Wait, what do you think I'm doing?"

"I think you're going to interrupt Jesse's date. You are, aren't you?"

"No," I say, my hand dropping from the door handle. "That would be weird."

"It would be weird."

"Why would you think I was doing that?" I ask. Do I look as desperate and out of control as I feel?

"Because you look like the girl at the end of the rom-com who is going to run to the airport to stop him flying away."

I take that to mean that I do look desperate and out of control but also cute, which is the best I can hope for. "Harper," I say, but then I have no more words. I want to deny it, but I'm struggling to lie to her. I'm scared the truth is all over my face.

She puts her hands on her hips. "What's going on? And don't say nothing, because I have eyes, and I can see the way you and Jesse have been looking at each other."

I am still jittery with hyped-up energy and I let the words flow out of me. "I know it's the worst idea and it's against the rules and it will probably be a disaster and you have no desire to live with a couple and you were very clear about that from the beginning and he's probably not interested and that will make it awkward, and either way you'll want us to move out, but I have all these feelings inside me, feelings I've never had before, and I have to do something with them and he said I could trust him and I want to see what happens if I do, if I finally trust *someone*."

Harper blinks at me, trying to absorb that sloppy overload of information.

"Okay. Okay. That's a lot. Let's take a breath. First off, I'm not going to kick you out," she says.

"You're not? But what about the rules?"

"What rules?" she says.

"Harper!" I say. How could she—how could anyone—forget about the rules. This is why you need an official binder. "The *house rules*. No pets, no romance, no unnecessary drama."

"Oh those," she says, and waves her hand. "Who cares about those. They're for, like, random housemates. You're one of my closest friends now."

"Oh!" I say, startled and delighted in equal measure. "You're one of my closest friends, but I didn't think you felt the same way."

"We hang out every day."

"Well, that could just be a housemate thing."

"It's a friendship thing."

I smile at her, and she smiles at me, and I think suddenly that maybe I don't need to tell Jesse anything. Maybe this is enough.

"So, you like Jesse," Harper continues, looking thoughtful.

"I like him," I say. And then, because just liking someone doesn't seem big enough to be dramatically running off to ruin their date, but I'm not ready to admit to the word "love," I add, "I like him a lot. I'm sorry."

"Don't be sorry! You feel how you feel. As much as I don't want to live with a couple, I do want to live with you both. You're my friends and I want my friends to be happy. And I'd rather you together than all angsty and pining for each other."

"Thank you," I say, still feeling emotional about her declaration of our friendship.

"None of this means I don't think it's a terrible idea."

"You think it's a terrible idea?"

"At best, it's a moderately bad idea. At worst, a total disaster."

"I guess I can operate on that scale."

"They're at that little bar a few streets over," she says. "I'll walk with you."

We step outside together. It's dusk, the sun is setting, the air is cold but not too cold, and I am about to do the bravest, stupidest thing I've ever done in my life.

THIRTY-SEVEN

We've been hovering outside the bar for ten minutes because I'm having second thoughts.

"You're right. There's no way this is going to go well," I say.

"No, you did not drag me out all this way to chicken out," Harper says. "Also, I'm cold."

"I didn't drag you, it was your idea to come! And Amber is your friend. You *want* me to ruin her date?" I say. Secretly, I am pleased that Harper is on my side over Amber's, even though I am objectively the villain in this scenario.

"Oh, she's still totally hung up on her ex." Harper waves her hand. "We had to really work hard to convince her to go on this date. She'll be fine."

"Oh. Well, now I feel bad for Jesse."

"A hot girl is about to tell him she's into him. He'll be fine."

"You think I look hot?" I say.

"You are smoking hot. And incredibly smart. You are too good for Jesse, too good for Henry, too good for Tristan, too good for any man, really. But if Jesse is the one you want, go for it. This is going to be the best night of your life."

"Wow," I say. "You are good at pumping people up."

"I know." She smiles. "It's kind of a specialty of mine."

I hug her quickly, steel myself, and walk up to the bar door.

Harper calls out, "Brooke!"

I turn, expecting her to say one final uplifting thing.

Instead she says, "I'm going to buy sweet-potato chips on my way home. Should I get extra for you?"

"No," I say, and it's the most rashly confident thing I've said all day, because if this goes badly, I'm going to want those chips.

I turn back to the bar, open the door, and walk in. My plan is to spot Jesse and Amber and to walk over and politely ask Jesse if I can speak with him, and then bring him to a corner of the bar, out of sight, and say something heartfelt, and then I'll go outside and wait for him to gently extract himself from the date.

And then we'll go home, hand in hand, and—

And what?

Go to his bedroom and have sex straightaway? With Harper sitting in the lounge? A love declaration *and* sex feels like a lot of levels jumped, all at once. But we already live together, so maybe it doesn't matter. I falter. I haven't really thought beyond the gooey feelings, of off-loading them onto him—*here, take all this*—to that part, the expectations, the rest of the night, the next day, and the one after that. My stomach drops. *No, no, no, focus on the now.* I'll never do anything if I have to plan out the days and weeks and months that come after it. We'll make rules, we'll make a plan, it'll be fine. Think back to what we told Tristan. We can make whatever rules we need, later. I can get it printed up, spiral-bound.

Be spontaneous, be spontaneous.

Maybe I'll just pull out my phone and make a rough plan

now, to show him, of how the relationship could progress, physically and emotionally, or a graph, a nice clean—

"Brooke?" Jesse says. He and Amber are standing in front of me.

"Oh hi!" I say, as if I am very surprised.

"What are you doing here?" Jesse says. I think his hand is resting on Amber's back and she's definitely leaning into him. Their body language is very *we are into this*. Oh God.

"Hi, I'm Brooke." I smile at Amber, mostly to avoid the question.

"My housemate," Jesse says.

"I remember," Amber says. "The one with the fancy fruit platter." She does not smile, which makes me smile more. Is it possible for your eyeballs to sweat? Because I think that's what is happening right now.

"We're just leaving to get something to eat," Jesse says.

"Oh, that sounds good," I say, as if I'm going to tag along.

Amber is looking at me like I might be a dangerous stalker, and she's possibly not wrong.

"Sorry, what are you doing here?" Jesse says again.

"Oh, um . . . ," I say, fumbling. My plan was to say, "Can we talk in private?" but those words don't arrive. Instead I say, "Someone crashed into your car."

"*What?*" Jesse says, looking alarmed.

"Not badly. But, um, you need to come home and give them your insurance details."

"I don't have insurance!" he says, looking even more panicked.

"You don't?" I say, slightly horrified.

"If they crashed into his parked car, why would they need *his* insurance details? It's their fault. Wouldn't you need their details?" Amber says.

"I'm not sure. You better come and sort it out," I say to Jesse. "They want to talk to you."

"Why did you come here, why didn't you just call him?" Amber asks. She's giving me an I'm-on-to-you look, and I'm not sure my lying can hold up under her scrutiny.

"My phone is dead, so I just ran here," I say.

"You were *just* on your phone, we saw you," Amber points out.

God, she should be a detective or a true-crime podcast host.

"I thought my phone was dead, but it was just turned off," I babble. "Look, it doesn't matter, just come." I pull on Jesse's shoulder. Amber is wearing very high heels, so I am betting everything on the hope she won't want to walk there and back.

"Brooke—" Jesse starts to say.

"He'll be back in ten minutes," I say to Amber.

"Not a problem, I can come too," she says to me, leading the way out of the bar, looking extremely comfortable in her shoes.

Fuck.

The three of us start walking toward the house, and I contemplate throwing myself in front of traffic. It's the only way to exit this hell of my own making.

Unless. If I text Harper right now, could she run out and bang up Jesse's car a bit? How far do I want to take this?

I think of one last desperate move that doesn't involve destroying Jesse's uninsured property.

"Amber, you can wait inside with me when we get there," I say. "Don't worry, we haven't seen any mice in a few days."

Jesse shoots me a look and opens his mouth to say something, but it's too late. The minute the word "mice" left my mouth she stopped walking.

"You know what? I'm just going to wait right here on this

bench," she says, sitting down on a bench seat on the footpath. She immediately pulls out her phone and smiles to herself as she starts typing a message to someone.

"I'll be ten minutes," Jesse says to her.

"It's fine," Amber says without looking up, and waves a hand. "Take all the time you need." Her tone is cold. I have officially ruined Jesse's date.

Jesse and I walk the rest of the way home together, and I am acutely aware that this is it, this is my moment, I only have one more block, time is ticking.

"What's going on?" Jesse says when he can apparently take the silence no longer.

"What do you mean?" I say, still stalling.

"You are very obviously lying."

"I'm not."

"So I'm about to walk around this corner and see my car all smashed up?"

"Well, okay, I was lying about that," I say.

"What the hell, Brooke?" he says. He shakes his head. I feel like I'm not putting my best self forward in this conversation.

"Look, I can explain," I say, but then I just keep walking to our house, and he follows me. We both stop when we get to his very-much-not-smashed car.

"Why did you come to the bar?" he says.

"I needed to talk to you," I say.

"Well, I'm here now," he says. "Talk."

I glance at the house and I can see Harper in her bedroom, eating her sweet-potato chips in bed and watching us like a show. It's very off-putting. She sees me looking at her and ducks behind her pillow. I turn and stand with my back to her, facing Jesse.

"Look, I know you're on a date with Amber, and you like her—"

"Is that what this is about? Because there's nothing serious going on between me and Amber. I'm pretty sure she was texting her ex-boyfriend the whole time we were at the bar. And that she's texting him right now. So don't worry. You have nothing to be jealous about." He folds his arms now, looking annoyed.

I almost yell, "I'm not jealous!" But it's a difficult position to argue at this very second.

"You said I can trust you," I say quietly.

"You can," he says, unfolding his arms, sounding exasperated.

"So I'm trusting you." I move closer to him, until we're almost touching. "I'm trusting you with what I'm about to tell you."

"Okay," he says, and he doesn't look mad anymore.

"I didn't want you to go on the date with Amber."

"Why not?"

I close my eyes, then open them.

"Because I have feelings for you."

"What kind of feelings?" he says, moving closer to me. His eyes are intense.

"I think . . . well, I think I'm falling in love with you," I say in a rush. It's the riskiest thing I've ever said, but it also feels *good*, in a dangerous way, in a euphoric way.

He stands there, just breathing, his brows drawn together the tiniest bit, a small line appearing between them. My heart wavers. It was too much. I'm ridiculous, I'm never trusting anyone again, I'm—

Then he steps forward and closes the distance between us.

"Good," he says. "Because I am so in love with you."

He puts his arms around me, and we stare at each other for a moment, before he leans down and kisses me.

My skin is tingling. My whole body is singing.

I'm full of love, I'm breathless with it.

THIRTY-EIGHT

We kiss on the side of the road for a few seconds until I remember that Harper is watching us and Amber is still sitting on a bench around the corner, and I step back.

"Okay. Okay," I say. "So, what do we do now?"

"Um," he says. "I better go back and talk to Amber."

We're both smiling and flustered.

"Are you still going to have dinner with her?" I say.

"No!" he says. "I'm going to tell her that . . ." He pauses. "Should I tell her what just happened? No. I can't say that. I'll think of something."

"Right. You'll think of something," I echo, but I'm not confident he will. Maybe I should offer to go with him and help. Absolutely not. I've done enough damage to their date already.

He turns to go and then turns back and kisses me quickly. My heart does a little flip.

"Good luck," I say. I almost say "I'll miss you," even though I'll be seeing him in about twenty minutes, but that feels like a lifetime right now.

He walks off, and I stand on the street alone, vibrating with the enormity of what just happened.

When I go inside Harper meets me in the hallway, grinning. "You did it!" she says. "It was like I was watching a movie!" She hugs me and offers me chips.

I eat one and hug her back simultaneously.

"So what now?" she says.

"I'm not totally sure," I say. They never show this awkward after bit in the movies.

"Should we celebrate?" she says, walking to the lounge room and flopping on the couch. "Should I call Penny to come over?"

"No, no, that would be too much pressure," I say. "Celebrating, I mean. Obviously, you can have Penny over."

"Are you guys fully together? Or just casual to start? Is he your boyfriend now?" Harper says, putting her feet on the couch's armrest and balancing the bowl of chips on her stomach.

"I don't know," I say. "We didn't discuss that." Her questions have made me instantly nervous.

"Well, what did you discuss?"

"Um." I chew on my fingernail, sitting down on the other couch and then getting up again. The whole thing is already feeling hazy. It was all so quick. We said we loved each other, didn't we? *Did we?* Yes. Sort of. What else did we say? I am starting to worry I hallucinated everything. "We didn't discuss anything. We just told each other how we feel."

"Okay. Good. That's a good start," Harper says.

"Right," I say.

"You'll figure it out when he's back," Harper says.

"Now I'm freaking out a bit," I say. "Are we together? What happens now? Who even says 'I love you' before knowing they're together?"

I'm pacing again, like I was on the phone with Lauren.

"You said you loved him?" Harper asks, eyes wide.

I nod. "Well, falling in love."

"Oh, that's not so bad."

"But it's still *bad*?"

"No! It's good. It's great! It'll be *fine*. Let me text Penny. She'll know what to do," Harper says reassuringly, but I can see a tiny seed of doubt in her now too. "Have another chip," she adds.

I hold the chip in my hand and walk in circles around the room.

"Maybe he regrets the whole thing," I babble. "Maybe I pushed him into it."

"You're making me dizzy," Harper says as I do another lap.

"What does Penny say?" I ask.

"She hasn't responded yet."

"That means she thinks it's a mistake."

"No. Penny's a total romantic. She'll be on board. Look! See? She just replied with about fifty love hearts." Harper holds up her phone.

This is lovely but it doesn't give me any guidance on what I should be doing right now or when Jesse comes back. I swallow down my urge to say this, because I am trying to convince Harper it will be very easy and low drama to live with a couple and, so far, I haven't been a shining example of this.

I sit down on the couch again and nibble at the chip. My stomach is churning.

"Do you want to watch a movie?" Harper says. "As a distraction."

"Sure," I say. I do not want to watch a movie. I have so much anxious energy inside me right now I could power a flight to the moon. Harper starts scrolling through Netflix, saying, "No, no, no, seen it, hate him, *really* hate him, God, there's nothing to watch, oh wait, what about this?"

"Looks good," I say without even registering what it is. I stare blankly at the screen, trying to formulate a plan for when Jesse returns, but my mind is refusing to be productive. It's gone mushy and only wants to replay the moment Jesse said, "I am so in love with you." Did that really happen? Yes, but I'm sure the universe is going to find a way to take it away and I need to be ready.

I hear the front door shut, and then Jesse walks into the room.

"Hi," I say, standing up and then sitting down again. Smooth.

"Hi," he says, sounding almost shy.

Harper looks between us, biting on her bottom lip. "Please tell me you were extremely kind and polite and groveling to Amber," she says to Jesse.

"I was," Jesse says. "I said sorry at least ten times."

I feel guilty, especially as I haven't even been thinking about Amber. Her date with Jesse has turned out even worse than my first date with Henry.

"Did you leave on good terms?" Harper asks.

"Yes, if you count her calling me a dickhead and then ringing her ex-boyfriend to pick her up as being on good terms. Oh, and she also said she only went on the date as a favor to you and Penny," Jesse says.

Harper makes a face and stands up.

"I'm going to go and call her and make sure she really is okay, and be extremely kind and polite and groveling to her myself."

"Should I send her flowers as an apology or something?" I ask. "Or a fruit platter?" For the good karma, if nothing else.

"No," Jesse and Harper say in unison, and then look at each other and smile.

"She'll be fine," Harper assures me, giving my shoulder a quick touch of support as she leaves the room, phone in hand.

Now Jesse and I are alone, and my mouth is dry. "So," I say, steeling myself in case he says he regrets everything. Or that he was caught up in the moment and it's too much, too soon. *Whatever happens, you can handle it*, I tell myself.

Jesse sits down next to me, grins, and then grabs me and pulls me down on top of him. I laugh, surprised. He hugs me to him and plants gentle kisses all over my face.

"I wanted to do that every time we watched *The Vampire Diaries* together," he says.

"You did?"

"Yeah. I did."

God, he's so cute. He's so cute, and he's kissing me so tenderly, and I'm going to ruin the moment with my insecurities.

"If you regret what happened, before, it's okay," I say.

He stops, confused. "Regret which part?"

"The, um, the telling each other how we feel part," I say. "If it was too much, if you felt pressured—"

"You think you pressured me into saying I'm in love with you?" he says. I feel a little shivery delight snaking down my spine at hearing the words again.

"I can be persuasive," I say.

He's smiling, but then his expression changes and he looks concerned. "Is this about what happened back at school? I know it still bothers you."

"It doesn't bother me. I have the map hanging in my bedroom," I say.

"I noticed," he says. "But that doesn't mean you forgive me. And you don't have to forgive me. I just want to know what you're thinking."

I open my mouth to automatically say I have forgiven him, and I realize that it's true. I have completely forgiven him. The memory still has an ache of embarrassment and pain, but I'm not mad at him anymore. That Jesse, fourteen-year-old Jesse, feels far away. So does fourteen-year-old Brooke. I feel a little bit sad for them both. I wish I could go back and tell them, "Just wait, it's all going to work out."

"I do forgive you," I say to him firmly. "And I trust you."

His eyes soften at this, and I can see it means a lot to him.

"But you don't believe I'm in love with you?" he says.

"I think that's the part I'm struggling with, yeah," I admit. I was so focused on telling him how I felt, I didn't spend any time thinking about how I would feel if he said it back. The intense joy of it, and then the aftermath of that joy, the worry that it might not be true and, if it is true, that it might disappear.

"Why?" he says.

I hesitate, and before I can answer, we hear Harper walking back down the hallway to the lounge room. I get up quickly, sliding off Jesse and moving to the far corner of the couch, because I don't want her to think we're going to be all over each other all the time. Harper gives me an is-everything-going-okay? look when she comes back in. I give her a quick smile.

"Okay, kids. Amber's fine. And I'm going to Penny's house tonight, to give you some time to figure everything out," she says. "Not that there's anything to figure out," she adds quickly. "I mean, to give you some new-couple privacy. Or, maybe not *couple*. I don't know if you're ready for that. Tell me what word to use when I'm back tomorrow!"

She turns and starts to walk back out.

"Wait," I say. I want to reassure her that we're going to be considerate, that we won't make things weird, that we'll do whatever she wants to make her comfortable. "Should we have a house meeting before you go? Just to, you know, make sure we're all on the same page and you're not stressed about anything?" I say.

Harper looks at me, her eyes warm. "I'm not stressed about anything," she says. "It's all going to be fine."

"Okay," I say, and then the front door clicks shut and she's gone.

I turn to Jesse. I'm worried he's going to jump straight back into our discussion from earlier, but he doesn't.

"Are you hungry?" he says. "Should we order something for dinner?"

And I relax, a little. A normal conversation. Almost like nothing has changed. I can do this.

After we've agreed on a Thai place and ordered, I stand up and hover, back to thinking of all the details we need to sort out and where to even start, and suddenly I'm chewing on my fingernail and about to start pacing again. Jesse stands up too, taking my other hand and pulling me toward him. I rest my head on his chest, and it feels so good that I close my eyes, all my muscles relaxing. His touch has an instant soothing effect on me. He runs his fingertips up and down my back, like he did the night of Harper's party before we first kissed, and it feels so good I make an involuntary *mmmm* noise in my throat.

"Are you freaking out?" he asks.

"A little."

"What about?" His hand slips under my top and he rubs a circle on my lower back with his thumb.

"We live in the same house," I blurt out. "We have to talk about how we're going to handle this."

"I know." He leans down and kisses my neck.

"Starting a relationship with someone you live with is like going from zero to one hundred," I say, letting my hair fall to the side so he has better access to my neck.

"I know." Still kissing.

"We can't escape each other." I nuzzle closer to him.

"I know. What on earth will we do?" He nuzzles me back.

"And I need this house. I have nowhere else to go. Neither

do you." I slide my hands under his T-shirt because I've been dreaming of touching his back, his chest, his stomach, all of him, and it feels unbelievable that I actually can.

"I know. We are trapped, together," he says, his nose touching mine.

"So, seriously, what do we do?" I say, pressing closer to him.

"We just . . . ignore it." He leans down and kisses me on the lips.

"I'm not really built for ignoring things," I say between kisses.

"I'm very good at it. Follow my lead," he says.

"You're corrupting me."

"How about this? For the next hour, we ignore it. Just one hour." He gives me his full-sparkle smile, dimple and all. I'm not made of stone. I cannot resist that face.

"All right," I say. "One hour."

He walks me backward toward his room, still kissing me.

THIRTY-NINE

I'm lying in Jesse's bed. More accurately, I'm lying on his mattress on the floor, because he doesn't have a bed frame. He doesn't have a bookcase. I'm looking around and realizing there's almost no furniture in this room at all. Not even a desk. His laptop is on the floor next to the mattress. He apparently just has a floor-based lifestyle and I never noticed.

I'm too scared to ask when he last washed his sheets.

Okay, rule one.

From tomorrow, my room will be the room we spend time in. I am not a floor person.

"Ta-da!" he says, walking in with our stir-fry and rice now in bowls and neatly presented on a tray.

Eating sloppy takeaway in someone else's bed should give me stress hives, but I am trying not to scare Jesse with all my anxieties in one go, so I am pushing that particular worry away. It is easy to calm myself about anything right now, because we've just spent forty-five minutes kissing and fooling around in his bed, and my brain is soft and squishy with pleasure. I can already feel myself becoming addicted to him, wanting to touch him, be near him, be next to him at all times.

We eat and chat, and I decide it's time to bring the topic around to the living situation because I can't hold off any longer.

"Okay," I say. "So. Are we—?"

"Are we what?" he says.

"Are we in a relationship?"

"Yes," he says, eating a piece of broccoli. "That's a safe assumption at this point."

"All right. Good. Good. We're together. We live together. We need to think through all the problems that could cause. Let me give you some scenarios, and you tell me how you think we should handle them." I push up my sleeves. I was cold and he gave me his blue hoodie to put on. It feels even more snuggly than I remember.

"This feels like a job interview," he says.

"It's more serious than that."

"Wait," he says, then leans over and puts on his glasses. "I'm ready."

I roll my eyes but I can't help smiling. Smiling might be my default for a while. His too. I notice he keeps grinning.

"Scenario one. We have a huge fight. We want to storm off and not talk to each other for days. What do we do?" I say.

"We do what you did at the start of the year. Hide out in our rooms and ignore each other but pretend to be normal around Harper, so it's not awkward for her."

"All right. You're not mad at me, but you're sick of the sight of me. You need space. What do you do?"

"Go for a long run." He scoops up some rice with his spoon, and a single grain falls off and into his bed. "What was the code word Henry said we used? Wackadoo. I'll say wackadoo and then go for a long run."

"You need more time away from me than that," I say, picking the grain out of his sheets and putting it on the tray.

"I'll say wackadoo and go and stay with my friends for a weekend," he says.

"Okay. You want to cheat on me but you can't bring anyone home. How do you do it?"

"Easy. I go to their place. Should I still say wackadoo before I go, or should we have a different code for that?"

"Jesse. I'm serious."

"Do you think these questions are a healthy way to start a relationship?"

"Yes. I do. I like to be prepared for the worst."

He puts his bowl down. "Let me give you a scenario, okay?"

"Okay." I fold my legs under me. "Go."

"I tell you I love you, and you let yourself be loved, and nothing bad happens." His voice is soft but his eyes are burning and serious.

"Oh," I say quietly. The way he said "I love you" just then, I might be thinking about that for the rest of my life. "That would be nice. But . . ."

"But?" he says, his expression gentle.

"But good things are scary." I don't know how to explain it better than that.

"Why?"

"Well, I might ruin it. Or you might get sick of me. Leave me. All the stuff I was talking about before. It's a big risk." I hate how insecure I sound. But it's better he knows now, before he truly commits to loving me, the fear that can rise up in me.

His eyes rove over me for a few seconds before he speaks. "Brooke. I need you to listen to me, okay?"

I nod and put down my food.

"I know I ruined it before, but I'm not going to ruin it this time. I'm never going to cheat on you. I'm not going to get sick of the sight of you. We'll probably argue sometimes, and we'll figure out how to deal with that when it happens. I know everyone says living together is a mistake. I know we're moving very fast. Maybe the worst-case scenario is in our future. But right now, it doesn't feel like that. Right now, I've never been happier. Have you?"

I pause.

"No. I haven't," I say. And I can, I can feel it, a wonderful warm happiness bubbling up from deep inside me.

"So," he says, giving me his cutest dimple-smile, "let's just be happy together."

FORTY

I put my hands on my hips and try not to shout. "It's not basket-ball. You can't move once you've caught the ball," I say.

"I'm not moving!" Henry says.

"You are," Penny, Harper, and I all say at once.

We're warming up for our first game as a mixed netball team. Harper, Penny, me, Jesse, Henry, Tristan, and Kendra. Penny is going to get a couple she knows to come along in future to be our substitutes, both tall girls who know how to play, but for today, it's just the seven of us. We spent a long time in our group chat talking about what our team name could be and deciding who would play in what position, and now I realize we should have spent some of that time going over the rules. Henry and Kendra have never played before.

We're five minutes until game time, and it's not looking good. I am mentally preparing myself to accept that we won't win our first game. Maybe we won't even win our second game. I will have a strategy in place by the third game, to head off any further loss.

Jesse jogs over to me.

"You look stressed," he says, grinning.

"This team is a disaster," I say.

He laughs. "Don't worry, you've got me. We can't lose."

"There's that cute little ego," I say, squishing his face. "But I'm not convinced you actually know the rules either."

"Did you see me intercept that pass before? I've got this," he says.

We watch Harper and Penny rapidly pass the ball back and forth before Penny pivots, shoots, and scores.

"Okay, *they've* got this, but we're going to help," Jesse says. He leans over and gives me a quick kiss on the forehead.

It's been a month since we got together, and it still feels wildly reckless and utterly wonderful. I'm sure both Mum and Nanna think it's a recipe for disaster, even though Nanna married her first husband at nineteen after knowing him for seven weeks and she says he was the best of all her husbands (she had three). Lauren thinks it's perfect, that I'm an intense person who needs to be all-in from the beginning. But she also said if we break up and I have to move home, I need to accept that I can't have my old bedroom back, because she's thinking of switching our rooms.

So far, no disaster has befallen us. We have some loose rules, at my insistence, but Jesse breaks them regularly. I'll say we should spend a night apart, and he'll agree, then at two a.m., he'll sneak into my room and say he's cold, and then he'll snuggle up against me and I won't be able to go back to sleep, but not because I'm spiraling with anxiety, because I feel a shot of giddy I'm-in-love happiness that's strong enough to keep my brain buzzing for an hour. We're up to season four of *The Vampire Diaries*, and he's helping me plot a novel that I'll probably never write but it's fun to talk about. I have finally convinced Harper and Jesse that we need more structure around our food shopping and chores, and they reluctantly downloaded the apps I suggested, but they haven't actually used them yet.

And I'm getting better about living in the moment. About ignoring my anxious thoughts and letting Jesse love me.

The netball team was Harper and Penny's idea, and inviting Tristan and Kendra to join kind of happened before I could think through the reality of it, and now we're hanging out and it's okay, maybe it's even nice. It turns out, the things I liked about Tristan as a boyfriend work much better with him as a friend. And Kendra, she's nice. And Henry, well, we're helping him develop his comedy set.

The umpire blows her whistle, a one-minute warning until the game starts. Jesse throws me the ball.

"Come on then, Captain, get your team in order."

I grin and lead him onto the court.

ACKNOWLEDGMENTS

A huge thank-you to my brilliant editor, Sarah Barley, and the wonderful team at Flatiron Books, including Sydney Jeon, Maris Tasaka, Cat Kenney, Devan Norman, Megan Lynch, and Malati Chavali. I am eternally grateful to have found a home with Flatiron. Thank you, also, David Forrer at Inkwell and everyone at Text Publishing, especially Jane Pearson, Kate Lloyd, Julia Kathro, Sophie Mannix, Ariane Ryan, and Anne Beilby. Thank you, designer Imogen Stubbs and illustrator Kitty O'Rourke, for the cover of my dreams, bringing to life one of my favorite scenes in the book.

Thank you to Emily Gale and Bronte Coates, for not only keeping me writing but making it a hundred times more fun than it would be on my own. Our writing group sustained me through the roller coaster of writing my second book—the panic, doubts, and second-guessing my ability to write anything at all, plus a pandemic, six lockdowns, early motherhood, toddlerhood, one hundred day care colds and viruses, Covid, and all the anxiety, joy, rage, gossip, kindness, and laughter we shared along the way. Forever my first and best readers, cheerleaders, book recommenders, and dearest of friends.

A huge thank-you to all my friends and family for your never-ending support and enthusiasm and love, it means so much. An extra-special thank-you to Mum, Dad, Carla, Andrew, John, Liv, Laura, Tom, and Maeve.

This book would not have been possible to write without paid childcare, so thank you to the excellent childhood educators who cared for my daughter so well through the last several years, including Zoe, Gaetana, Katie, Purti, Naama, and more.

Thank you to all the readers of my first book, *It Sounded Better in My Head*. Every review, every social media post, every lovely email, I have treasured them all. A very special thank-you also to the glorious booksellers around the country who hand-sold and promoted it, I am indebted to you all.

Thank you to Taylor Swift for releasing two very good albums in 2020 that helped me find Brooke's voice. And to everyone who ever worked on *The Vampire Diaries*, for giving Brooke and me the Salvatore brothers to enjoy.

Thank you to Dan, who, when my day job, parenting, the pandemic, and writing were all too much, encouraged me to take a risk and helped me rearrange our lives to create the time and space I needed to write this book. And asked every day with cheerful enthusiasm, "How's the writing going?" even though I never responded well to that question. Love you.

Finally, thank you to my daughter, Abby, who—while I can't say made writing *easier* exactly—has brought so much love, joy, humor, chaos, and happiness to my life. You've made my world more interesting, more intense, more wonderful than I could ever have imagined.

Lian Hingee

Nina Kenwood is an award-winning author living in Melbourne, Australia. Her debut novel, *It Sounded Better in My Head*, was a finalist for the American Library Association's William C. Morris YA Debut Award, has been published in six languages, and was optioned for film. *Unnecessary Drama* is her second novel.